Daughters of the Gentry, Book One

JENNIE GOUTET

Development edit by Jolene Perry at Waypoint Authors

Proof edit by Theresa Schultz at Marginalia Editing

Illustration by Sally Dunne

Cover Design by Shaela Odd at Blue Water Books

To my daughter, Juliet

CHAPTER 1

Philip Townsend descended the stairs at a clipping pace, his hand skimming the broad railing and his feet clattering on the narrow wooden treads. He skipped the last step and landed on the threadbare Oriental rug that had been in place for as long as the Townsends had owned Boden House. Mrs. Mason, who'd held the role of housekeeper since his mother's death, paused at the entrance to the dining room to stare, a tray of Boden's finest china in her hands.

Philip's good mood threatened to flag under Mrs. Mason's vacant regard that always seemed to mask belligerence. He knew he didn't need to answer to her, although she had held the position since he was a lad of fourteen. Nevertheless, he found it difficult to greet her with an air of authority.

"Good morning, Mrs. Mason. You are washing the tea service again, I see."

"Ay. 'Tis the only way to keep the set from becoming caked with dust," was her reply, although she evaded his eyes when she said it. She must have been using the tea service again for her own personal enjoyment.

"I trust you have not had any more misfortunes?" Philip strove to keep the edge out of his voice. After all, the service was blessedly large, and goodness knew he had little use for it as a bachelor.

"Only a saucer, Mr. Townsend." Mrs. Mason ducked her gaze and shifted the teapot to the center of the tray. "Now the set has matching cups and plates, it does. What with there not being enough servants to keep Boden running proper, these accidents are bound to happen."

"Well." Philip absently flicked the riding crop he held against his leg, then flinched at the sting. "That obstacle is sure to be cleared as soon as Miss Dawson arrives on Friday. She will set all to rights."

The housekeeper only tightened her lips at the reminder of Philip's blessedly capable, angelic cousin, Sissy, who would arrive in two short days at Boden House to serve as mistress until Philip stumbled upon a suitable candidate for a wife. Mrs. Mason would not like it as Sissy was sure to impose order and did not flee from the protests of fractious servants the way Philip did.

He turned into the library without another word. From there, he heard Mrs. Mason cross the dining room and enter her small sitting room to the left of the butler's pantry. A pantry that currently had no butler to fill it. The cups rattled violently on the tray as she turned to close the door behind her, and Philip held his breath. There was no corresponding crash, and he released it in an exhale as he crossed the library toward the informal sitting room. In it lay the main door to the outside. No footman stood in attendance, of course, but at least Jim had the insufficiency of servants as an excuse for his absence from his post. The lone footman was, at present, one of only five male servants, and the other four were employed on the land and in the stables. Boden's challenge of inadequate or inefficient servants was becoming pressing.

Outdoors, an untidy garden stretched before Philip with weeping silver lime trees serving as tall, stately sentries at the park's limits. Beyond the front garden, the land was flat and faded in color but for the yellow-green leaves on the trees dotting the countryside. However, the late August sunlight sent a shimmer of golden beauty to the landscape that could not help but restore Philip's cheerfulness. He was of a naturally sanguine disposition, and therefore the increasing challenges of running a household as a bachelor could only dampen his mood for so long. After all, Sissy's arrival with her mother promised an end to Philip's troubles, and her brother would spend the first month with them as well. Theo was his favorite cousin, if not his favorite person altogether.

Philip's gaze roamed the shaggy lawn adjacent to the stables and carriage house. The stables were extensive, and it was his goal to fill them. For now, however, they held only his prized stud, a matched pair, his roan gelding, and two dray horses. He entered and went to stand between the stalls of the latter two and held out his palms with sections of an apple in each. The Shires gobbled them up before bending their heads to sniff at his coat.

Philip laughed. "Don't be greedy, fellows. A man's pockets are only so big and there are six of you."

He inspected the Thoroughbred's eyes next, as he stroked his muzzle, then called out over his shoulder to the groom who was readying Philip's gelding to ride. "His eye contagion appears to have resolved with the treatment."

"Ay," the groom answered. "The hot poultice thrice daily, though he didn't like it."

"I'm sure he didn't." Philip gave the site one last look, then leaned over to kiss the horse's forehead—a spontaneous gesture, but not one that made him feel foolish. Although Crown Glory had yet to prove himself, the stud had already turned a small profit by siring a local foal, besides being a handsome stallion with a surprisingly sweet disposition. Philip wanted him in the best of health.

After greeting his chestnut pair, Thunder and True, he strode over to where Jim held the reins to his gelding. Philip gave his last bit of apple to the roan, who was named Poker-Up for the way he averted his head when pouting, and swung into the

3

saddle, urging the horse out of the stables. By force of habit, he directed the gelding to the northern end of his property where an idea that involved diverting part of the Waring River had taken hold of his mind. Doing so would irrigate a particularly dry stretch of land to the south, turning it into a field for growing corn. The contemplated project was a knotty endeavor as the public road split a portion of his property, and he would need to cross the main road in order to accomplish it. Downstream was the Coning mill. He would make certain his plan did not affect the mill's operations.

Philip approached the open field, south of where the river cut through Horncastle and his own land as well. Before him, a thick mass of brambles formed a wild hedge of late-blooming blackberries that were delicious when he remembered to have them picked. On the other side of the river, the woods stretched as far as he could see, providing tempting shade in the hot days of late summer. It was not a place he was welcome to enjoy. The owner of the woods, Mr. Alfred Bassett, and Philip's late father had been at odds for most of his life, and the cool relations had outlasted the death of his father.

He was working out how to dig the canal, and what series of pipes needed to be installed under the road to accomplish his purpose, when a flash of light blue cloth caught his eye, now partially hidden by the brambles. The cloth gradually revealed itself as a dress, and it was with some surprise that he recognized the figure which filled it. He had not crossed paths with little Miss Honoria Bassett since his return to Lincolnshire, and he had drawn the conclusion that she must surely be away on an extended visit—although with their families' unresolved tension, it was not precisely something he could have gone to inquire about.

Miss Bassett was little no more. She turned at the sound of his horse, and he saw a heavily laden basket almost slip from her fingers. Then his gaze rose to her face and stayed there. She gave a surreptitious swipe at her lush mouth, but it did not hide the telltale stains of blackberry juice. Philip was torn between a desire to laugh and an unexpected acceleration of his heart. *That* was not something he was prepared for. But it was impossible to deny that she had changed in the three years since he had seen her. As a girl, she had been rather forgettable; as a young lady, she drew one's attention and kept it captive. Her neat, stylish gown fit like a glove and was as fine as anything he might see in London. Her eyes sparkled under her poke bonnet, and her cheeks glowed in harmony with her red hair.

Philip redirected his gaze to the row of blackberry brambles. This would not do. Had he not known Honoria under the most informal terms since she was an infant? Even if their fathers had maintained a distant relationship, their mothers had been friendly enough until his own mother had died. And what was more, the neighboring siblings Augustus and Christine Grey, who resided at Farlow House when in Lincolnshire, counted them both as close friends, adding to their intimacy. There was no room for anything like desire in his acquaintance with Honoria. He therefore quickly repressed the wayward reaction, though it was the likely cause of him speaking with more starch than he might otherwise have.

"Good morning, Honoria. Miss Bassett, I mean to say. You are out early." He made a point to look behind her, drawing his brows together. "And unaccompanied?" Why *was* she unaccompanied? Any man could come along and be tempted by the same vision that had met Philip—one of fruit-stained lips and sunkissed skin that disappeared enticingly into a neat little bodice ... Another man might not have a sense of honor.

Honoria lifted her chin. "I do not need the company of a servant to pick blackberries on my own property." She flushed slightly, adding, "Well, technically your property, I suppose."

Another surge of laughter welled up in Philip. Six years his junior, Honoria had always been an incongruous mix of fierce practical stubbornness and ... a sort of innocence and vulnerability she had apparently not lost on becoming a woman. And she had certainly become a woman in the years since he had last seen her. Even her eyes had grown larger as her face thinned, and her small waist brought her curves into greater relief.

Philip looked away. "Yes, well, as you say, these fields belong to me. As such, I cannot account for what you might be doing in them." He allowed his face to remain severe, although his voice trembled slightly with the laughter that bubbled underneath the surface. He returned his gaze to her just as she whisked her own smile away.

"Well, Mr. Townsend." She put her free hand on her hip. "I say you ought to be ashamed of yourself to let these berries go to waste the way you do each year. I've decided to intervene. I am sorry to say this, but if you cannot direct your servants to pick and preserve the berries, then someone better had."

Philip knew she meant the words playfully, but they hit close to the mark. It was a sobering reminder that not only was his estate desperately short of servants, but the ones he did have little respected his authority. That was hardly her fault. It was his own father who had sunk his already meager fortune into excavating a mine that had turned up empty, leaving the estate in financial distress. When Philip glanced again at Honoria, she was waiting for him to respond, her expression hesitant as though she feared having offended him. He relaxed the crease that had formed in his brow.

"Perhaps you will have the goodness to bring me a crock of blackberry jam when you have done preserving them." The crease returned. "That is, if your father will permit it."

"Why, sir, you may rely upon it." Honoria smiled as though her father were not the terrifying man Philip knew him to be. The Townsends might have the larger estate and be in possession of an old family crest, but the Bassetts held prime land between two rivers and owned the mill that served five surrounding villages. As the magistrate, Mr. Bassett was well respected both in town and in those villages that depended on him, unlike Philip's own father, who had scarcely cared for his own tenants and had never been well liked. Philip doubted whether Mr. Bassett would allow his only daughter to bring anything, even something as innocent as a crock of preserves, to the heir of a family with which there was an impossible breach.

A silence ensued, and Honoria shifted her basket to her other arm. Philip took hold of the pommel and prepared to dismount. "Shall I carry that for you?"

"No," she replied quickly. "You are most kind, but it will not be necessary." He suspected the reality of their families' situation had at last dawned on her and that she was imagining what her father would say if she allowed Philip to cross their land.

"Well," he replied, not wishing to leave the first friendly conversation he'd had in days but having no excuse to stay, "I wish you will make free use of the berries, so that I might not be accused of allowing shocking waste to occur on my land."

"There are no accusations amongst neighbors," she replied, smiling. "Only helping hands."

Philip tipped his hat and rode away, wondering at the unexpected encounter and the likelihood of seeing her again, when their paths had not crossed even once in the six months since he had returned to his estate. While her parting assurance had not been entirely true, it was a pleasant idea nonetheless.

CHAPTER 2

Honoria perched the heaping basket of blackberries on her hip and opened the back door with her free hand. Entering the airy kitchen painted in yellow, she deposited the basket on the rough wooden table before grinning at their cook and popping another fat blackberry in her mouth.

"That's quite a harvest, miss." Mrs. Sands went over to examine the berries and clucked her tongue in satisfaction. "This'll make us a fine blackberry tart for dinner tonight, and we might have ten jars of preserves besides. Was there any more to be had?"

Honoria wiped her hands on the work apron she had taken, which was now stained beyond remedy. She untied it and set it on the stone slab at the far end of the kitchen. "Plenty. There are enough berries to fill two more baskets like it, I daresay. I shall have to return."

She walked over to the sun-filled room adjacent to the kitchen and reached up to test the herbs that hung upside down to dry. The room beyond that held the undercroft where their root vegetables were stored, and beside it was her little apothecary with all manner of remedies she oversaw herself. She might be young, but she had an appreciation for the art of healing that had seemed to skip the generation of her mother to pour directly into her. Perhaps it was just as well, since her mother would not have had the energy to travel around their town to attend to various illnesses, whilst Honoria seemed to have it in unlimited supply.

"I shall run up and see if Mother needs anything," she told their cook as Mrs. Sands pulled the day's game toward her and began plucking feathers with swift, efficient movements.

Honoria darted up the two stone steps from the kitchen of their medieval home to the main floor and strode across the Great Hall. The term had become a family joke, as the hall was not very great in size, but her grandmother had named it so, proud to serve dinner where the noble guests of centuries past had gathered to eat. On the four sides of the room, tall white pillars supported a first-floor balcony, and when one lifted one's gaze, the doors to the bedrooms above were visible beyond the railing. Her favorite part of the hall was the nook nearest the kitchen, where six narrow windows holding diamond-shaped panes stretched to the ceiling, crowned with stained glass at the top. Even when there was little sun, light shone through the glass, projecting the latticed and colored patterns on the stone floor.

Honoria crossed to the morning room where the clip of her boots gave way to the muted sound on the oakwood herringbone floors of Weeton Hall. At the far end of the morning room, a large rounded alcove held another tall set of windows—this time with no stained glass. In its center, chairs and two sofas were placed in a cozy circle, and there her mother sat with a novel on her lap, looking as contented as she might with such an untaxing program of pleasure before her. There could not be a more felicitous home in all of Lincolnshire, Honoria thought. Not in all of England.

"Mama, we shall have blackberry tart for dinner. I knew I would find a harvest at the edge of the Townsend estate, and I was not disappointed. All was nearly lost with this summer's drought, but it took only that bit of rain last week to plump the berries up to just what was needed." She kissed her mother, who had turned her cheek upwards, then sat on the chair opposite. "Good morning," she added as an afterthought.

A smile lit her mother's face, and she closed her book, marking the page. "You would not have needed to inform me you went blackberry picking. I can see that for myself."

Honoria touched her fingers to her lips. "I look a fright, do I? Such a shame Philip Townsend had to ride by just then and see me in such a state, when we had not crossed paths in ages." She thought back. "I believe the last time was in the company of the Greys before he left for London and they removed to Bath."

"Philip Townsend." Mrs. Bassett lifted an eyebrow at her daughter, revealing a glimpse of her quiet humor. "Indeed a shame. Especially since the shrubs are on his property, are they not? My dear, although Mrs. Townsend once said we might pick the blackberries there anytime we liked, she is no longer here to countenance it. And it is perhaps not quite what your father would like."

Honoria would not have bothered to respond to so unimportant a detail had her mother not added with an indulgent smile, "Although if Amelia Townsend had had her way, the blackberries would by now be the joint property of you and Philip."

Honoria pinched her lips tight and came near to glaring at her mother, ignoring the fact that even in her own heart she had found Philip unexpectedly pleasing to look at. His hair was cut long. Its honey color could almost be described as feminine were it not for the decidedly masculine square jaw framed by the thick waves. And he had been easy to talk to. With him, she wasn't tongue-tied the way she was with Augustus Grey. Then again, she supposed that was only natural. Few men could hold a candle to Gus.

"Mama, I cannot imagine what prompted you and Mrs. Townsend to decide your children would be a suitable match whilst we were still in the cradle. Unless that is the sort of thing one did back then. These days, arranged marriages are not at all the thing. One likes to have a choice in whom one marries." A fuzzy image of dark, windswept hair and a teasing, heart-melting smile filled her mind.

Mrs. Bassett laughed. "You must forgive us our youthful optimism, then. When we saw our babes playing together so sweetly —or rather, I should say little Philip looking after you so attentively when you were an infant—and the two of us such intimate friends, we could not help but imagine a happier future for you both."

"Well." Honoria had taken her mother to task often enough on the matter that there was no point in belaboring it.

She nevertheless did. One never knew whether one had protested the idea enough to kill all lingering hope. "It was a whimsical notion to have arranged our match, to be sure. But the reality is that we are not at all suited, which you must surely see by now. Why, Papa would never permit it. And Philip and I are no longer in each other's company—there is little enough opportunity when we don't even belong to the same parish."

Her mother sighed. "I suppose I gave up the notion once your father and Mr. Townsend had that falling out over the mine."

Losing interest in the all too-familiar subject, Honoria glanced over at the tray on the table near her chair and spotted a small stack of letters sitting there. She reached over and plucked the one on top. "It's Christine's handwriting. I have been waiting for word from her." She considered the neat scrawl and ran her fingertips lightly over the folded paper. "I do hope these six months have allowed her to bear the loss of her mother. I know they were not as close as you and I are, Mama, but it is, after all, her mother."

Mrs. Bassett sent her a sympathetic look, then set her book to the side. "Before you begin reading it, I am afraid I have some unpleasant news."

At this, Honoria looked up without breaking the seal. She was sure it must be that the expected delivery of cloth to make over the curtains in the drawing room had been delayed again.

They were beginning to fear the pattern they'd chosen was not available at all.

"Your father will have to travel to London next week, and he will be gone for over a month. He could not put it off." Her mother studied her face as she added gently, "He will be unable to squire us to Lincolnshire for the Stuff Ball this year."

Honoria froze in dismay. The Stuff Ball was Lincolnshire's most important event, gathering society's prominent members. The annual ball had begun twenty-five years ago with the aim of supporting the Lincolnshire wool merchants. Attendees were required to purchase locally dyed and manufactured wool for their outfits, and they were always bought new since the elected patroness chose a different color for the ball each year. Honoria had been working on her gown ever since the Assembly had settled on green.

Last year, yellow was the chosen color for the event, which had been fatal. In green, she would shine as no tint better suited her complexion. Furthermore, the Greys were expected to return to Horncastle in the near future. There was every likelihood that Gus would attend the Stuff Ball, even if he might choose not to dance with his mourning so recent. She would appear in a becoming ballgown, marking the first time he would perceive her as the woman she now was. Honoria had looked upon this convergence of signs as a mark of providential favor.

"And Samuel?" she asked as soon as the words would come. Tears threatened at this unwelcome news—tears she thought wholly unbecoming. She would not become one of those females who cried over a ball. "Can he not return from London and escort us? He has nothing better to do with his time."

"Your brother will not be able to come home as planned. His letter arrived in this morning's post, informing us that he has pressing matters to see to in London." Mrs. Bassett reached over to squeeze Honoria's arm. "At the very least, your father will be able to meet him in London while he is there."

This was no consolation, and Honoria forced her words out through gritted teeth. "I knew it. That is just like Samuel. He will not leave off his pleasures, even to represent our family at the Stuff Ball. What happens here is more important than in London. After all, this is where he will live when he marries, and it is about time he thought of that." The last bit she said without any real conviction. Her brother was a notorious flirt and had always said he would not marry until he was bored enough to settle down.

Her mother sighed and shook her head, and Honoria saw for the first time the disappointment she attempted to hide. "You must not judge your brother harshly. He is young and will want to see something of the world before he comes and takes over management of the estate and the mill. There is time enough for him to attend next year's ball."

Honoria did not trust herself to answer. At least she could not do so without grumbling, so she remained silent. It was not as though *she* had any choice about either managing an estate or going off to enjoy a season. No, with her mother laid up with rheumatism, Honoria was fully running a household for which she would not always be mistress and had no choice whatsoever about spending her time in London or Lincolnshire.

Her mother perfectly read her thoughts. "I know you are disappointed. We shall have to find some other way to amuse ourselves. And, of course, we may rely on Mr. Grunden to oversee the estate while your father is away. Him, and your industry, my dear Honoria."

"Well, of course you may rely on that," she replied, suppressing a sigh over her heedless brother.

The sounds of Mr. Bassett entering the house reached them, and Honoria fell silent. In another minute he had entered the room, and he glanced at her face before coming over to place a kiss on her cheek. "Well, my pullet. You've heard the news then. I knew you would not be best pleased, but I cannot delay my trip. There is a committee got up to discuss fixing the grain prices, and my voice needs to be heard. I will be representing this part of the shire."

He clearly expected a response, so she managed a quiet, "I

understand, Papa." She would not complain about her brother any longer. Instead, she turned her attention to the letter she held, and her father went to sit by her mother, who reached over to pluck a short stalk of wheat from under his collar. "Let me see what Christine has to say."

Christine Grey, and her older brother Augustus, had been an inseparable part of Honoria's childhood. Philip Townsend was of an age with Gus and she with Christine. As such, the four of them had often gathered together in company. That was before Mrs. Grey contracted an ailment that no doctor had been able to identify, and which took them to Bath where they saw any number of specialists in trying to find a cure. There they had settled for three years, with Gus returning alone to Horncastle for short visits to oversee his estate—the only bright spots in Honoria's quiet life when she could somehow contrive to see him. Now that Mrs. Grey had finally succumbed to her illness, Christine and Gus were expected to take up residence once again in Lincolnshire.

She slit the seal and unfolded the starched paper, scanning the lines eagerly. "They're returning for good!" She looked up with bright eyes, at last finding something to rejoice about. "There. Sam can stay in London for all I care. Christine is to be here in a fortnight. I only hope her spirits will not be too oppressed." Any wondering about Christine's brother, Honoria kept to herself.

"As do I, my dear. Mrs. Grey suffered for years, so perhaps the end has brought them some measure of relief. Her children will know that her suffering is over." Mrs. Bassett rubbed her knees as though the thought called to mind her own discomfort.

Mr. Bassett took his wife's hand in his and held it there. He had only once been able to accompany her to Harrogate to bathe in the waters, but it was not enough to grant any lasting change to her condition. Honoria knew that nothing harassed her father more than his inability to bring his wife relief.

"I want to make a present for Christine for her arrival." Honoria leapt up and started for the door, taking Christine's letter with her, then turned back with a sudden idea. She looked at her parents anxiously. "Do you ... do you suppose if the Greys are to go to Lincolnshire for the ball, I might go with them?"

"I am not convinced they will wish to go when they are in half-mourning," Mrs. Bassett said, after exchanging a look with her husband. "Even so, it will not be right without a matron accompanying you."

"Do you think not?" Honoria's spirits plunged anew. "I suppose you are right."

"I am almost tempted to write to Samuel," her father began, and Honoria held her breath. But he merely shook his head. "It will be as well that he is with me in London so I might introduce him to my associates there. It may be our last opportunity to both reside there at the same time."

Honoria did not trust her voice to be cheerful, so she merely nodded and exited the room, turning to climb the winding staircase. Her bedroom was one whose door faced the balcony in the Great Hall, and she entered it now, abandoning the idea of reaching for her sewing basket. She had been working on an embroidered cushion that she was now determined to give to Christine. But that would have to wait until she could restore her frame of mind to something more hopeful. She sat and grabbed the nearest embroidered cushion at hand—the first she'd attempted that was too ugly to give away—and hugged it to her chest.

If Gus did not go to the Stuff Ball, did she still want to go? She supposed so. It was too exciting an event to miss, especially with *such* a gown as she had. But then, whom did she know well enough to request an escort? No one that came to mind, except perhaps the Mercers, long-standing residents of Horncastle she had known all her life. They were intimate enough friends to the Bassetts to willingly take on the service if they were planning on attending, but the latter was far from certain. She did wonder if Philip Townsend would go, but as he could not serve as her escort, she would not waste time thinking of him.

It did seem a coincidence that on the very day she learned of

Christine's return, Honoria would cross paths with Philip after such a length of time. Her relationship with Philip was an odd one. To all appearances, they had none. His mother and hers had been intimates, but Mrs. Townsend had died young of influenza, severing that connection. Their fathers were not on speaking terms—or had not been before Mr. Townsend's untimely death due to a partial collapse of the mine shaft he had dug. Before his only remaining parent departed from the world, Philip would be away at school for months at a time. And in the years afterwards, he had gone off to London, leaving his house and estate in the hands of servants. However, before that, in those early years when the Greys were living in Horncastle, they spent afternoons in each other's company playing games, riding, and teasing like siblings while their fathers pretended the friendship did not exist. Fortunately, Honoria's interest lay in quite another direction than Philip Townsend, so she did not have to choose between breaking her father's heart or her own. It was just as well that her affections were engaged elsewhere.

Musing over the simple pleasures of her youth turned Honoria's thoughts to more hopeful avenues. She would take up her embroidery now. There was little enough time, and she wanted to have it ready for Christine's return.

The rose damask armchair was placed in the corner of her spacious room in such a way that allowed her to face the large window overlooking the brick-enclosed garden. She settled there with her sewing basket and glanced out at the stone pond tucked between the yew hedges, the fountain trickling at the end of it. As she selected a purple thread, it occurred to her that the return of Christine and Augustus Grey would evoke the days long past, where laughter and play were central to their lives, ball or no ball. Perhaps it would not matter that Samuel had not come, for her time would again be filled with friendship. Perhaps more than friendship.

Gus. The thought of him brought on a wistful sigh. As children, before he was of an age to care about girls, he gave her every bit of attention he gave his sister whenever they were together. Except he teased her in ways he did not tease his sister, tugging the end of her hair and tickling her. And he was kind, too, offering her smuggled sweets and putting his arm around her shoulders when a torn stocking brought tears to her eyes. Not even Samuel had paid any attention to her that was not forced upon him—or taught her how to put a bridle on a horse or a worm on a hook. Not that fishing was a genteel occupation.

Philip had been a steady presence as well, but he had always been consumed by the sport. Gus, on the other hand, had managed to devote as much interest in her as he did in sport, so that she felt quite important in his eyes. It was therefore not difficult to imagine that he might grow to love her.

Honoria bit her lip. It was a shame Gus would not see her in her first ballgown as a lady, and of such an exquisite fit and color. She had been sewing tiny crystal beads, one after the other, into the neckline, fueled by her hope that he would see it. And now all that effort would be to no avail.

She chose another color and squinted at the eye of the needle to thread it. Who knew? Perhaps his interest in her as a potential match would develop before the ball, and if he did go, he would find it insipid without her there. He would then be inspired to rush home to declare his newly discovered feelings. Why should she not hope for such a thing?

CHAPTER 3

The day was dawning cool despite being early in September, and Philip was in the stables preparing for his morning ride when he heard the sound of hoof-beats cantering in approach. He wasn't expecting anyone until the following day, and he looked up in curiosity and then surprise.

"Yes indeed, coz. It is I." Theo Dawson reined his horse in and swung down from the saddle.

Philip handed the reins of his gelding to the groom and strode over to his cousin. He held out his hand and seized Theo's arm as they shook. "I did not look for you until tomorrow. Did you leave your poor sister and mother to suffer the journey unescorted?" Philip teased, knowing Theo would do no such thing.

"Ah." A flash of discomfort filled Theo's features, which left Philip with a mild sense of foreboding. "Come. Leave off your riding for a bit and spare me an hour of your time. Has the breakfast been cleared? I did not eat at the inn, hoping you would provide me with better fare."

Philip signaled to his groom to unsaddle the horse and walked at Theo's side into the soft daylight, their boots crunching on the leaves that had started to fall early after a dry summer. "You thought you would get better fare here than at an inn? I did not take you for such an innocent."

Theo chuckled. "Mrs. Mason still rules the nest then?"

"Yes, and she has chased off Cook. We've had to hire someone from the village to fill in temporarily until Sissy arrives. I've warned Mrs. Mason that there will be changes afoot when my cousin has taken up residence. She did not like that, I can tell you."

Theo met Philip's laughter with a weak grin. "About that ..."

Philip stopped and faced his cousin, all humor gone. "About that? About what? Tell me you are not bearing ill tidings." A fear gripped him. "Your mother has not been laid up again? I told Sissy we would employ every effort for my aunt's comfort. She needed only endure the journey once, and then she could make her home here."

Theo held up his hands, stopping the flow of words. "My mother is in the best of health. Well—as good health as she can be, considering her age and ... disposition. Sissy is as well. In fact, my sister could not be better." He paused, and Philip waited in wary silence, now certain that a piece of bad news was forthcoming. "Thing is, Sissy had an offer and was married in a fortnight by common license. She's already on her way to Cornwall where her new husband lives."

For a minute, no words came to Philip. He steered his gaze past Theo to the broad stretch of yellowing lawn to his left, then dropped it to the ground.

"I know it's not what you were expecting."

"Why did she not write to tell me of it?" Philip asked in a surge of indignation. Now his plans were overset, and there was no solution he could think of. It was not as though there were a ready supply of unmarried female relations with a gift for management to apply to. He had been counting on Sissy to restore his household to some semblance of order.

"Come," Theo said. "Let me have a pot of ale and something to eat. Then I'll ride with you. My last inn stop was only an hour away so I'm not overly fatigued."

"And yet you did not push through last night and sleep here."

"What, in damp sheets?" Theo grinned.

"You were afraid to tell me, weren't you?" Philip moved forward again, his humor partly restored by his natural temperament and partly by the pleasure of seeing his cousin.

"I was," Theo replied baldly. "But it was mainly the sheets. I know you have an indifferent housekeeper, and I was likely to sleep better at the inn."

"Which is not saying much."

"We'll get Mrs. Mason sorted out. I'm still staying for the month, you know. I can help."

Philip sent his cousin a look heavy with irony. "You're just as reluctant as I am to put yourself in the way of trouble. No, I shall be stuck with her forever, I foresee." He sighed, and Theo only laughed.

They entered the house and made their way to the heavily draped breakfast room, which still had the dishes in place, although Philip had breakfasted an hour earlier. The eggs were hard and cold, and the ham was dry. In truth, the spread hadn't been much more appealing when it had arrived fresh. Theo looked it over with distaste before choosing from the rolls and ham. "This is meant to be coffee, I suppose," he protested when he sniffed at the pot.

"Right you are. But I may be able to get you something more tolerable." Philip went over to the wall where the frayed bellpull hung and rang for a servant. A short while later, the servant girl from the village, who was acting as temporary cook, came in and took away the coffee pot with its offending contents, promising to replace it with something fresh. While they waited, he poured some ale from the pitcher and set it in front of Theo. "I warn you, it won't be chilled."

"Of course not. You are lucky I am not more fastidious," Theo said in between bites.

As Theo broke his fast, they spoke about Sissy's wedding. It was to a widowed lawyer with four children, the eldest a year older than Sissy. Although it had not been a love match, Theo said his sister had thought herself past praying for and had received the offer gratefully. Their mother was to live with them to assist with the widower's younger children as soon as they had completed a short honeymoon.

The news of Sissy's marriage caught Philip entirely by surprise. His cousin was not pretty in the traditional sense, although it was precisely her practical nature that made her such a perfect candidate for mistress of his household, at least in the short term. He had been happy enough to put his own idea of marriage off while there was the promise of his cousin running Boden. But now ...

"Well then," Theo said, wiping his mouth on a napkin. "Let us take a turn about your estate. It's been two years since I've come, and I am anxious to see what plans you're getting up, now that you're resigned to managing the estate yourself."

Philip got to his feet and waved for Theo to follow. They retraced their steps through the library and the sitting room, before exiting into the weak sunlight as Theo recounted news from the rest of his family. Once they had returned to the stables and had the horses bridled, Philip directed their path to the river where he was contemplating the irrigation project. He could ask Theo's opinion on the likelihood of getting a return on the crops in the newly watered field. Although Theo ran the family's textile mill, he was curious and intelligent and had a gift for improving whatever project he applied his energy to.

"I can see your mind is taken up with this disappointment," Theo said as they rode, casting a glance at Philip, then looking up as the wind rustled the leaves above them. "But your house will not be in such a mismanaged state forever. What you need is a wife."

Philip let the silence stretch between them before answering. He knew this, but he had been hoping not to rush the matter. Choosing a life's mate was not a decision to make in haste, and he could not do it in that cold, calculating way some other gentlemen seemed able to do.

"I know I require a wife," he answered at last. "But my need to settle someone as mistress of Boden House is too urgent to have that woman be her. I can't choose a wife like I choose a horse."

"Your selection of horseflesh is not all that quick," Theo said drily. "I don't know that it has to be so very complicated either. Look at Sissy. She went to one ball, danced with the fellow twice; he came calling, and the matter was settled in less than a month. It need not take the eternity you seem to think."

"Is that so? If you had to marry in haste, would you have an appropriate candidate at the ready?" Philip lifted an ironical brow, knowing the answer. Theo was no closer to the marital state than he was.

"Oh, I'm certain if my hand were forced, one woman would distinguish herself from the rest." When Philip gave a huff of disbelief, Theo continued. "Listen. There are plenty of pretty faces, and one fine figure is as good as another. Apart from a decent dowry and the ability to run a large household, you need only consider how able she is to hold an intelligent conversation."

"And how likely she is to cut up my peace."

"Now, this fit of the dismals is unlike you." Theo clucked his tongue. "I expect you'll have remembered some way of approaching the matter reasonably before we sit down to supper and will be able to eat in tolerable cheer. Those woods in the distance are yours? Ah no. They're bordering the other bank of the river."

Philip nodded. "That's the Waring. I was thinking of diverting it to the field here on the left, and this is what I wanted to show you. The soil here was once fenland, and it's full of sandy loam. It drains too quickly for the corn I wish to grow."

They approached the river and Theo narrowed his eyes against the sunlight, pointing to their right. "But this is a public road, is it not?"

"'Tis. It makes the operation more complicated."

Theo reflected on this, then pursed his lips. "You will need some sort of pipe or cask that can be dug under the road. You've probably already figured that out. But you'll have to control the amount of water so it doesn't flood, of course. It's not a light project you're contemplating. I won't ask if you're up for the challenge, knowing you, but ..." He trailed off.

"But you wonder whether there's not a simpler way to bring my estate to solvency," Philip finished for him.

Theo grinned. "Something like that. Then again, you've always worked harder than I've ever had the inclination to do. Your stud farm project?"

Philip shook his head. "Crown Glory is not yet paying off, although I expect him to. That must be a goal for the long-term as it won't answer my need for ready cash."

He studied the soil, contemplating how he could control the flow of water, when his gaze lifted to the stretch of brambles ahead. It brought to mind his last encounter with Honoria, and he wondered idly if it would be another several months before he saw her again. Something about her pleasant face and conversation made him wish it was sooner. Their brief meeting had been reminiscent of happier times, when their mutual friends, the Greys, were still in Lincolnshire. He would not allow his mind to dwell on the more recent, physical changes that had overtaken her, lest it travel down forbidden paths.

As if the force of his nostalgia and desire had conjured her, Honoria rounded the hedge of brambles and came into view. He could tell by the way she lifted her gaze cautiously that she had been conscious of their approach. And even at this slight distance, he could see a blush tint her cheeks as he nudged his horse forward to greet her.

"I have taken to heart your words about the blackberries," she said with a slight nod at the nearly full basket. "Although I fear I should be ashamed of myself since this is the last of them, and they are not mine to pick."

Philip couldn't help the smile that spread at her shy acknowledgment. "I meant it. As you said yourself, the berries were going to waste. I hope you were able to put the first harvest to good use." He gestured to Theo. "This is my cousin, Mr. Dawson. Theo, this is Miss Bassett."

"A pleasure," Theo said.

"Mr. Dawson." Honoria curtsied then fingered the handle of her basket, allowing her gaze to sweep the field on her right, seemingly at a loss for words.

"My cousin is staying with me for the month," Philip explained to break a slightly awkward silence.

Honoria turned her bright smile to Theo. "Well, then. You shall sample my preserves. I promised Philip I would bring some. I mean to say—Mr. Townsend. We grew up together, and I forget we are no longer children at times."

"You must not mind me," Theo replied promptly. "I am not one to insist upon formality. And I would be delighted to try your preserves. It seems I have arrived at a fortunate time."

At this second mention of her promise, Philip began to believe she would indeed find a way to bring him a jar, despite her father's known antipathy. The thought filled him with warmth—and it would make his dry bread more tolerable.

"Well then, Miss Bassett." He raised his hand to bid farewell, before being struck by the fact that she was once again alone. Shifting in his saddle to peer around her, he frowned suddenly.

Before he could speak, Honoria forestalled him. "A servant could not be spared. I know that is what you are about to say, Phil. But I assure you, I am in perfect safety. I've been running about in this area since I was a girl."

But you are a girl no longer, Philip thought firmly. However, he held his tongue and tipped his hat. "Then I shall not take the high-handed approach of telling you what to do—again." Honoria gave him a dimpled smile and turned back to the brambles, reaching out to pluck one berry and toss it into the basket, following it with another. He and Theo rode on, allowing their horses to pick their way up the incline from the field.

"The blackberries would have to go if you created an irrigation system. They will not thrive in soil that is overly wet." Theo steered his horse to the public road that ran alongside the river.

On the far side, the mature birch and elm trees cast a green and gold shaded canopy. "It would be a shame."

"A small price to pay," Philip responded. "Blackberries will not bring in the income I need to restore my estate."

They were well out of earshot now, and Theo said in an even voice, "They seem to have netted you a fine candidate for a wife, however." Philip did not pretend to misunderstand his cousin's meaning and lifted his brows in surprise. "Honoria?"

"Is that her name?" Theo replied mildly. "It suits her. She's perfect for you. A young lady unafraid of hard work, despite her obviously gentle breeding. And she is fine to look upon with her ginger hair, you must own."

Philip chuckled humorlessly. "Her father would never allow it. He and my father were as near mortal enemies as gentlemen could be. Mr. Bassett did not appreciate the mine excavation my father attempted that turned the land bordering his into an eyesore, and I believe my father lost few opportunities to question how much of a gentleman he could be when his estate ownership traced back a mere generation."

"An unfortunate distinction to make when your father married the daughter of a merchant."

"My father was nothing if not consistent," Philip replied in a dry tone.

"Surely her father cannot object now," Theo protested after a space. "It was not as though you had any say in what projects your father attempted, or what feather-brained ideas he had about the qualifications for a gentleman—" Theo turned on his saddle, chagrined. "I apologize."

"Accepted." Philip was not hearing any disparaging ideas about his father he had not entertained himself.

"Besides," Theo went on, "what could be more advantageous than having a neighbor for a son-in-law?"

Philip shook his head. Something warm in his chest buzzed at the thought of such a simple match, but his cousin did not understand. "Trust me. Mr. Bassett has a long memory."

They rode on a little farther, discussing the idea of

installing dikes and the placement of such in the canal. Just when he'd thought the subject of Honoria Bassett had been exhausted, Theo broke a silence that had fallen by glancing at Philip and saying, "But I do think she would make you a good wife."

"Too much water has passed under that bridge," Philip replied firmly. It was a shame, perhaps, as she did possess every-thing a man might want in a wife, but as it stood ... "She is simply not an option."

THE DAY SISSY should have arrived, Philip and Theo got up early to go shooting. The morning fog had only begun to lift when Philip raised the end of his musket to the sky and waited. Theo paused a moment at his side before doing the same. At some unseen movement, Philip's setter rushed forward with loud yaps. The flock of birds that had been nesting in the trees took instant flight, and the sound of both Philip and Theo's muskets exploded.

"I believe that one was mine," Philip said as one of the birds dropped to the small pond and the dog ran to retrieve it.

"I think it must have been," Theo agreed. "Shall we try for another?" He reached for his bag of powder and Philip did the same.

"We shall have to go to a different part of the woods. We must have chased off all the birds in the area." He glanced around at the vegetation near where they stood. "Unless there are still some grouse to be had."

Theo was about to answer when the sound of a horse's whinny and its rider's soothing words reached their ears. The branches of a young tree were pushed aside and a grin broke out on Philip's face, as they both exclaimed at once.

"Grey!"

"Augustus Grey, by my life!"

"In the flesh." Gus swung down from his horse and came

forward to greet them. "You cannot be surprised to see me, though. You must have known I would return."

They shook hands with Gus by turns. Not only was he Philip's neighbor, but the three had also been friends from Harrow. In fact, it was Gus who had introduced Philip to his own cousin. Theo's father had not been keen on his sister's choice to marry Philip's father—an impoverished landowner—and had made no efforts to introduce the cousins though they were of the same age. Once presented at Harrow, however, the trio became inseparable—Philip and Theo even more so because of their blood ties.

"I am sorry for your loss," Theo said when their initial greetings had died down.

"As am I," Philip said, and after a spell, added, "I *had* hoped you might return, but I could not say how long you would remain with your uncle, or whether you would remove there permanently as you do depend upon his fortune to some degree. You aren't the best correspondent, you know."

Gus grinned at the last comment before sobering. "Thank you for your condolences. It was a relief for my mother to reach her end, I think." He went to take hold of the reins of his horse, who had drifted away. "My uncle offered us residence for as long as we wished it, but after six months we thought it time to see to the matters of my property. Christine was anxious to return to a place that was familiar to her. She wrote of our arrival to Honoria, who I thought must have told you."

Philip became aware of the dog at his feet, who was panting with his prize in his mouth. He reached down and patted his dog before taking the game and slinging it into the pouch on his horse. "Honoria and I don't spend much time in each other's company. Come, let us walk. We shall have to find a new place for sport, and you may as well tell us what you've been up to."

Skirting further mention of the loss of his only remaining parent, Gus began to complain about the state of their house, which had suffered damp due to the neglect of his servants. He stopped short mid-discourse. "Theo, what in the blazes are you doing in Lincolnshire? Last I heard, the textile mill required you to be on hand at all times."

"I have a capable foreman now," Theo replied. "I can leave things in his care for the time it takes me to visit an esteemed cousin." Philip sent him an appreciative, mocking grin, and Theo went on. "In truth, I was to accompany my sister who was going to take up residence at Boden, along with my mother. Sissy was to keep house for Phil."

Gus sent Philip an inquiring glance. "Considering a match, are you? There is only one outcome to be had of such an arrangement." He threw a playful punch at Philip's arm, who raised his eyes heavenward.

"Sissy is three years my senior. I can assure you a match was the furthest thing from either of our minds."

"In any case," Theo interrupted, "Sissy is married now and can no longer be of assistance to poor Phil here. I came to break the ill tidings."

They led their horses out of the trees without giving much thought to where they were headed. The slight chill of the morning had been replaced with the warmth of an early September day. They had already bagged their dinner for that night, if his makeshift cook did not burn it, and did not precisely need to continue with their sport.

"Well, fellows, I did not merely come for an idle visit. I stopped by to extend an invitation for a little supper party Christine and I wish to host to reconnect with our friends. When I saw you were not at home, I determined to go riding and look for you. Therefore, you are cordially invited—both of you—to our house Thursday next."

"We shall have a good meal for once," Theo said, sending a belated, rueful glance Philip's way. "My apologies again for another thoughtless remark."

"Apology accepted. You have spoken only the truth." There was little his cousin could say that would ruffle Philip.

When they reached the open pasture, the men swung onto the horses they had been leading and began to ride toward

Philip's house. It felt like the most natural thing in the world for them to be together again, although the trio had not been in company in the three years that Gus resided in Bath. As they rode toward Boden, Philip could not help but take a cheerful view of the future. Despite the fact that he had, at present, no prospect for mistress of his household, he had his friends. And that was no small thing.

CHAPTER 4

Honoria knocked on the door of Farlow Manor, her heart beating in trepidation and excitement. She was happy to see Christine most of all, but she could not help but wonder whether Gus had changed in the year since she'd last seen him. Then again, he had been a man for some years now and change would not be so noticeable in him as it would hopefully be in her. Perhaps he would at last discover she had grown into a woman.

The formal sitting room lay to the left of the main door, and Honoria peered into it through the window panes that bordered the door. Christine stood on a chair dusting the top of a painting, and when she turned with the feather brush in hand to direct the maid, she caught sight of Honoria outdoors. She nearly toppled from the chair but righted herself before hopping off and rushing to the door, her newest pug darting in front of his mistress.

"My dearest Honoria!" Christine's reserve rarely permitted her to show an excess of emotion, but as her oldest friend, Honoria was privileged to witness it.

She hugged her tightly and pulled back to look at her. Oh, Christine had changed. She could see it now. There was a somber light to her eyes that hadn't been there before, but Honoria would do all in her power to add joy to her friend's existence. "It is *so* good to see you," she said, hugging Christine again before shoving the cushion she had embroidered into her hands. "It is not as fine as your needlework, but I made this for you."

She reached down to greet the golden-colored pug, aptly named Guinea, whom she had learned about from Christine's letters. It was impossible to imagine her friend without a dog at her feet.

"*Oho*! What's this?"

Honoria knew that voice and, forgetting momentarily about the new addition, she slowly turned. Her heart had not obeyed her directive to remain unaffected and demonstrate to Gus just how poised she was. Instead, it flopped around inside of her like a fish that found itself on dry land.

Gus looked much the same, except that his thin, boyish frame had turned stouter in a way she could only describe as the masculine ideal. He kissed her on the cheek and followed this with an appreciative look up and down. The familiar lopsided grin set Honoria's heart to beating again. "Well, little Miss Bassett. You've grown into even more of a beauty in the year since I've lain eyes on you—if you will accept such a fulsome compliment from someone who has known you your whole life."

I will accept anything you give me. Tongue-tied, she turned to Christine and repeated herself for lack of inspiration. "It is so good to have you back. Both of you." She glanced again at Gus, a quick fleeting look in an attempt to mask how nervous she was. This was no time to appear the foolish girl, hopelessly in love. This was the time to show him that she would be the perfect candidate for his wife, now that he had come back to Horncastle to stay.

"Come sit down," Christine said. "We've had the Holland covers removed in most of the downstairs rooms, but as you can see, we still have quite a bit to do to remove the dust and make these rooms livable. And there's that patch of damp on the ceiling that I don't know what to do with." She beat the sofa cushion before allowing Honoria to sit. "I had your note that you would come and had a tea tray readied. We don't have much to offer, but at the very least we sent Tim and Becky to purchase the essentials to fill the larder, and I brought back a fruited blend of tea from Bath. It was my uncle's favorite."

"You've turned to wearing half-mourning, I see," Honoria observed. "You did not speak of it much in your letters, but how are you bearing up?"

Christine sighed and exchanged a look with her brother. "I suppose better than six months ago. After all, my mother had done with a life of suffering towards the end. And there is something of a relief in going into half-mourning, which I decided upon before removing to Horncastle. When one has mourned for some time, one longs to fold the grief and put it up in silver paper the way we can with black clothing. Even if we feel guilty for doing so."

Honoria nodded, adding nothing. She had never so much as suffered the loss of an animal she had affection for. "I hope you will use me shamelessly in putting your house to order. I have a deal of time on my hands now that my herb garden is just as I wish it and the harvest is behind us."

The maid entered the room carrying the tea tray and set it on a small table. Gus had wandered into the formal sitting room to retrieve his snuffbox while Christine was responding to her question. Now he returned and waited as Christine poured a cup of tea and handed it to Honoria, who was on intimate enough terms to serve herself a lump of sugar. She paused with the sugar nips in hand. Perhaps she might show Gus how careful she was with household provisions. He must surely appreciate an economical wife. Yes—she would drink her tea black. She restored the sugar nips as he took his own cup and sat.

"Well," Honoria said after a minute, with only the clink of spoons and cups on saucers to be heard, "you will not know any of the village gossip, so let me be the first to tell you that there is a young and very pretty widow newly established in Thimbleby." She had cause to regret her choice of news when Gus looked up, an interested light in his eyes.

"Pretty, you say?" He stretched his legs forward carelessly. "I might have to seek an introduction. Can you provide one?"

Honoria returned a tight smile. Augustus Grey had not spent any considerable time with her in three years, and he was more interested in some widow he'd never met than he was in her? Even if she could have provided an introduction, she would not make it that easy for the widow. "Not I. My mother was not well enough to call on her and determined upon sending a card so that Mrs. Northwick would feel welcome." The tea was bitter without any sugar and she swallowed quickly, then coughed as the heat poured down her throat.

"What did her husband die of?" Christine asked, nibbling on a piece of seed cake that had been set out with the tea.

Honoria shrugged, cross with herself for bringing up pretty widows when Gus appeared to be hanging on every word. "Old age, I am told." Eager to change the subject, she took a deep breath. "I don't suppose you are to go to the Stuff Ball next month?"

She saw Christine glance at her brother and added, "Perhaps it is too soon to ask when you've only just arrived. As for myself, I am unable to go as it stands. My father must journey to London, and Sam will not be returning to escort us. As you might guess, my mother's rheumatism would make such a journey impossible without my father to see to all of the usual comforts."

"Perhaps the Mercers might go," Christine offered. "Or Mr. and Mrs. Billings."

Gus set his teacup on the table and went over to stir the fire that was starting to burn low. It was early in the season for chimney fires, but the room held the chill of one long unused. He added a log, sending up a curling plume of smoke. "I shall leave you both. I've to attend to the stables and see that the horses have been exercised. You may talk dresses and balls to your heart's content in my absence."

Honoria managed a smile but felt her hope fade as he exited the room. His pleasure in seeing her again could not keep him in the house more than a quarter of an hour into her visit. Did he not care for balls? Well then, she would have been just as happy —if not happier—had he invited her to visit the stables with him. She could have told him if the horses were in good health. She might possess only the most basic knowledge of healing animals, but it was enough that two tenant farmers had requested her advice. Not that this was something Gus could have known when he did not remain around long enough to learn it.

Christine pulled Honoria's thoughts back to the present. "As for the Stuff Ball, we have not yet decided. It is not only the mourning ... One of our challenges is that we have not had time to acquire any Lincolnshire wool, and we would have to have our garments made rather quickly. It's not an impossible feat, but it has made us hesitate with all else we must do."

Christine's reticence came as no surprise, as Honoria knew how important it was to her that everything be perfect. Whatever her friend undertook came about after great deliberation. She was therefore pleased to hear her add as she refilled their cups, "However, it has been some time since we have seen the good people of Lincolnshire and our particular friends. It would be a shame to miss it."

"I own"—Honoria reached for the sugar nips and plopped two lumps into her tea—"that it would be vastly agreeable if you were to go. You could tell me all about it, and it would be almost as good as if I had been there."

"Well, while we muse on that, let us think of more immediate things," Christine said. "As our very first engagement back in Horncastle, we would like to invite you and Philip Townsend to dinner. And I have learned that Philip's cousin, Mr. Theodore Dawson, is visiting. He must receive an invitation, of course. I will request that Mr. and Mrs. Mercer come to serve as chaperones for us."

"So, you think the Mercers might go to the ball?" Honoria questioned, her thoughts on the greater project. Then she shook her head. "No, they did not go last year. They said they had grown too old for the journey and the late night of dancing."

Christine cleared her throat. "The dinner we are hosting, Honoria?" She lifted an eyebrow. "May we focus on our homecoming first before we talk about trips to distant towns?"

Honoria smiled sheepishly. "Forgive me. Of course we may. As you know, when I set my mind to something, it is very hard to give my thoughts a different direction."

"The more things change, the more they stay the same." Christine pulled the cushion Honoria had made for her from between Guinea's paws. "I have planned for dishes of prepared pike and venison, but will you help me come up with ideas for the removes? It is time I learn to keep house, now that we are here and mean to stay. My uncle had a formidable housekeeper, and she decided everything, so I've had little practice."

"It is what I love above all things," Honoria said. "I wonder if we might procure some turtle for soup since it is growing cool. And we must have a blancmange. Have you a pencil?"

Christine nodded and jumped to her feet, showing a rare flash of eagerness. "Let me also take you to see our dishes. We can determine which set will be best to put out."

In her enthusiasm for the new project, Honoria abandoned the dilemma of how to get to the ball in Lincoln for the present. Perhaps with her assisting Christine, Gus would notice how well she arranged the table and consider her for another role than a second sister to tease. If she could catch his eye here, going to Lincoln would hardly hold any importance.

Then again, she reflected, if she knew anything of Gus besides the goodness of his heart, he was a dedicated flirt; nothing was more likely to seal his regard for a woman than a little competition from other men. If he went to the ball without having truly noticed her first, he might fall under some woman's spell there and become smitten. She had such a short time to win his heart before he left!

WHEN HONORIA RETURNED HOME, she stopped short at the entrance to the drawing room. Sitting on their jonquil-colored sofa next to Mrs. Bassett was a slender young woman whom Honoria did not know. Golden-blonde tendrils peeked out from under the rim of a black bonnet, and the contrast of her somber clothing against her creamy features only added to her charm. It could be no other than the widow she had heard spoken of. For a moment, Honoria froze at the entranceway. Mrs. Northwick, if indeed it was her, was a rare beauty. It would appear that Gus would not need to go to Lincoln to run up against a pretty face to turn his head.

Her mother gestured for her to enter. "Come in. I would like to introduce you to Mrs. Arabella Northwick. Mrs. Northwick, this is my daughter, Honoria."

As the widow stood, her petite frame was tight with what seemed like years of worries, though her smile was sincere and warm. She and Honoria exchanged curtsies.

Honoria gestured for Mrs. Northwick to resume her seat, then glanced at the empty table. "Mother, shall I call for tea?"

"I have already seen to it," her mother said. "Your father had not left for the mill when Mrs. Northwick arrived, so he called Perkins for me." She smiled at her daughter. "Do join us. You are sure to be more interesting company for our young visitor than I."

Mrs. Northwick clasped her hands together. "Mrs. Bassett, in our introductions, and I suppose in my nervousness, I have not yet thanked you for your kindness in having a card sent to my house. I hesitated to return a visit, since your health does not permit much activity, as you so kindly explained. At the same time, I did very much wish to make your acquaintance."

Honoria's mother answered with disarming warmth. "You were right to come. We did not wish to be backward in our attention, although I was unable to make the trip to see you. It can be difficult to come to a new community. I hope the local families have been welcoming."

Mrs. Northwick did not quite meet Mrs. Bassett's eye. "There have not been many visits forthcoming, I am afraid."

Honoria darted a surprised glance at the widow. She was sure her family had been one of the last ones to meet her. "That surprises me, knowing the people of Horncastle." She gave a puzzled laugh. "They would visit for no other reason than out of pure curiosity. They must not know you are here."

Mrs. Northwick smiled and gave a small lift to her shoulders. After a pause, she added, "My deceased husband's brother accompanied me to Lincolnshire to assist me in settling down, and he told me not to fret over the lack of visits. As soon as he meets the gentlemen in the area, he will request introductions to their wives on my behalf."

"Will you be going to the Stuff Ball in Lincoln?" Honoria asked her. "Surely you have received an invitation, because it gathers everyone of note in the shire. You will meet everyone there."

"I have received an invitation to that, at least. To own the truth, it is an event I both look forward to and dread," Mrs. Northwick said, her lips pulling upward to add lightness to her words. "I am charmed by the idea, but as you said, I will meet everyone there. That cannot be but intimidating. And you? Will you go?"

Honoria looked at her mother before shaking her head. "It will be our first year to miss it, but it is simply not possible. My father must make a last-minute trip to London, and there will be no one to escort us."

Her mother reached across to Honoria's chair and clasped her hand on the armrest in a gesture of sympathy. "I have made the journey in the past, but without my husband here to see to all the details, I fear it will be too much for me. I can manage some exertion but not what I was used to."

"Well," Mrs. Northwick said reflectively, "I have been looking for an auspicious moment to put off my blacks, and I am

37

thinking this might be the appropriate occasion. I could not attend without doing so anyway, since I understand we must appear in green. In any event, my time of mourning has been over for some months."

Mrs. Bassett asked the question that Honoria had been longing to ask. "If this is not an indelicate question, perhaps you might wish to tell us more about your husband? If doing so brings pleasant rather than painful memories."

Mrs. Northwick's face shuttered and Honoria sensed that, as tactful as her mother was, it was not a subject that brought any pleasure to the widow. Nevertheless, after a moment she met their gazes. "My father arranged for my marriage to Mr. Northwick. He was in need of an heir, and my father ... did not find having a daughter living at home a convenience, I'm afraid."

"I understand," her mother murmured as Honoria stared at Mrs. Northwick in mute sympathy. At least her own parents would never force her into a marriage she found distasteful. And contrary to finding her superfluous, they appreciated her and told her so often.

"Do you live on your own?" Mrs. Bassett asked.

Mrs. Northwick appeared to relax somewhat. "For the moment, I live on my own in a large, rambling estate, although I hope to have my son brought to me soon. He is with his nurse in London. My brother-in-law insisted that the nursery was not yet ready to receive my little David and that my presence was needed to supervise its renovation. Indeed, it was in a sorry state ..." Her voice trailed away. "Mr. Northwick has taken up residence in the dower house should I have need of him." A flash of discomfort passed over her features as she said this, and Honoria wondered what could have occurred to put it there. It seemed there was more than one point of difficulty in being a widow, especially one that had no family to rally behind her.

Perkins entered carrying a heavy tray, and Mrs. Bassett indicated for her to set it in front of them. Honoria darted to her feet to prepare the tea. "Even if we are not to meet at the Stuff Ball," she told Mrs. Northwick, "I hope we might meet often in company here in Horncastle. I must be younger than you, and as an unmarried woman am not in a position to sponsor you in our society, but I do know everyone and will be happy to make whatever introductions I can."

"That is very kind of you." Mrs. Northwick gave her a genuine smile that turned into a chuckle. "I feel I must confess, Miss Bassett, that I am only eighteen, although I am a widow and have a child."

Honoria stared at her. "Eighteen? Why, I am nineteen! I am older than you then."

"So you see," the widow said. "I shall be grateful for your sponsorship." She hesitated, adding, "And I would be very satisfied if you called me Arabella. That is ... if you wish to."

"Then do call me Honoria," she replied. When the visit came to an end, and Mrs. Basset had bid their guest farewell, Honoria walked Arabella to the front door. There was something about her situation that hinted at unspeakable difficulty—something about Arabella's attempts at bravery that made Honoria long to support her. "I hope you will consider me a friend, and that you will call if you should need anything."

"A friend," Arabella said softly. "I would like that." From her expression, Honoria had the distinct impression that she had not many of those.

CHAPTER 5

The dinner at Farlow Manor occurred the following week, and Philip drove his black-hooded tilbury into the courtyard of the Greys' home with Theo at his side. They were dressed in evening clothes, and he was glad that local society's eye for fashion was more forgiving than London's. He had not been to the tailor since he'd left Town, if one did not count the coat he was having made for the Stuff Ball. Even Theo had entered into the spirit of Lincoln's annual ball, though he had never before attended one. It had been a simple matter to procure an invitation for him since the ladies outnumbered the gentlemen.

"I had not contemplated a trip to Lincoln during my stay with you," Theo said, when he had ended his soliloquy about why his waistcoat should be made from a different wool than his coat. "But since I'm in the shire I may as well go to Lincoln, and what better reason than to attend the ball? From there, it will not be so very far to Mary's house. I am not without hope that I might convince you to accompany me there and extend our visit." Mary was another one of Theo's sisters, whom Philip had never met. At ten years Theo's senior, she married when Theo and Philip were still in school and, unlike Sissy, had never been home at the same time that Philip visited.

"There's time enough to decide that as the ball draws near." Philip alighted and handed the reins over to the Greys' servant. His gaze roamed to the open stable, where he ran an appraising eye over the horses Gus had had sent from his uncle's stable just outside of Bath. There was a new Thoroughbred mare Gus had boasted about, and Philip was eager to see how she held up on a hunt. This was a passion he and Gus shared which allowed them to remain close despite fundamental differences in personality. They were both of them sports-mad. If one proposed a venture, the other was sure to accept.

The main difference was that though they were each responsible for estates of varying sizes—Philip's three times as large as Farlow Estate—Philip was much more likely to take a personal hand in the management of his. Then again, Gus's father had not frittered away his inheritance through unwise investment schemes, and whatever money he lacked for pleasure was made up for by his loose-fisted uncle. Philip's plunge into adulthood was not by choice.

A footman opened the door, and Christine came forward as they were ushered in. The Greys' house possessed an intimate layout with the formal sitting room and morning room both visible from the main door. Despite the lack of grandeur, Christine had managed to decorate the house with an elegance and polish that Philip would probably never acquire in his own larger home.

She smiled and curtsied before them as Theo bowed at his side. "Miss Grey, I have heard much of you over the years." He wrinkled his brow as though chasing a memory. "I believe 'quiet sort' and 'great gun' were your brother's terms when he mentioned you."

This caused Christine to laugh out loud, which was rare enough, and Philip had to admire how Theo set people at ease. He bowed in turn. "That sounds like something Gus would say. But Horncastle has been quiet without you, and you have certainly made your mark. We are all glad you have come back."

He glanced around the room and saw that they were not yet

complete, as neither Honoria nor the Mercers were in attendance. A knock sounded behind him, and he turned and caught sight of a rich nut-brown cloak through the paned glass.

Honoria stepped through the door, bringing with her a waft of cool evening air. She turned to her maid, saying, "I will let you know when I am ready, Maggie," before greeting Christine with the warmth of old friendship. Philip stood the nearest, and she dipped into an informal curtsy before greeting Theo with more ceremony, asking him how he was enjoying his stay at Boden House. He murmured a reply about how favorite cousins made it easy to bear the smoking chimneys, eliciting another laugh.

Gus entered the room and moved to join them, and if Philip had not been looking at Honoria, he might have missed the change in expression. Her eyes widened, and a blush filled her cheeks before she looked away. He had once suspected she held a *tendre* for Christine's older brother, and it appeared the years had not diminished the attraction. Gus bowed before Honoria, then leaned down to whisper something in her ear, causing Philip to speculate whether he also had some interest in that direction.

But Gus would never do for Honoria. He was much too lazy for someone so industrious. Once the infatuation had worn off, he would only make her life miserable. And as much as Philip was fond of Gus, he had too much esteem for Honoria to wish such a thing on her.

A servant brought in glasses of sherry, and Gus moved over to hand them to the guests as Honoria rested a hand on Christine's arm. "I've been meaning to tell you. I have met Mrs. Northwick. My mother sent a card welcoming her to the neighborhood, and she paid us a visit in response to it."

"Is she indeed as pretty as she is reputed to be?" Gus cut in. "Shall I have Christine visit her?"

"Yes, quite," Honoria said, her voice clipped. "But a woman's measure is not the sum of her looks." She turned back to Christine. "I found her to be a pleasant person to talk to. I am sure there is much to her story, but she disclosed very little of it."

Christine nodded thoughtfully but said nothing further until he and Theo had stepped away from the conversation, and then he heard her tell Honoria, "When we lived in Bath, it was difficult to make new acquaintances. My uncle was prosperous but not precisely fashionable. It can be a lowering thing to find no invitations or cards waiting for you when you return from a walk or the Assembly rooms. I think we should extend some northern hospitality to her." Honoria murmured her assent.

"I will need to show you the new Baker rifle I acquired," Gus said, drawing Philip's attention. "It's deadly accurate. As fine a shot as one could wish."

"But not quite a hunting rifle," Philip said. "Not with a bayonet. What did you purchase it for?"

Gus shrugged. "It's not made for hunting, but I practice with it anyway. You will not believe from how far away you can hit your mark. You and Theo will have to come shoot with me."

There was another knock on the door, and Mr. and Mrs. Mercer arrived, completing their circle at last. Mr. Mercer greeted the ladies, then crossed the room, allowing Philip to introduce him to Theo.

"I am from Newark-on-Trent," Theo said in response to his inquiry, and was then led to compliment the beauty of the Wolds, which was precisely the thing to say to the elderly Mr. Mercer. He had grown up in its hills and thought no part of England could be finer.

"Mrs. Mercer, we are ready to sit down to dinner. May I show you and your husband where I've placed you?"

Christine led the small crowd into the dining room, where a spread of dishes awaited them that included two tureens of soup, a plate of venison, and what looked like pike. Honoria was seated directly across from Philip, and he was able to see her animated face as she spoke to Theo. She showed no shyness as he helped her to the dish in front of her, but asked him about the textile mill she had overheard him talk about to Mr. Mercer. When Mr. Mercer dropped his knife, she leaned down to retrieve it without waiting for the footman, then made sure he had everything he needed before returning her attention to Theo.

The ladies left the gentlemen to their port following dinner. The men lingered in the dining room over the empty glasses, finally moving as a group and finishing their discussion by the door. After a few patient minutes waiting for a conversation that didn't concern him to end, Philip was the first to join the women in the drawing room. On one side of the room, Mrs. Mercer sat with Christine, holding her hand in a bolstering gesture and speaking in low tones. It seemed to Philip that she was comforting her on the loss of her mother, and he refrained from interrupting.

Honoria stood in contemplation before the massive fireplace that had enough room to roast an entire sheep, and probably had centuries earlier. She stared, unmoving, at the painting above it, and Philip stared at her, wondering what she was thinking. Just as he was about to ask, she turned to look at him, her face creasing in an inviting smile that made him take an involuntary step toward her. Behind her, the fire roared with the fresh logs that had been added, whose damp caused the flames to crackle.

A spark flew out from the fire, and Philip opened his mouth to give a word of warning for Honoria to draw away, when a burning ember fell off a log and rolled out of the fireplace. Before he could quite comprehend what was happening or have time to react, the ember touched the bottom of Honoria's skirt on the side, and a tongue of fire shot up the light cloth at terrifying speed.

Honoria shrieked when she felt the scorching heat, and Philip launched himself on her, pressing her to the floor as he threw his arms around her to break the fall. With his body covering her own, he smothered the flames of her skirt and felt the fire penetrate his own clothing to the skin. He hissed at the pain on his inner thighs and calf and pulled to the side to get a better look at her dress. The fire had only been partially extinguished, and in panic, Honoria rolled over and tried to crawl away. Philip seized her ankle to hold her, then beat the rest of the flames from her skirt with his hands.

When he saw that he had extinguished everything at last,

and that she was no longer at risk, Philip sank back, trembling. The men had heard Honoria's cry and rushed into the room, everyone speaking at once and Guinea barking and running in circles around them. But Philip and Honoria were frozen in place as they held each other's gazes, and an unspoken current passed between them. In another minute, Gus was at her side, helping her to rise. She looked at him blankly, clearly in a state of shock. Philip stood as well and faced her, and it was then that he felt the pain in his hands and legs and looked down. Honoria followed his gaze to his hands.

"You have burned yourself." She glanced up at him, her voice hollow. Her hair had come undone and waves of it fell softly around her face. "I can help you."

"Do not fret about me. Are ... are you wounded?" He did not mean to be indiscreet, but he could not help but notice where her skirt was in shreds. She followed his gaze and leaned down to part the burnt cloth and examine where her own stocking had been singed away. She turned to block his view of her leg, but he was quite certain it was an angry red.

"No." The word was spoken almost inaudibly, but she shook her head to strengthen it. "I am not injured in any significant way. You were quick to assist me." She looked at him, her gaze catching on his hands. Reaching forward, she turned his palms upwards to inspect them, her touch gentle and firm as she cradled the backs of his hands. "You appear to have sustained the worst of it. Please allow me to dress your wounds."

Philip was uncomfortable with the attention, but his hands throbbed and clamored for relief. "Very well. If you know what to do." He would not mention his legs, one of which had been burnt more badly than the other. He was not sure he would be able to bear having her touch him there.

Mrs. Mercer was laid prostrate on the reclining sofa, with her husband standing over her and fanning her face. Guinea, who had done with running around the room in the excitement, was now panting at the foot of the sofa. Christine had gone white and appeared undecided as to whether she should attend to

Honoria or Mrs. Mercer. But she broke out of her spell when Honoria turned to her, her voice still sounding hollow to Philip's ears.

"Will you have your servant bring cold water? As cold as you have. And we will need honey. And oil of rapeseed." As Christine gestured for the servant to come, Honoria added, "And clean linen strips. But the water first."

When the bucket was brought, Philip plunged his hands into the cold water. The relief was immediate, but that only brought to his awareness more acutely the pain in his thighs. Honoria hovered over him anxiously, and when he looked up at her he managed a smile.

"You must sit, Honoria. You have suffered a shock." Gus pulled a chair over to her, allowing her to remain at Philip's side. Christine had overcome her initial dismay and brought Honoria's cloak, holding it at the ready to cover her damaged skirt.

She ignored Christine's ministrations, and at Philip's side, stared into the brown wood barrel where his hands appeared stark white in the icy water. "The pain is more manageable, is it not?" He nodded, his eyes on her, and she added, "I wish it were possible to remain like this, but I shall have to put a salve on your hands, and when you remove them from the water, the pain will return."

"I can bear it."

The conversation had resumed in the room, although threads of it touched on what had just happened, with Mr. Mercer recounting an amusing anecdote in an obvious effort to lighten the mood. Theo came over to put his hand on Philip's shoulder for a brief moment, but he soon stepped back again as though fearing he might somehow make things worse. When the servant reappeared with the rest of the requested supplies, Christine hurried to take them from him.

As Honoria reached for the cloth strips, she glanced down at Philip's legs. "Oh! You are burnt here as well. But not as badly. How did I escape more serious injuries?" She turned her large eyes to him. "You must have taken it all on you."

Philip looked away. He could not hold her gaze. He shuddered to think what might have happened if he had not been there at just that moment. If he had remained with the men in the dining room ... Until a short while ago, Honoria Bassett was nothing more to him than a little friend from the village where he grew up; but now from some unfathomable place, a root of determination sprang up and cleaved his heart in two. One that proclaimed she needed and deserved to be protected. *From every ill* was the thought that flooded his mind.

She set the supplies on the floor in front of her, with the strips of linen on her lap, then looked around with a furrowed brow. "I am sorry. I forgot to say this, but I will need a clean wooden bowl and a spoon as well." Christine gestured to the servant, who rushed away again to do her bidding. Honoria gave a nervous laugh. "I must still be flustered. It is not like me to forget things."

"You are not usually the victim I think," Gus said, coming back to stand at her side.

"No. Never." She gave Gus a fleeting smile then looked down to smooth the linen strips on her lap as Philip studied the variety of emotions that flitted across her face.

The servant was back moments later, and Honoria spooned some of the honey into the clean wooden bowl, then set it down and poured in the oil, which came out quickly and spilled on her dress. She looked over at Christine, who was watching the procedure, and gave a weak smile. "The dress is ruined anyway."

Honoria stirred the salve, and bent down to tug at the remaining tights that were underneath Philip's breeches to give a clearer view of the wounds on his calf of one leg and part of his thigh on both. He was too shocked to react, as he had supposed she would tend only to his hands.

Using the spoon, she began to spread the ointment gently on his burns, and Philip didn't know where to set his gaze while she did so. He had sworn he would not let her treat his legs, but she had not asked him before she began her ministrations. It seemed the Mercers were familiar with this side of her, because they did not protest the indecency of it. Or perhaps they, too, were in shock.

His hands were submerged in the cold water and his legs burned, both from the injury and from the gentle strokes she used to cover the wound with ointment. With the same delicate touch, she wound linen strips around each leg, covering both the burns and where his stockings and the lower part of his breeches remained in place.

By the time she had knotted the cloth strips neatly, his head was spinning from the weariness following the excitement and her unexpected tenderness. He had not had anyone fuss over him since his mother had died.

"I am afraid it is time to bind your hands," she said.

He pulled them out of the water and held them, dripping, palm up in front of her. She put her hand under one of his to hold it, and again there was that gentle touch that would have stolen his breath had his hands not begun throbbing again with pain. She carefully spread the ointment over the first hand. He fought to keep from making a sound, though the touch pained him. However, she could read the expression on his face.

"I am sorry," she said, as she finished applying the ointment and began bandaging the hand. He didn't respond and she started on his other palm. He was grateful for the quiet conversation around them, as he could only focus on what she was doing and the relentless pain. He was not capable of conversation himself.

"There. Done. It should heal thoroughly. I only hope the pain will not last long. You must keep it bandaged." Honoria looked up at him, a tiny smile lighting her face. "Thank you for saving my life, Philip."

"Of course." Philip willed himself to hold her gaze, smiling at her despite the awful throbbing in his hands and now the lesser throbbing that he was aware of on his legs. "Always."

CHAPTER 6

Honoria arrived at home, her cloak covering most of the damage the fire had done to her dress. She paused outside of the drawing room, where she could hear the quiet voices of her parents, having already come to the decision that she would not tell them about the episode. When her father was a boy, he had lost a beloved sister to a fire, although Honoria knew very little about the details. He would be appalled to learn what had happened tonight. It could only bring up memories better left buried. And as he would be leaving the next day, perhaps the thought of something happening to his only daughter might cause him to cancel a trip she knew was necessary. Or he would leave with a heart full of apprehension. She would not do it.

Upon entering the drawing room, she found her parents sitting together on the sofa and enjoying their last night before her father left on his journey. Honoria smiled at the familiar sight. "I am come home. Good night, Mama. Good night, Papa."

"How was your evening?" her mother called out as she turned to leave.

"Delightful." Honoria paused at the door. "I believe I have worn myself out from all the emotion."

Her faithful maid was waiting for her near the kitchen. On the carriage ride home, Maggie had already tidied her hair and promised to dispose of the dress. Honoria had not been entirely truthful when she declared there had been no hurt done to her leg and murmured for her maid to bring honey, oil, and linen strips to her room without discussing it with others.

The skin on her leg smarted and stung, but she had not wished to expose her calf in full view of Philip and the rest of the company. In the privacy of her room, she parted the hanging tatters of her dress to examine it. A large patch of skin had turned red on her leg, and blisters had formed. Not as much as the burns on Philip's hands or legs, but enough that she would need to treat it. It would take time for the skin to heal.

A soft knock on the door was followed by Maggie poking her head in, then entering holding a bundle. "Here you are, miss. I've brought everything you require. Shall I hold the strips for you?"

Honoria shook her head. She would not like having someone hover about her when she was managing her own hurts. "Thank you, Maggie. You may retire. I will not need you."

When her maid left, Honoria went about mixing the salve, applying it before she bound her leg with practiced hands, as though the wound belonged to someone else. But after she had washed her hands and face, braided her hair, and slipped into her nightshift, she laid down and pulled the covers over her, keeping her legs in the open air because she couldn't bear even the pressure of the quilt or the heat that seemed to emanate underneath it. It was then that she began to tremble uncontrollably. Earlier that evening, in the shock of the moment, the weight of Philip's body pressed against hers, the bewildering pain she could not make sense of, she had put all fear aside. But now, alone in her room, she could not help but think what if ... what if ...

What if she had been burned worse—enough to be disfigured? What if she had died? And here she had been worrying about a ball.

Her leg pained her, but she could not toss and turn. Eventually, the fatigue of anxiety overcame her, and she was able to fall asleep. As she was drifting off, Honoria wondered whether Philip was able to sleep with the pain of his own, more serious wounds and wondered when he would be able to ride again. It was something he loved to do but now could not do so for a fortnight at least. This last thought was somewhat misty as she began to drift off to sleep—as was the idea that she knew an uncommon lot about Philip who had become all but a stranger to her in the years since he had reached adulthood.

The next day, the sight of the bright sun streaming through the trees, and the fresh smell of autumn air that crept through the window when she opened it, restored her frame of mind. She dressed quickly, the burns paining her slightly less, and went down the stairs as servants piled luggage in the entranceway.

"Papa," she called out, just as he was about to round the corner of the library and enter the drawing room. "I came to see if you needed anything before you left."

Mr. Bassett stopped in his tracks and came over, where he put his arm around her, kissing the top of her head. "No. Nothing, my dear. Just don't fall in love with anyone while I am gone. You know I want to be here to approve your suitor and chase all the rakehells away." He winked at her. "And take care of your mother, but that I know you will do."

Honoria smiled, biting back the peevish words that if he hadn't insisted on leaving for London right at this juncture, he might examine every single gentleman who stepped forward to claim her hand at the Stuff Ball. It was an unfair accusation, however. He had not chosen the timing of his trip to frustrate her.

She went outside and stood at the entrance, watching the servants pile two trunks on the back of the coach and place her father's portmanteau, a smaller trunk, and a basket of food inside the carriage. Her mother was in the drawing room, and Honoria allowed them to have their time together. After all, if it pained her to see her father go, how much more difficult must it be for her mother, who was also invalid from her rheumatism and unable to move about freely. Which reminded Honoria: she needed to collect more stinging nettle on the path near the woods. Her supply to make the infusion to alleviate her mother's pain was running low.

In a short while, Mr. Bassett came outside and gave his daughter a last hug before climbing into the coach. A servant held the iron gates open as the coachman pulled out of the courtyard and onto the main street. Honoria followed to the gate and lifted her hand as she watched his carriage go over the stone bridge of the River Bain and out of sight.

So that was that. It was never as jolly without her father at home. There was nothing like the comfort of being all together as a family. Samuel's absence she was used to, as he had gone from university to London with only a brief stay in Lincolnshire. But her father was a solid, reliable presence in their world. He had a blustery temper at times, but he loved them fiercely.

I had better seek out Mother.

Mrs. Bassett sat in her usual chair, with a blanket over her lap and a book on top of it, which she stared at with unseeing eyes. When Honoria walked into the room, her mother whisked away the expression of melancholy and assumed an air of cheerfulness. "Now it will be just the two of us. We shall have to contrive to keep ourselves occupied. What are your plans for today?"

"I have promised Philip Townsend and his cousin to bring some of the blackberry preserves," she answered, taking the chair next to her mother's. She would not mention the jar of healing ointment she planned to bring as well. "It is the least I can do when the berries belong to him, so I hope you will not forbid it."

"You have waited until your father left to ask, however," her mother observed, with a twinkle in her eye.

Honoria laughed. "I suppose I did. But really, Papa would have made a big fuss, and all for nothing. It's just preserves. It is not as though I am planning to marry the man."

"Well, as long as you have Maggie with you, I suppose it is all right," her mother replied. "I should not like to openly flout your father's authority by encouraging a friendship with Philip Townsend, but even your father will own that you've long been in the habit of spending time together whenever the Greys are here. Speaking of which, you hardly spoke two words when you came home last night. Tell me more about the dinner."

Honoria had remained firm in her conviction not to tell her mother about the mishap or her ruined dress—it would only distress her. It was challenging to smile in a way that was natural, but she made the attempt. "It was delightful to be once again in Christine and Gus's company. Philip was there, as you might guess, and his cousin Mr. Dawson as well, who has shown himself to be an agreeable gentleman. He is staying with Philip through to the Stuff Ball, and from there he will go on to visit his sister, I am told."

"It is a shame you must miss this year," sighed Mrs. Bassett. "Well, do give my regards to Philip when you see him today. Even though our families are not supposed to be on speaking terms, his mother was very dear to me. Did you find out if the Greys will be going to the ball?"

"They are undecided." Honoria allowed a frown to touch her lips. "And the Mercers have concluded they are too old to make the trip."

"A sentiment I can relate to," her mother said ruefully. "I must be twenty years their junior, but my movements are as stiff as a woman of eighty." She fingered her faded ribbon bookmark. "I have not given up all hopes of your being able to attend. Even your father has said that if we can find the right situation, perhaps you will have your fun after all. He wondered if we might apply to the Cranshaws."

But Honoria had heard that the Cranshaws would not go because Mrs. Cranshaw was in the family way. She had racked her brains but could not think of anybody else who could serve in the role of chaperone—no one that they knew well enough to ask—so she did not allow her heart to hope. It was almost enough that her father wished a solution might be found.

When she and Maggie arrived at Boden House, Honoria's gaze roamed the square brick structure with its three floors of evenly spaced windows—seven per floor. There was a stone urn holding a brown fern plant under the portico, and the front door was tucked deep into the walls of the house. She had not been to Boden since she was a small girl and their parents were still friendly. She had certainly never come on her own with only a maid in attendance. However, she had given her word, and the blackberries did belong to Philip. It would be wrong to take them all and not spare even a jar for him. Besides, she had an obligation as a healer to see how his wounds fared.

When she knocked, it was some time before a servant admitted her. It was long enough that she glanced at Maggie, keeping her criticism to herself, but Maggie's pursed lips showed she was of the same mind. The servants at Weeton Hall were irreproachable, and the staff at Boden could learn a thing or two from them. Once inside, she took in the interior at a glance, only now remembering that his house also opened into a comfortable sitting room. But unlike Farlow Manor, there were no window panes to reveal the inhabitants to any curious onlookers. Before long, Philip entered the room where she stood.

His hands were still bandaged, and when he approached her, the stiffness of his movements was barely discernible. "Honoria, you came. I was sure you would not—that your father would not permit it." He glanced at her maid. "But are you sure this is entirely correct? I have no female relative here to receive you."

"My mother has given me permission to bring you the jar of preserves I had promised," Honoria replied, her heart fluttering when she looked at his bandages, remembering what might have happened had Philip not been there—remembering the protective weight of his body on hers through her searing pain. "I thought I might see to your burns while I am here. I've brought some additional healing ointment."

Philip glanced at his hands briefly, then turned his intent gaze on her, cocking his head to one side. "And how are your own injuries?"

54

She frowned. "I told you I had none. Or none to speak of."

He folded his arms, then winced at the pressure on his hands and dropped his arms to his side. "I don't think you are telling the truth. It is impossible I would suffer burns and that you would have none."

Honoria sighed and hugged the preserves and healing ointment to her chest. "It is nothing worth mentioning, I assure you. Yours, however, will take some weeks to heal. What will you do about your horses?"

This brought his gaze up, a surprised expression in his eyes. "Why do you ask about my horses?"

"Because I know you value them, and that you love to ride and will not be able to do so with injuries to your hands and legs," she replied, her words coming out in a breathless rush. "They will need to be exercised, of course, and I am guessing Mr. Dawson will perform the office? I remember when word came that you bought your Thoroughbred stud. Even my father approved of your choice, though he is still not ready to send you a gilded invitation—unfortunately," she added with a laugh.

Philip shook his head, smiling, as Theo entered the room. "Miss Bassett, I thought I'd heard that we had visitors. What a pleasure to see you. I hope you have recovered from your ordeal last night."

Honoria held up the large jar of blackberry preserves. "I came as promised."

Mr. Dawson grinned, revealing a playful, boyish side to him. Upon closer study, he did not much resemble Philip but there was a family air. Philip had golden hair, and Mr. Dawson was darker, but they both had an aquiline nose and a firm set to their chin.

"I shall take this and save poor Philip's hands from the pain of carrying it," Mr. Dawson said. Maggie had sidled into the room behind Honoria to stand near the mantelpiece in the back, and he went to set the preserves there. "Come to think of it, I don't think he even likes blackberry preserves."

Honoria laughed as Philip shot his cousin a wry look, then

waited until he returned his gaze to hers. "Will you allow me to examine your hands?"

He hesitated, then gestured for her to follow him to a sofa in the comfortably faded sitting room. He sat across from her and put his hands on his knees, palms upward.

Honoria carefully unwrapped the linen strips that she had bound around Philip's hands the night before. The exposed skin was red and full of blisters—larger ones and more of them than what she'd suffered on her own leg. "I don't believe we should wash the wounds yet, but Mr. Dawson, if I can prevail upon you to procure some fresh linen strips, I should like to apply more salve and rewrap them."

Mr. Dawson had been staring at Philip's hands in horrified fascination, but at this he straightened and gave a nod. "I shall see that Mrs. Mason provides us with what is needed."

He left the room, and as the seconds ticked by in silence, Honoria cradled the backs of Philip's hands as she examined the skin and tried to ascertain the seriousness of the burns. When she looked up and met his gaze, there was something in his look that confused her, so she slipped her hands from underneath his and sat back. "I must see to your legs as well."

Philip shook his head firmly. "My legs are perfectly fine. There is no need to examine them again. The wounds are likely not much worse than your own."

"Nevertheless, the bandages should be changed just like the ones on your hands," Honoria insisted.

Philip gave her a cutting look. "As you can see, I am wearing breeches over the bandages. Would you have me stand and take them off?"

Honoria presumed he was trying to embarrass her, but when it came to healing, she did not get embarrassed. "I suppose the buttons would be difficult to manage with your hands as they are. I can wait while you call your valet and have him attend to you."

She glanced up and saw the slightest flush on Philip's cheeks. "I employ no valet. And I have no intention of removing my breeches. You will have to content yourself with healing my hands." Mr. Dawson walked in carrying strips of linen, and he stopped short at Philip's words, a look of astonishment on his face. If anything, Philip only grew more red.

"Stubborn man," Honoria said to no one but herself. Let Mr. Dawson make what he might of that statement.

"Only stubborn about certain things," she heard Philip retort under his breath.

Mr. Dawson stepped forward with the strips of cloth. "It was not as difficult to find Mrs. Mason as I feared it might be, and to my surprise she was able to hand over what was needed. Here you are, Miss Bassett."

Just as she had the night before, Honoria lay the strips over her skirt. She applied fresh salve, before carefully binding his hands in such a way that was protective but not overly tight. "Would you have a pair of scissors nearby?"

His hands held captive in hers, Philip gestured with his chin toward the writing desk. "In there."

Mr. Dawson went to retrieve a pair of scissors that ended up being as dull as any she had ever used, and she sawed at the excess cloth until she was able to cut it. "Well, the bandage is not as neat as I should like it to look, but it will do. The important thing is to keep the wound from becoming infected."

"Let us hope it will not come to that," Mr. Dawson replied.

Honoria stood and caught Maggie's eye. "I shall leave you now. I hope you enjoy the blackberry preserves. If there are any problems with the bandages, you must send word and I will come immediately."

Philip stood when Honoria did, and he accompanied her to the door, allowing Maggie to exit first. Honoria turned to face him, and he lifted his hands revealing the bandages she had just tied. "Thank you, Honoria."

The sound of her Christian name on his lips sparked a strange sensation inside of her—like that of falling. She couldn't make sense of it, especially since he had said her name before throughout the years they had known each other. It was certainly not the wild heart-fluttering she had with Gus, so it couldn't be any kind of infatuation. It must simply be attributed to the leftover sentiments of a shared moment that had been fraught with danger. She smiled and answered him with a simple nod before slipping out the door.

CHAPTER 7

"I 'll bring the jam to the kitchen," Philip said when the door closed behind Honoria. He went over to the mantelpiece to take it, balancing it carefully between his chest and the part of his left hand that smarted less. He had an unexplainable urge to be alone with his thoughts, and as he descended the stairs, tried to sort out why his mind seemed wrapped in wool regarding Honoria. It was as though there was a thought he was meant to pull out and examine, but it was too elusive, and this metaphorical veil blinded him to any very concise idea, except an overall awareness of her loveliness.

His burns pained him. Honoria had not provided him with any further treatment to soothe the pain, but it wasn't his wounds distracting him. It had been that gentle way she had of cradling his hands in hers as she examined them—the efficient manner she had of bandaging the injury. Her touch was calming, and the sensation of being taken care of was not one he was used to. He found he quite liked it.

Had his mother been so tender? He could not remember, and as he had never had a sister, he could not say if this was characteristic of the female sex or something particular to Honoria. If her father had not held on to his aversion for Philip's family, she could have been a sort of sister to him—although he could not claim the direction of his thoughts to be brotherly. Her request that he remove his breeches was outside of enough, her skill in healing notwithstanding.

When Philip returned to the sitting room, Theo threw down the newspaper he had been reading and got to his feet. "Let us take your chestnuts out with the tilbury and give them some exercise. We can then see how your men are getting on with digging the canal."

"A capital idea," Philip said with a cheer that sounded forced to his own ears. He needed to clear his head. "I must thank you for exercising Crown Glory this morning. Your visit was timely in more ways than one, since you are able to do all I cannot. If only you had brought me your sister, all would've been perfect."

Theo smirked in response. "I am beginning to think it was providential my sister did not come. This lack of a ready house-keeper is forcing you to realize it is time to settle down."

"This again?" Earlier, Philip had thrown his hat on the side table, and he went now to pick it up. He pushed it down on his head with a pat, then gritted his teeth. Clearly, he needed more than bandages to remember that his hands would not be healed for some time. "Your insistence is beginning to be tiresome. Let us talk instead of *your* settling down."

"There is no urgency. *I* don't need to run an estate," Theo shot back cheerfully. "Perhaps you should hire more servants to prepare the house for the eventuality of a permanent mistress? Who knows? If Miss Bassett does not catch your fancy—and I'm not entirely sure she does not; after all, rescuing a damsel in real distress is a quicker path to love than many a ball and stilted drawing room conversation—nevertheless, if you are determined to remain blind, then surely some other woman will catch your eye. Perhaps at the Stuff Ball."

Philip was eager to change the course of this exchange, but there was truth in one thing at least. "Yes, I need to see about hiring servants, and as poor as the estate is, it does have the funds for one or two more, at least. But servants require someone to give them direction. And I am not confident in Mrs.

Mason's capacity for the role. She can barely see to her own duties."

An indignant squawk rose from the stairwell, and Philip knew his words had carried beyond his intention. It was his luck, of course, that Mrs. Mason would have been within earshot when his tongue was ill guarded. "Come. Let us go to the stables."

Theo allowed the conversation to turn to indifferent matters as they had the tilbury readied with Thunder and True harnessed, and he took the reins. Philip climbed in, using his hands as little as possible. He would have been frustrated at the pain and his lack of ability to drive were it not for the fact that he had managed to save Honoria. Every time he suffered from the burns, he remembered that.

"All this talk of my finding a wife," Philip said as they drove in the direction of the river. He narrowed his eyes and glanced at his cousin before bringing it back to the project visible in the distance. "You're not bored and inventing an excuse to leave early, are you? You've been here less than a fortnight."

It had only taken that first day with Theo, talking late into the night about the irrigation project, for Philip to decide it was time to begin. After all, they had quite a stretch to dig before the ground froze and made the work impossible. His solicitor recommended a young man by the name of John Coates as engineer, and it had been easy to find men who were looking for work, including a navvy who specialized in digging canals of more consequence than his. In just a few days, they had dug a stretch of an eighth of a mile alongside the road that ran parallel to the river and had already installed two basins that would serve as dikes. The pipes under the road that permitted the river water to enter the canal would be put in last. Coates had given instructions for gates to be inserted into the dikes to prevent the canal from overflowing. Philip wanted a certain amount of surface water to keep the soil moist, but he had no wish for it to revert back to the swampy fenland it once was.

"Bored? No. It is a little slow here," Theo admitted, his

61

friendly smile removing all offense. "As much as I enjoy our late-night card games and those few times we've gone out shooting with Gus, life in Horncastle moves at a slower rhythm than I am accustomed to. However, it does suit me, both the lifestyle and the society. I wouldn't mind another night such as the one we had at the Greys. Well, I suppose except for Miss Bassett catching fire."

Philip shuddered at the memory, and brought the conversation along more pleasant lines. "Maybe you should move here."

"Someone has to run the family mill, and if I passed the task off to my brother, even supposing he wished to do it, I would have nothing to live on." Theo's voice lost its light tone, and Philip wondered how suited his cousin was to the mill his father had bequeathed to him. But his brother, Anthony, was young still, with another year of school ahead of him and what Theo said was true besides. A man needed something to live on.

Philip dropped his gaze to his neatly tied bandages. "Society *is* pleasant in Horncastle, although I have known most of them my entire life, except for this elusive Mrs. Northwick we have yet to meet. From what I gather, not even Gus has managed to win an introduction to the widow."

"They've made progress," Theo said.

Philip pinched his brows in confusion at Theo's reply until he realized his cousin was looking ahead at the start of the canal they were quickly approaching. The workers had indeed made progress. He would have to measure, but it looked to be as long as a quarter of a mile by now. In the distance, faint shovelfuls of earth flew from where the men dug. "I do believe I will have a field ready for planting as early as spring."

"I believe so. Shame I won't be here to see the water diverted into the canals," Theo said, laughing suddenly. "Your country ways are rubbing off on me. At my father's mill, I stand about while the steam engines clatter and cotton floats. As much as I am born and bred to textiles, what I wouldn't give to spend more time outdoors in the open country."

Philip shook his head with a grin. "So not quite as slow as you claim."

"Only slow where the absence of the fairer sex makes—"

"Ah, look. There's Mr. Mercer." Philip was out of the carriage as soon as it had come to a stop. The gentleman had come to measure the progress at Philip's request, and he went over to him now.

"How good of you to come, sir. Has Mr. Reid given you his opinion yet on how much the diversion will affect downstream?" Both Mr. Mercer and Mr. Reid were gentlemen farmers with land on the edge of the Wolds, and they had served Philip as advisors and father figures since he'd begun to take an active hand in his estate. Mr. Reid, in particular, had experience in irrigation methods.

Mr. Mercer lifted his hat to Theo, who was sitting on the tilbury. "Afternoon, Dawson. Philip. Burns healing all right?" At Philip's nod, he turned his gaze back to the men working on the canal. "You say the land on the other side of the public road is yours as well?"

"Yes, up through to where it meets Mr. Bassett's woods. When my ancestor acquired the land, he bought it with the public road already in place. My property extends to the river but no farther."

"I crossed paths with Reid yesterday, and he plans to pay you a visit, but he's busy at present. After coming to see the project, he's confident your man, Coates, knows his work," Mr. Mercer said. "The basins and the dikes you're putting in place are not overly deep, which will prevent too much of the river water from being diverted. Therefore, it should not greatly affect things upstream." Mr. Mercer stepped back to allow a man to push a wheelbarrow past their group. "This was an ambitious project, but it seems it will work. However did you come up with the idea?"

Philip looked down, unable to hide his smile of satisfaction. "I fell into conversation with a gentleman from Spalding when I was in London last year. He explained how he had created a system like this for one of his fields that was prone to drought, and I realized that something like that might work with mine. I only wished to have your advice to be sure I would not be doing something that risked changing the landscape or weakening the river's current."

"But you did not wait for our advice before beginning to dig," Mr. Mercer said in a dry tone that masked humor.

"I had not time to waste," he replied as Theo hopped down from the tilbury to join them.

"Ah, the impetuousness of youth." Mr. Mercer chuckled.

"I would not have begun diverting the water without hearing both your and Mr. Reid's opinions." Philip looked ahead and squinted against the sunlight. "Mr. Mercer, you will have to excuse me. I fear they are digging at an angle rather than removing that thick brush."

He went over to speak to Coates, who explained that he trusted the advice of Tom Hull, the older man of bent, wiry stature, who had been a career navvy but could no longer do the hard work of digging the large navigation canals. He led Philip over to where the tangled knot of roots lay visible in the trench. "He tells me the canal walls will hold better if we deviate rather than uproot."

"Ay." After this monosyllabic confirmation, Hull hurried over to pull a wagonload of dirt that workers were pushing up a makeshift ramp. Philip stayed to see the progress until Mr. Mercer arrived at his side with Theo and proposed they come by and taste Mrs. Mercer's shortbread.

The following day, he and Theo were just finishing their breakfast when Gus appeared in the dining room, either having been let in or taken it upon himself to enter. "You'll both be attending the Stuff Ball in Lincoln, is that not so?" he asked without preamble, taking a seat at the table and reaching for the pitcher of ale.

"Yes, both of us. Why—are you?" Philip had assumed Gus would not attend because of his recent period of mourning and return to Horncastle.

Theo, lounging in a chair with his boot on the wooden footrest of the table, tugged off a cluster of grapes from its stem and popped one into his mouth before responding. "Following the trip to Lincoln, I'm trying to convince Philip here to accompany me to visit my sister in Leicester. I'm sure there's room for another if you'd like to join us."

"Well, I do think I will take my sister to the ball because she's pining to go. But it would not be wise for me to stay away from Horncastle for too long. The few tenants I have seem to have forgotten my existence." Having finished his ale, Gus leaned back and crossed his legs in front of him. "A quick jaunt to Lincoln should not be problematic, and I own to having my own reasons for wishing to attend the ball."

Theo lifted an eyebrow. "The widow?"

Gus laughed. "Perhaps. It has been some time since my prospects for pleasure have been anything but to frequent watering holes packed with aged residents. I'm finding any company under the age of thirty to be attractive."

Before he could think better of it, Philip was pushed by an internal impulse to ask, "What do you think of Honoria?"

Gus turned confused eyes on him, and Philip realized that after such a sudden question he would need to elaborate, though he did not wish to betray what he suspected—that Honoria's heart was for the taking if Gus was interested.

"Well, she is your sister's closest friend, and I imagine she must be continually at your house. Have you ever considered her?" Philip asked. It seemed the room had taken on a strange tension once the question was out, but Philip thought it might only be from how interested he was in the answer. Perhaps it betrayed something in himself.

Gus shrugged at last. "I don't know. She's a pretty little thing. Perhaps she has some odd notions, but to be honest, I've never really thought much about her in that way."

"Odd notions?" Philip raised an eyebrow. "There's nothing odd about her."

"I suppose not." Gus was silent for a minute and picked at

65

the fringe on the arm chair. "She traipses about town on errands of what she calls healing. A woman practicing any form of medicine is not something I can recommend. She'd best leave that to the sawbones. And truth be told, I've had enough *healing* to last a lifetime in Bath."

Philip suffered a prick of annoyance. "Her healing came in handy when I was covered with burns."

Theo, likely recognizing from Philip's tone that he was about to say something provoking, hastily interrupted. "You said you've come with an invitation?"

"Ah, yes." Gus sat upright. "Why don't we set out for Lincoln together? We can stop along the way for a picnic. Christine was very keen on the idea when I suggested it." Gus didn't seem to have noticed Philip's irritation and grinned with no hint of self-consciousness. "Mrs. Northwick will be going apparently, and I thought we might invite her to join us as well. After getting an introduction to the widow from Mrs. Reid, I've not found any way to further our acquaintance. This picnic could be just the thing."

"A capital idea," Theo replied, glancing at Philip.

Philip suspected that Gus's interest in traveling caravan lay in the widow rather than in their own company. "With my burns still healing, I cannot ride with you. But there is no reason we can't travel together. Theo, you'll need your horse in any case. I'll take the carriage, and have Jim drive."

"Well, that's that, then." Gus slapped his hands on the table and stood. "Fishing anyone?"

Theo looked at Philip and shrugged. "Why not?"

Two weeks before they were to set out for Lincoln, Philip and Theo went by to invite Gus for a game of cards. Christine opened the door and stepped back, allowing them to enter.

"I am to understand that we will travel to Lincoln together,"

Theo said, bowing his greeting. Christine smiled and answered with a nod.

"It will make for a merry party, will it not?" As soon as the words left Philip's lips, Honoria entered the room from the corridor that led to the kitchen and service rooms behind. She was carrying a bundle of simple ivory cotton and had three pins pinched between her lips. Her eyes immediately sought out Philip's bandages, which gave him a jolt of recollected pain that mingled with his pleasure and surprise at seeing her.

Honoria removed the pins from her lips and tucked them into the cloth. "I have been wishing to visit you and see about the burns, but I did not dare come again without an invitation." She smiled up at him, and it struck a soft blow to his heart making him temporarily forget the pain.

"You need not wait for one," Philip replied with such promptness that it was followed by a flash of embarrassment. He had sounded too eager and was sure everyone would notice. He forced his voice to deepen when he added, "I must ask you for the measures of that ointment you put on my hands so I might have some more made up."

"May I take a look to see how they are healing now?"

Philip made a show of reluctance, but he was anxious for her to take his hands in hers once again and soon agreed. They moved to a set of chairs on the side of the room while Theo drew Christine into conversation about what sorts of improvements they were making at Farlow, pulling her out of herself with all the ease of a man who was genuinely interested in others.

Honoria carefully unwrapped the bandages and studied the injuries while Philip studied her. She scrunched her nose in concentration and he watched, fascinated at the changes in her expression. At last, she shook her head. "It's not healing the way I had hoped. Does it still pain you?"

"Not overly much," Philip said carefully. It still pained him, but as he did not know how long such a wound generally hurt, he could not say if it was in the realm of normal or not.

Honoria looked up at him and the little frown between her

eyes did not disappear. "You needn't put on a front with me. I fear there might be an infection forming. I will clean it now and reapply more salve, but if it still pains you in two days, I believe you should send for Mr. Blackwell."

"If you think it necessary."

Gus walked into the room, and as Honoria's back was to him, she did not yet notice. "I'm just going to make up some salve and fetch water and clean linens so that I might bind it again." She released his hands and stood, turning and coming flush up against Gus.

"Playing doctor again, Honoria?" Gus took her hand in his, and from where Philip sat, he had a clear view of them both. Honoria's expression was conflicted between joy at his taking her hand and annoyance at his dismissive comment.

"Has Christine told you of our plan? The idea to ride to Lincoln with Phil and Theo and stop for lunch?" Gus released her fingers and winked at Philip.

Honoria pasted on a smile. "Yes, it sounds most diverting. It is a shame I cannot join you."

"Ah, is that so? Indeed a shame." Gus lifted his hand to greet Theo before turning back to her. "Well, let me not keep you from tending to poor Philip here."

Philip had not realized she would not be attending the ball. The prospect of going seemed to dim with the news. And why had he never noticed how dense his friend was when it came to women? Gus said all the wrong things.

"Right." After a brief conference with Christine, Honoria slipped away to fetch what was needed.

Gus took the seat she had been occupying, crossing one leg over the other. "I believe we did the right thing by proposing this picnic. Now I just need to pay a visit to Mrs. Northwick to see if she will join us."

"I understand she has her brother-in-law to look out for her. I am not sure she will require our escort." For the first time in his friendship with Gus, Philip's voice held a sharp edge.

Gus dismissed the brother-in-law with a shrug. "I'm sure he

will be keen to join us as well. Perhaps he will wish to play the gallant to Christine. In any case, we cannot let a small issue like that prevent us from attempting the plan. I can just see it now. The pretty widow settled with us on the blanket, taking grapes from my fingers—"

"I will need my chair back." Honoria had returned with the linen and other supplies, and her voice was clipped.

Gus got up without a word, then glanced at Philip's open wound. "That is looking ugly. Perhaps you should get it looked at."

When he left to join Theo and Christine, Philip leaned in to murmur, "I would trust any wound in your care. Don't listen to Gus."

"He treats me like a little sister, but I am a woman grown." Honoria's obvious irritation did not extend to her ministrations which were exceedingly gentle. Philip had difficulty concentrating with the delicate way she washed and dried the wounds, applied the salve, and held his fingers as she began to wind the strips around them. "And I am very good at healing. Even Mr. Blackwell said so."

"You are," Philip agreed. He waited in silence while she finished wrapping the linen, and this time she had sharp scissors to trim the edges. She tied a knot and tucked the ends into the bandage. "Why are you not attending the ball?"

Honoria darted a glance up at him, then gave a sad shrug. "My mother is not well enough to go, and my father and brother are not here to accompany me."

"It's a shame. I should have liked to dance with you."

She met his gaze for a long moment, and although it seemed his words had brought her pleasure, he could see her thoughts were divided and that part of them she kept hidden from him. "I would have liked that."

CHAPTER 8

Honoria entered the drawing room carrying a small basket of almond biscuits, covered by a white cloth, which Mrs. Sands had just finished baking. "Mama, I have decided to visit Arabella Northwick. Might I have your permission?"

Mrs. Bassett stood beside her chair, one hand on the armrest and the other holding her lower back. "Of course you may go." Her voice was thick with pain.

"Oh! You are standing with no one here to help you." Honoria rushed forward, irritated with herself for not having come to check on her mother earlier. Grasping her arm, she led her back to her chair. "Did you not ring? I would have come to you had I heard something."

Her mother sank into the chair and paused for a moment to catch her breath. "I did not wish to disturb anyone. My book was just out of reach, but I thought it not so far I could not manage. Perkins forgot to hand it to me when she assisted me earlier, and she is now laid up with a headache." Mrs. Bassett leaned back and closed her eyes. "It is troublesome not to be able to move about freely, but please don't let my pain hinder you from your visit. Mrs. Northwick will be delighted to receive you, I am sure."

Honoria pulled back to look at her mother and bit her lip, thinking for a moment. "I will just fetch you some nettle tea before I leave, and make sure Perkins has some headache powder. I hope the infusion will make you more comfortable. I have harvested as much nettle as I could find and now have it drying. There should be enough to last us through the winter."

Without waiting for an answer, she hurried off to ask the cook to put water on to boil, and after bringing some headache powder to Perkins, brought the medicinal drink to her mother. "I'd like to see if I can make this into a salve as well—one that won't sting. I will try that later tonight, and we can put it on your knee first to see if there is any improvement before we attempt it on your hands." Honoria leaned down and kissed her mother on the cheek, then went over to retrieve her basket.

"See that you bring Maggie with you. It's farther than most of your visits, and even if it is a countryside you know well, you must not go unescorted."

"Yes, Mama." Honoria went outdoors where Maggie was already waiting for her, her thoughts dwelling on her mother's condition. Her boots crunched on the gravel as her mind calculated how long she should steep the nettle to retain its healing powers while entirely removing the portion that stung. This thought naturally led her to wonder how Philip fared and if his wounds had started to dull in pain the way hers had. She hoped he had taken her advice and consulted the doctor. Maggie followed her in silence to the stables.

"You've had the carriage harnessed, Jeffrey. Well done. This will save us time." She handed her basket to her maid and climbed into the small covered carriage. Maggie entered and pulled the door closed behind her as the footman leapt onto the driver's seat and clicked for the horses to move forward. Honoria settled in for their forty-minute ride.

They had ridden over the bridge and into the countryside when the sound of hoofbeats galloping to overtake the carriage reached her. The village was small enough that she could not resist peering through the window to see who it was. A bolt of

71

excitement shot through her, and before she could think the better of it, she called out.

"Gus!"

The noise of the wheels on the road drowned her voice and he didn't turn, so she leaned out of the window and called again.

"Augustus!"

Gus had been on the point of veering away from the public road to cross the open stretch of land that accessed the Waring River on the other side of it. Having at last registered his name, he wheeled his horse toward her carriage, and she called out for the servant to stop the coach while she waited for him to approach.

"Honoria, you little minx. What are you doing calling out after gentlemen on a public road? When are you going to act like the young lady you are?" His face was creased in a teasing smile, but his words bit. She couldn't help it if her pleasure at seeing him led her to yell out his name. And she *was* a woman. He had only to open his eyes and see that her dress fit her quite differently than it had when he lived here three years ago.

She refused to let her mood be cast down. "Well, Mr. Grey. When you and I have been in the habit of riding around the country together for as long as I've known how to ride, one occasionally forgets. But you are glad to see me, are you not?"

"Of course! I'm always glad to see you." He glanced over his shoulder at the river. "I am to meet Philip and Theo for some fishing. Where are you going?"

"I'm to visit Mrs. Northwick," she said, watching his face for a reaction. If she had hoped to see none, she was disappointed. He turned his horse more fully toward the carriage and peered in at her.

"Oh, *are* you now? I wish I might go with you. I don't suppose ..." He screwed up his handsome face as he thought. "No, it wouldn't do. You and I are not related, and I should not visit her without receiving some encouragement. Do you think she might attend the little dance party the Flynns will have next week?"

72

Honoria strove for a pleasant tone. "I am not sure she has been invited, but I will see if Mrs. Flynn has sent her an invitation before I bring up the party to Arabella."

"Arabella? Why—you two are on intimate terms. What is a mature widow doing with a chit like you?" He grinned at her, and she could not resist the urge to respond.

"I'll have you know that I am a whole year *older* than she is." Honoria knew her face was flushed with indignation, and it frustrated her that this evidence of her feelings was not something she could control.

He raised his brows, whistling. "Are you? Well, one would never guess it." He looked back over his shoulder again. "I must leave you now. Do me a favor and tell Mrs. Northwick I send my regards." He didn't wait for a response but tipped his hat before turning his horse toward the river.

Honoria would not pass on his regards. She pressed her lips together to keep her resentment from boiling over into hasty words. Maggie said it for her anyway. "He 'us allays looking out for himself, he is. Handsome though he be," she amended.

Their carriage started forward again, and Honoria reflected that he had not always looked out for himself. She didn't think he had been so self-absorbed when they were younger, although perhaps she had just been naive. But no, whatever he had given as little gifts to his sister, he had given to her as well, though they were of no relation. And he had always shown interest when he spoke to her, although he did not seem to do so as much now. But those memories made it difficult to give him up, although he gave her little enough hope. There was still a chance his eyes would be opened toward her, and that when it happened, it would change him.

Her carriage pulled through the tall iron gates into the courtyard where Arabella lived, past a sign that labeled it as Penwood Estate. The beige stone house stretched ten windows across. Its façade would have been impressive enough, but as a square structure with windows on all sides, it was imposing. Abutting one end was a small row of houses Honoria assumed were for the servants. The gardens in the front of the stone arch and to the right of it were kept up admirably, although there was little activity of gardeners or servants bustling about. Honoria sent Jeffrey to find the carriage house, which was most likely through the brick archway to the left, then walked with Maggie up to the front door and knocked.

As she waited, a crunch of boots on the small yellow stones sounded behind her. She turned to see a gentleman approaching, dressed in modish attire with gleaming top boots and a rifle-green coat. His clothing was particularly fashionable for Lincolnshire, and she wondered how she must appear to him. She suppressed the unconscious urge to tuck her hair more precisely under her bonnet and began to wish she had worn one of her better dresses. It was not often she had a chance to impress a handsome man who had not known her from the cradle.

"Good afternoon, miss. George Northwick at your service." He bowed then started up the steps toward her, his lips pulled up in a friendly smile.

Honoria curtsied. "Honoria Bassett. Mrs. Northwick is not expecting me, but we are newly acquainted and I wished to pay her a visit." She stopped short of asking whether Arabella was in. Although he must surely be her brother-in-law, she could not imagine that he could be on overly intimate terms with the widow when he could not be much more than ten years her senior. It would not be seemly. Arabella had said he was staying at the dower house.

The door opened and they both turned to face it. Inside, the housekeeper glanced at Honoria and curtsied. "I beg your pardon, miss. The footman was called away." She then saw Mr. Northwick and curtsied to him as well before returning her gaze to Honoria.

"I am Miss Honoria Bassett. Mrs. Northwick knows me, but here is my card."

"Yes, miss. I will announce your visit." The housekeeper paused to look at Mr. Northwick.

"Do that. You may inform her I will not be staying long," Mr. Northwick said as though her words had been meant for him. The housekeeper turned to enter the drawing room, leaving them to wait just inside the entryway. "I like to come over at least once a day to ensure that Arabella has everything she needs."

"I understand." Honoria stood quietly, unsure of what to say next. It was rare that she was at a loss for words, especially mere pleasantries, and she could not tell if her reticence was due to his being a stranger or because she found him a particularly intimidating stranger. He was certainly an attractive one. She glanced behind her at Maggie.

She ought to say something in reply. "Where do you come from?"

"My brother and I were originally from Norfolk—a bit like our name, I suppose." Mr. Northwick laughed, turning his clear eyes to her, and she fought the urge to look away. That would reveal her disquiet too readily. "Josiah was my father's firstborn, and I was born to my father's third wife, so although we are the only two, there was a great difference in age between us. He bought this property with the intention of setting up residence before passing it on to his heir, but fate had another plan."

"I am sorry," Honoria murmured.

The housekeeper returned. "Mrs. Northwick will see you now."

Honoria turned to follow her, sticking close to Maggie as Mr. Northwick trailed behind. The back of her neck tingled in awareness of his proximity. When they entered the drawing room, this sensation gave way to frank admiration of what was before her. The tall ceilings drew the eye upward, and the room itself was lavishly decorated, with gilded frames on the wall, a mounted pheasant on a side table whose long tail balanced in the air, and a collection of sofas and chairs in the middle. The fireplace on one wall was framed with decorative blue and white Dutch tiles.

"Honoria, what a pleasant surprise it is to receive your visit."

Arabella stood from where she had been seated on the sofa and walked over to greet her. She was as warm as she had been when paying the Bassetts a visit, but there was a reserve to her now that had not been there before. "George." She nodded at her brother-in-law with less warmth, then gestured for both to sit.

After they had all taken their seats, with Mr. Northwick claiming a spot on the sofa where Arabella sat, she turned to Honoria. "I feared that the distance might be off-putting for a spontaneous visit, so I can't tell you how glad I am to receive you. I had just been considering the idea of sending you a formal invitation."

"I am not bothered by a bit of distance," Honoria assured her. "I did wish to see how you got on."

"So kind of you," Arabella murmured. "I have everything I wish for, now that my son David has arrived with his nurse." She did not look at her brother-in-law as she spoke, and Honoria feared that they were excluding him from their conversation.

"That is splendid news. May I meet him?" She turned slightly to include Mr. Northwick, but the gesture was in vain as Arabella continued to avoid her brother-in-law's eyes.

"I believe he will have woken from his nap by now. I will ring for a servant to tell Nurse to bring him to us." Arabella got to her feet, and Mr. Northwick stood as well.

"I will just greet my nephew and then leave you. I came for that purpose." He smiled, but Arabella only met this gambit with a slight curve of her lips which quickly disappeared—a smile, it seemed—to keep him at arm's length. Of course, Arabella could not marry her deceased husband's brother, but he would surely prove himself useful to her. Why did she not warm to him?

It would have simplified matters if Gus had known she were not available, Honoria thought with an inward sigh.

Arabella went to the bellpull and when the servant came, conferred with her. A short while later, the nurse appeared carrying a little blond boy who could not have been more than a year old. He tucked his head into the nurse's neck, apparently still sleepy. Arabella went to reach for him, and with visible reluctance the nurse handed him over.

"He is a darling," Honoria said. She would have gone over and slipped her finger into the tiny hand curled into a fist, had Mr. Northwick not moved closer to Arabella and reached over to pat the child. The gesture seemed perfectly natural for an uncle to his nephew, but his proximity was perhaps overly familiar for his dead brother's wife. Arabella shifted away, almost imperceptibly.

After exchanging a few more commonalities and having satisfied himself that his nephew was well, Mr. Northwick took his leave. A silence settled in his absence before Arabella turned to the nurse. "Mrs. Billings, I will call you if I need you." The nurse frowned in response but nodded and left the room.

Now alone, Honoria went to sit beside Arabella and reached out her hands for the boy. "May I? Just for a moment? I adore babies."

Arabella smiled and handed David over, pulling at the bottom of the dress that covered his chubby legs. Honoria could not resist planting a kiss on top of the sweet boy's head as he reached up to pull on a chain necklace she wore.

"It seemed to me that—"

"Do be careful—" Arabella said reaching for her baby's hands to free the necklace.

They both stopped and looked at each other with a smile, and it was Honoria who spoke first. "Do not worry. My necklace is sturdy and will not break." She breathed in through her nose before continuing. "I could not help but notice that you appear more ill at ease when Mr. Northwick is nearby."

"Oh! I ..." Arabella seemed at a loss for words, and she absently straightened the baby's bonnet. "Mr. Northwick is all that is good. I must be thankful for the care he has taken of me and David since my husband's death."

Honoria nodded and remained silent. It was not very convincing, but she could not force a confidence. A lull appeared in the conversation as she attempted to think of a new thread of discussion, but Arabella spoke again.

"I just do not wish for our names to be too closely linked together. I suppose that is silly of me since we share a name, but as a widow, and particularly a young widow, I cannot be too careful. George does not seem to regard the risk in the same light, and I find I must keep him at arm's length."

"I understand." Honoria did not know how she could help, as it seemed a complex issue and she had not even the wisdom that came from being married. She wished she could offer something more than platitudes.

David began to cry, and when Arabella could not console him, she rang for his nurse to come. After he had been taken away and the widow ordered tea, Honoria remembered the biscuits her maid had handed her before going to the kitchen. They took tea together, and Arabella exclaimed over how light the almond biscuits were, but Honoria did not stay for any great length of time. Something in Arabella seemed to have deflated after Mr. Northwick's departure as though he had left a burden of constraint behind. Honoria's presence felt like an invasion of the widow's privacy.

CHAPTER 9

A broad swath of finely woven Lincoln wool, dyed a rich olive green, was spread across Honoria's herringbone wood floor. She and Christine knelt in an unladylike manner on the floor beside it as they discussed how to lay the pieces of pattern in such a way as to ensure the cloth had a consistent sheen throughout the entire gown. The dress was for Christine, and although they had sewn the lining, they had yet to tackle the most difficult part.

"If you move this pattern piece to this corner, you will be able to fit both of those pieces on the larger area." Honoria showed her what she meant and sat back and watched as Christine began to pin them in place. "My gown was nearly finished. There were only the rest of the glass beads to be added and the hooks in the back."

"I do wish you were able to come. As much as I long to see our old friends at the ball, it will not be as amusing, or as comfortable, without you. There"—Christine searched the floor around her—"we are ready to begin cutting."

Honoria handed her the scissors. "I suppose Gus will meet some enchanting heiress and fall in love at first sight."

Christine did not look up from her labor. "Gus is the wrong

match for you. I haven't changed my mind on that count in our years away—as much as I would like to have you as my sister."

"You are just blinded to the idea of a match because we are both familiar to you. But marriages in the context of what is familiar are the very best."

There was only the sound of the scissors cleaving bits of cloth in neat strokes until Christine was ready to say more. "A match where a lady must throw herself at a man's feet in order to gain his notice is far from the very best."

A resounding knock from the front entrance interrupted this unpleasant truth, and Honoria leapt to her feet and went to answer the door herself. Before she exited the room, she leaned back in to say, "One day you will fall in love, and I will be much more supportive than you have been to me."

Christine sat back on her heels and regarded her in full sincerity. "Honoria, I am truly on your side. Even more so than I am my brother's side. I want for you someone who deserves you." Honoria did not respond, but the truth in her friend's words needled.

The footman was coming from the dining hall at just the same time, but she waved him away. "I will answer it. Be so good as to have Cook make up a tray of tea and some of the short-bread she made earlier and bring that to us." She opened the door and discovered Arabella waiting on the other side of it in a dress of mazarine blue wool. Her expression was a mix of dimpled pleasure and shyness.

Honoria opened the door wider, stepping back with a smile. "What splendid timing. Do come in and meet my friend Christine Grey. She has only heard of you until now, although I understand you have already been introduced to her brother."

The crease in Arabella's brow lightened at Honoria's welcome, and she stepped in. "I had been hoping to find you at home and that you might not be occupied. I did not expect the additional pleasure of meeting someone new from the village. My acquaintances here are still so limited. Her brother—is Miss Grey related to Mr. Augustus Grey?"

"Christine is Gus's sister," Honoria replied, watching Arabella carefully. She was piqued at herself for the jealous feelings that arose, but Arabella showed little reaction to the news.

"Is your mother at home?" she asked as she followed Honoria through the library and back into the drawing room.

"You will always find my mother at home," Honoria said. "Today she has been feeling well and is walking in the garden with the help of her maid. Well—her maid and a darling little cane my father had sculpted for her for when he's not here to lend his hand."

"How thoughtful." Arabella's expression was wistful. "I am happy to hear she is doing so well."

Christine had removed herself from the floor and was now seated on the sofa. The green cloth was carefully folded with the remaining patterns pinned in place and set beside her. The cut cloth had been bundled and put on the table.

"This is Miss Christine Grey. Christine, I'd like to present you to Mrs. Arabella Northwick, and if you are both in agreement, I propose we use Christian names."

Christine stood and curtsied. "It's a pleasure."

"Delighted," Arabella said with a friendly smile as she returned the curtsy. She then looked over at the material folded on the sofa cushion. "I imagine this must be for the Stuff Ball considering its color. Is this for you?"

Christine glanced at Honoria. "It is. I had not intended to go as we are not so long out of full mourning, but the event does fall around the time when I had intended to put off my blacks. I believe with this dark of a green, we shall be observing correct half-mourning. Of course, we shall not dance. Or...at least I will not. I cannot answer for my brother."

"You are echoing my own thoughts," Arabella replied. "A year has come and gone, but I have found the black clothing a comfort until now and have not wished for anything more colorful. I've contemplated attending the ball only because the color is not too shocking a departure from black. I managed to have a dress made up that is both pretty and discreet."

Honoria gave a resigned smile. "As we were discussing when you arrived, the only thing missing in all this delight is my own participation. I have finally accepted that I will not be able to go, and I'm deriving a somewhat"—she let out a feeble laugh—"unsatisfactory pleasure in assisting Christine with her dress since there is no point in finishing my own."

"*Hm.*" Arabella reached down to finger the fabric. "The texture of this cloth is quite nice. Honoria, the Stuff Ball is actually what I came to speak to you about."

Sensing that there might be exciting news afoot, Honoria gestured to the chairs and sofa. "Please, do let us sit."

As Christine pushed aside the fabric to make room for Arabella, the footman came in with a tray of hot water and a plate of shortbread biscuits. Honoria hurried to the cabinet to retrieve the tea leaves, anxious to know what Arabella could possibly have in mind. Everyone remained quiet while the footman arranged the cups and plates on the table and Honoria allowed the tea to steep.

When he finally left, Arabella took a sip of the tea she had been given and set the cup on its saucer without a sound. "The reason I asked if your mother was at home was because I wished to speak with her on the matter of chaperoning you to the ball—or have you speak with her, if that is more to the purpose. I know we are new acquaintances, but as a widow it will be considered perfectly respectable. We can share the room at the inn. And I am to have the escort of my brother-in-law. I will also have my maid, the nurse, and my son with us in the coach, so although it won't precisely be a peaceful trip—"

Honoria clapped her hands together and sent Christine a look brimming with excitement. It was returned, their momentary tension forgotten. "I must ask my mother. I cannot think she would deny me such a pleasure—not with all the people we know in Lincoln, and those coming from Horncastle. And with your escort, there can be no objection."

"Then you may travel along with our carriage and join us on the way for a picnic," Christine added.

"Oh, yes." Arabella stopped short awkwardly. "I believe your brother spoke about something like that when we crossed paths at the haberdasher's shop."

Honoria did not wish to hear more of Gus's contact with the widow or have further reason for Christine to think Gus was not a good match for her. "I must ask Mama. Will you wait here while I go find her?"

"Of course." Arabella lifted a piece of shortbread from her plate and turned to Christine. "Must one's jewelry also be in tones of green for the ball?"

"It is not required, but many choose to wear items in matching tones."

Honoria, relieved that the conversation had shifted away from Gus, went outside and found her mother sitting on one of the iron benches whose armrests finished in the form of sculpted pointers about to set off for the hunt. Her eyes were trained on the fountain at the end of their rectangular pond before she lifted her face to the sun, her expression a look of pure pleasure.

Not wishing to startle her, Honoria approached quietly and sat beside her, drawing her mother's hand in her own. She detailed the plan that Arabella had proposed, attempting to minimize her excitement so that her mother would see how reasonable such a proposal was.

Mrs. Bassett brought her gaze forward to the bubbling fountain, the look of peace unfading. "Well then, I cannot think of any objections. Does Mr. Northwick seem an honorable man?"

"I ..." This was not a question Honoria was prepared for. She had some doubts that were only based on Arabella's reactions to him but kept those to herself. Nevertheless, she could not lie. "I do not know him, Mama. But I will not leave Arabella's company. We will stay in the same room, and the nurse will be in the adjoining room."

Her mother searched Honoria's eyes, then smiled and nodded. "Very well—*oh*!" She cut off suddenly when Honoria put her arms around her mother, patting her arm. "You will have a lovely time."

"Thank you, Mama. I am so very grateful." She hurried back into the room to tell her friends the good news.

Arabella clasped her hands on her lap. "I am delighted to hear it. I will enjoy the trip so much more in your company."

Christine came over and hugged Honoria. "This is most excellent news. I will have to tell Gus."

For one delicious moment, Honoria allowed herself to imagine Gus's look of enchantment when he saw her in her gown. She would be like an emerald sparkling in the candlelit ballroom. Her thoughts then spun to all there was to do to be ready in time. It was as well the Flynns had canceled their dance party as Mr. Flynn had contracted a lung infection and would not be fully mended before Thursday. She would need every spare minute. "Where have you taken up lodgings in Lincoln?"

"Mr. Northwick has arranged for us to stay at Ye Olde Whyte Swanne and has done all that is necessary for our accommodations."

"I believe that is where we are staying as well," Christine said. "And if I am not mistaken, Philip and Mr. Dawson have taken rooms there, too."

Honoria's heart beat as she thought about the possibilities and what this ball could mean for her and Gus. She set her teacup down and pressed her hands to her cheeks. "Oh dear. I had better get started on my dress again. I have much of the embellishments yet to do."

CHAPTER 10

The morning's peace was interrupted by the sounds of a carriage rolling into their courtyard. "Honoria," Mrs. Bassett called out from the foot of the stairs.

"Coming, Mama. Tell them I shall be right down." She turned to her maid who was strapping the leather trunk closed. "Go see where Jeffrey is. He should have come by now."

"Right away, miss." Maggie hurried out of the room, and Honoria stuffed two more books into her portmanteau along with her healing bag that held the most basic necessities. She never went anywhere without that. She then rushed over to get her small sewing kit to slip into her reticule. When the footman arrived, he swung her small trunk on his shoulder and headed for the stairwell. Honoria was not long behind him and she exited into the fresh air, her breaths coming out in puffs in the early October weather.

Arabella stood beside Mrs. Bassett at the entrance and waiting beside the carriage was Mr. Northwick, who held the bridle of his horse. She nodded in his direction. "I believe you remember Mr. Northwick, my brother-in-law."

"I do," Honoria replied. "Please accept my thanks for coming out of your way to fetch me. It has only added to your journey, and it was kind of you." Mr. Northwick nodded his acknowledgment as Arabella murmured that it was nothing to speak of.

Honoria turned to her mother, searching her gaze for any hesitation, although she hoped she would find none. "Are you sure you will be well without me, Mama?"

"You need not worry about me," her mother replied. "Besides, I have received a very thick letter from your father only this morning. I shall be quite content catching up on his news as it is not often that he writes such a lengthy epistle. Go ahead, dear. It is only for two days, and it is my wish that you will enjoy yourself."

Honoria threw her arms around her mother, hugging her gently so as not to crush any joints that might be sore. Although Mrs. Bassett was using her cane, she appeared more stout than she had in some time. The nettle tea and poultice had proven to be quite effective, and Honoria hoped her mother would continue to improve.

"You had best get started if you want to have enough time to dress before the ball tonight." Mrs. Bassett hugged her one more time, then Honoria moved to join Arabella.

"The Greys are to meet us here," Arabella said, as they walked toward the carriage. Scarcely had she uttered the words than the Greys' carriage clattered over the bridge and rounded into sight with Gus riding beside it. When they pulled up, the greetings and introductions for Mr. Northwick had to be made before they could start off again.

Christine was holding Guinea whose paws were resting on the open window. He panted at all the commotion, looking ready to leap out of the carriage. Honoria waved at Christine and Guinea both, then pulled back in to ask, "Where will we meet with Philip Townsend and his cousin? Are they not also traveling with us?"

"I believe we are to meet near Mr. Townsend's estate," Arabella replied, smiling at her son who sat between his nurse and her maid across from them. She waved a large wooden ring, then handed it to him when he reached for it.

That made perfect sense as Philip's estate was in the direction of Lincoln. They began moving, and Honoria watched the
scenery go by from their carriage, anticipating the sight of him
as it would mean their party would be complete and they could
then begin their journey over the Wolds. Before long, they
reached the path leading to his estate, and Honoria noticed for
the first time the long canal that had been dug alongside the
road. She frowned when she saw that the blackberry brambles
had been completely uprooted.

"What?" she breathed. Her stab of disappointment was
quickly replaced with a sense of indignation that Philip had not
even bothered to tell her he would be removing the brambles.
Had he been more opposed to her picking them than he let on?
She would have to ask him what his purpose had been in digging
the canal, as it surely couldn't be of greater good than blackberry
preserves.

Philip's carriage was now in sight and heading their way,
with Mr. Dawson on horseback beside it. The occupants of the
three carriages called out greetings rather than delay their journey, and they set out at a decent pace to Lincoln. Honoria's
chagrin over the loss of the blackberry brambles gave way to
enjoyment of the scenery passing before her. She loved this
portion of the journey as it took them through the Wolds—the
gently undulating hills that were bright yellow with rapeseed
set against a blue sky in the spring, and which were now
showing patches of red as the autumn leaves turned. When
they were on top of one of the hills, the valley stretched before
them with an occasional farmer's house perched amidst the
pasture.

Just before the village of Bardney, they stopped for their
luncheon, choosing a small area off the public road with a few
trees that lent some shade. There was plenty of space in the
middle of it to set their picnic, and Christine and Arabella's
maids worked to spread out blankets and place the dishes of
their small feast, while Christine scolded Guinea for showing too
marked an interest in what was being offered. Through the gap

in the trees in front of them stretched a meadow on an incline, and there was a row of hedges separating two fields.

At Honoria's left, Mr. Dawson insisted on serving Christine, while Philip eased himself slowly to the ground. He appeared to be gaining more use of his hands, but it wasn't always a simple matter to do things like sitting and getting back up again. Gus sat, leaning back on one hand as he breathed in the autumn air that carried wafts of smoke from someone burning leaves on a hidden farm nearby. Honoria peeped at him under her lashes and chose a seat at his side. He gave her a friendly smile, then turned his eyes to Arabella, who was standing next to the blanket where her baby sat. Her attention was absorbed by the boy's efforts to reach forward to grasp at a twig.

"You look enchanting, Mrs. Northwick." He smiled at her and Arabella, now focusing her regard on him, looked conscious, her color heightening.

Turning from a scene that brought no pleasure, Honoria's gaze crossed that of Philip's, and she looked away again. She was irritated by him for no good reason, irritated by the loss of the blackberries, by Gus ... and she was afraid that Philip could read what was in her mind.

Mr. Northwick had been watching Gus's interaction with Arabella, and he now called her attention to David. "Mrs. Northwick, I believe you oughtn't to leave your son unattended. It cannot speak well of you as a mother, and you would not wish to give our new company a wrong impression."

Philip's cousin Mr. Dawson darted his head up at Mr. Northwick's rebuke, and he glanced at Arabella with a frown. His gaze then went to the child who, at present, was sucking on the wooden ring then waving it. Mr. Dawson seemed to assess both Arabella and her brother-in-law as she hurried to sit beside her son.

"Of course. How careless of me," she said, picking up the baby. She kissed him. "But you are perfectly all right, are you not?"

Honoria's heart was troubled. There was something heavy in

88

the way Mr. Northwick ordered his brother's widow about, and it was not something she had ever witnessed. Her own family was far from perfect, but at the very least there had always been an underlying respect and affection between its members.

Philip bent down and took little David's hand in his own. "You have a fine son, Mrs. Northwick. He does you credit."

Arabella could barely lift her eyes to meet his, but she murmured her thanks, and his words seemed to have soothed something inside her—reassured her. The flash of irritation Honoria had felt towards Philip was replaced by a strong urge to go hug the man despite the berries. He had seemed to know just what was needed. She may not have been thrilled that Arabella had captured Gus's full attention, but she did not want her to be ill at ease.

When the food had been distributed and everyone began eating, Christine asked, "How much farther have we to travel?"

"We are not quite halfway there," Gus answered. He then directed the rest of his conversation to Arabella. "But we will arrive well before five o'clock so you will have time to ready yourself for the ball. I assume you have a gown in the appropriate Lincoln-dyed wool?"

"Why, of course, Mr. Grey," Arabella said softly before catching her brother-in-law's gaze. She dropped her own like a spark that had been snuffed, then remained that way throughout the meal, although Gus tried to draw her out of her tongue-tied state. The only time she came to life was when Honoria or Christine addressed her. Honoria was still trying to puzzle this out when Philip was at her side, leaning down to address her. She had not seen him get up.

"Would you like to take a turn with me? I am not yet able to ride. And it's hard for me to sit still for so long. You will be doing me a service."

She brushed the grass and twigs from her palms that came from leaning back and stood. "Why, if it's a service I'd be doing you, then you need say no more. Besides, I have something I wish to ask you. Or, rather, two things."

"I am all yours." Philip held out his elbow and she slipped her arm through it. The natural path wound around the trees, and as they followed it, she began to relax. It accomplished little to worry just now about Gus, or about Arabella and the strange hold Mr. Northwick seemed to have over her. She would turn her thoughts to things that concerned her more nearly at home.

"Have you seen Mr. Blackwell for your injuries?"

"I did," Philip replied, walking at her side as comfortably as though they had long been in the habit of doing so. "He does not think the wound has turned infectious, and in fact it appears to be improving already. He praised your abilities and I agreed with him fully."

"Oh!" A flush of pleasure went through her at the compliment. They walked for a bit, and he waited in silence for her next question.

"What is the purpose of this canal you've fashioned, and why did you dig up all the blackberry brambles? Was it because you were displeased that I had picked them?" She felt him pull away to look at her in surprise.

"What? No, of course not. I meant what I said about the blackberries. It's only that I needed to dig the canal for irrigation purposes. I want to improve the return on the field next to it."

"Ah, I see." She supposed if she were a man she would want to know all about how such a venture worked. Instead, she mourned the loss of the fruit. The brambles were mature and could not be easily replaced, and was there not a return to be had on those as well? She was about to bring up the argument when Philip cleared his throat in what sounded like uncharacteristic nervousness.

"I am sure it is entirely out of place for me to speak on a certain matter, and I only hope you will excuse such forwardness out of consideration for the years we have known one another," Philip began. She looked at him curiously but he continued to face forward, avoiding her gaze. "I cannot help but notice that you seem to have a *tendre* for Gus."

His words came like a stunning blow on an intimate corner

of her heart she had thought quite hidden. Honoria turned away to stare at the meadow, her cheeks hot from embarrassment. The fact that her face was an open book to her feelings piqued her even more than his presumptuous observation. "You are right. It is forward of you," she said at last with emphasis.

Philip shifted at her side, a slight limp she had not noticed growing pronounced. It was a moment before he spoke again. "Forgive me. I should not have brought up such a private matter. It was wrong of me." He walked on without looking at her. When he said no more, Honoria was forced to prompt him.

"But to what end did you bring it up? Did you wish to ... encourage me or warn me away?"

"It is not my business to warn you away," Philip replied. "But neither can I encourage you. Gus is the best of creatures, but I have never known him to settle on a woman seriously. In fact, the most attention I've ever seen him give to one in particular is for Mrs. Northwick. I suppose I do not wish to see you end up hurt."

Honoria picked up her pace until her own burns began to chafe, and she realized that it might not be comfortable for Philip to walk faster. "So not only do you wish to mortify me, you wish to crush my dreams."

Philip groaned and at last turned to look at her, offering a weak smile. "I suppose I've made a mull of it. I tend to do that on all delicate matters. I should not have said anything, and I do ask your forgiveness."

Honoria struggled with her pride for a minute, then relented, turning to humor for refuge. "Well, you could have bartered for my forgiveness if you'd had any blackberries to spare, but now ..." She tipped her nose upwards.

Philip laughed at her side. "I see now that I have much to learn in the business of bartering. If only I had not been so hasty in building that canal, I might still have some counters left to gamble."

CHAPTER 11

After they had completed their lunch, the maids packed up the remains of the picnic and stowed it in the carriages. Mr. Dawson went over to Arabella, who was still seated beside her baby, and held out his hand. "May I assist you, Mrs. Northwick?"

"Oh!" Her cheeks grew pink, but she allowed him to pull her to her feet. When he let go, he leaned down to pick up David and tickled him under the chin before returning him to his mother. Then he reached down again for the toy and handed that to her too.

"Thank you," she whispered and turned toward the carriage as Honoria folded the boy's blanket that remained on the ground and followed her.

The carriages journeyed onward. David stretched out and fell asleep at an angle between the maid and his nurse, while Honoria exchanged quiet conversation with Arabella, telling her about the past balls and some of the people she was likely to meet. Eventually, they both fell silent, Honoria lulled by the rocking motion and the pull of fatigue.

David continued to sleep on, and Honoria began to notice his flushed color. She feared it was not from the natural exhaustion of being outdoors but rather from the beginnings of a fever.

She leaned across the seat to feel his forehead, causing the nurse to stir in her seat and look down at the baby. Arabella watched the interchange and swallowed nervously. "He looks feverish." She looked at the nurse. "Do you not think so?"

The nurse pulled him more firmly on the seat between her and the maid. "You're his mother, ma'am. Surely you must know best."

Honoria brought her gaze up to the nurse, astonished at the surly tone in her voice and the fact that she could be so heartless concerning her own charge. How could Arabella abide such a person caring for her boy? Nevertheless, any reprimand for the nurse's behavior would have to come from the boy's mother, as it was not Honoria's place to do so.

Arabella ignored the disrespectful tone and reached forward to touch the boy's forehead. "He is hot."

"I do believe he is feverish," Honoria admitted. "The sun is growing lower in the sky, and we must surely be in Lincoln soon. We can get more adequate care for him there."

She looked through the window to rally her thoughts, torn between concern for David and worry that they would have to miss the ball. Of course, she wanted to give Arabella the support she so clearly needed, but to have all her efforts to attend the ball come to nothing was almost more than she could bear. There was the nurse, but after her unfeeling comment, Honoria did not trust her to properly care for the boy in his illness. She turned her mind to the problem of the fever, remembering that her grandmother recommended valerian for children in case of fever, rather than the white willow bark generally prescribed.

"Perhaps I should try sal volatile," Arabella said, doubtfully.

Honoria shook her head. "He is sleeping, and he should continue to do so. The scent would only wake him. When we arrive at the inn, I will administer some valerian." She silently offered up thanks for her grandmother who had taught her to always carry the essentials with her.

"Miss, if you don't mind my saying so"—the nurse sat upright and sniffed—"you'd best be letting those of us with more experience care for the wee one."

"But I do mind." Honoria challenged the nurse with her gaze, her hesitation to get involved forgotten. She turned to Arabella. "I have experience with healing, and I think if we can get him to swallow some valerian, he will rest more peacefully and the fever will go down. I've a tincture of it with me, and I believe we should bathe his temples with lavender water and put wet socks on his feet to draw the fever." Arabella brought her worried eyes to her child, then nodded in agreement. The nurse turned to the window, her mouth clamped shut.

It was growing dark when they arrived at the inn less than an hour later. Mr. Northwick came to the door of their carriage to help them to alight.

"David is feverish," Arabella told her brother-in-law breathlessly. She did not wait for his reply but hurried into the inn next to the nurse who carried the child. After a second's pause, Mr. Northwick gave a sharp order to the groomsman then stepped into the inn behind them.

Honoria had not noticed anyone from the rest of their party as they were led up a narrow staircase to the first floor. They must have been separated during the long ride. Once inside their room, she glanced around. A small fire crackled in the fireplace, providing warmth and an aspect of cozy cheer. Some effort had been made to decorate the walls, and the two beds looked to be clean. Next to the door was a small room for the maid with only enough space to walk around the bed and for her to lay her effects at the foot of it. There were two beds in the main room, and the nurse's quarters could be achieved by accessing an adjoining door. This was larger than the maid's.

Arabella fluttered behind her boy but allowed the nurse to bring him into the room where she and the boy would be staying. Mrs. Billings laid the boy down on the bed, then Arabella turned to Honoria. "I am very sorry but I will not be able to leave him to go to the ball tonight. I hope you will understand."

Honoria swallowed, refusing to permit her disappointment

to gain hold, and touched Arabella's arm. "Do not think of it. The most important thing is for your son to regain his health. As soon as David is awake we can administer the valerian. I will just fetch the lavender and water for bathing his temples—I am sure the kitchen will have some."

She exited the room, hoping she would cross paths with Christine since she did not know in which room her friend was staying. Instead, she met Philip, coming flush up against him in the narrow corridor. He put his hands out to halt her forward progress and kept them there as he searched her face.

"What is it?"

"David—Mrs. Northwick's baby boy is feverish. I must fetch some hot water and lavender from the kitchen, and I was hoping to find Christine as well."

Philip seemed to realize he was holding on to her, and he dropped his hands. "What will you give him?"

She met his gaze, grateful that he seemed to assume she would know what to do, rather than thinking she should leave the healing to trained doctors. She explained what treatment she proposed as he listened attentively.

"Why don't you go to the kitchen and I'll fetch Christine for you? I'm sure I can find out where she and Gus are staying."

Honoria shot him a look of gratitude. Their faces were very near as she did so and only then did she notice how much space he took up in the cramped corridor. "Could you? She would be a real support to me."

Philip began to walk away then turned back. "Will you have to stay with Mrs. Northwick tonight while she watches over her boy? You would miss the ball after all this?"

Honoria shrugged, hiding her regret. "I am not sure. I am certainly prepared to do so."

Philip nodded and left on his errand, and Honoria shoved down the lingering disappointment, refusing to let it waver her determination. She went down to the kitchen and was given a larger quantity of lavender than she needed with promises that hot water would be sent up. When she returned to the room,

David was tossing restlessly, and Arabella's shoulders were tight with worry.

Honoria rubbed the lavender buds into the bowl she had been given, and as soon as the servant arrived with the hot water, she poured it over the buds and set the mixture to soak. The baby started to fuss, then cry, and Honoria pulled the valerian tincture out of her portmanteau that was lying beside her bed. "Let us see if we can get him to drink this."

They succeeded in encouraging him to finish the medicine, and as soon as the lavender was cool enough, Honoria took a cloth and gave it to Arabella, who bathed his temples in hesitant strokes. Finally, the nurse could stand it no longer, and she took the cloth from Arabella and undressed the boy, applying the lavender water to the rest of his body. When she was done, he quickly fell into a sleep that appeared to be more restful.

All of this had taken an hour, with Mr. Northwick knocking once to inquire after the boy. Arabella looked up from where she was sitting on the bed and said, "You should change if you're going to make it to the ball."

"I don't need to go—" A knock sounded at the door, and Honoria came into the adjoining room as the maid opened it.

"Christine, you have come at last. I began to fear that Philip could not find you." She was relieved to see her friend's diminutive form.

Christine peered into the room where David was sleeping and lowered her voice. "We were separated on the journey from the rest of the train, and Gus got lost, I am afraid. We only just arrived a half hour ago." She gave a tentative smile to Arabella. "It appears as though you have got him to rest."

Arabella left David in the nurse's care and joined them in the main room. "Honoria found something that I hope will keep him quiet for the time being—at least long enough for you to attend the ball. It would be a shame to come all this way and not go. Of course I must stay behind, but I was hoping Honoria would be able to attend with you."

"Nothing could be easier. My brother will escort us," Christine said, then paused. "And Mr. Northwick? Will he attend the ball?"

Arabella's expression was hard to read. "I will encourage him to do so. But Honoria, you must go. I will be unhappy if you do not."

It took little persuasion for Honoria to agree to what she so eagerly wished to do. "Very well. Please take a pair of David's stockings and soak them in lavender water and put them on him, covered with thick wool socks if you have them. It will help to draw off the fever." She leaned in to whisper, "And don't let the nurse stop you from doing it."

Arabella smiled weakly. "I will do as you say."

She returned to her son's bedside, and Honoria retrieved her gown from the maid who was holding it at the ready. She followed Christine to her room, where her maid helped Christine first with her hair then turned to take over Honoria's attempts to do her own.

Now fully dressed, Christine looked down at Honoria's gown, her lips quirked. "It will not do to spend too much time in each other's company. I am afraid your emerald green clashes sadly with my olive. I suppose such a thing is not so problematic when the color chosen is something like blue, for instance."

Honoria grinned through smarting eyes as the maid pulled a comb through her hair. "But it can be even more problematic when the color is red, as it was two years ago when you were in Bath. Let us just thank the committee for sparing me that color. You could pull it off without a problem, but for me it was dreadful."

They had just finished the last touches when Gus arrived at the room to escort Christine to the ball. He raised his eyebrows when he saw Honoria in her room but did not ask her why she was there. "My, don't you both look nice."

It was tepid praise, especially being lumped together with his sister. Honoria was beginning to fear that Philip and Christine had been right. She was wasting her energy setting her cap after a lost cause. This fear was enhanced when Gus made a show to search behind them. "Where is Mrs. Northwick? Is she not with you?"

"She was unable to come because her son is sick," Christine said. At the words, a variety of emotions flit across Gus's face, disappointment being chief among them, and his sister did not allow Honoria time to reflect on her hopeless cause. "Shall we be off?"

Christine's room was off a different staircase, and it led directly to the front entrance where the carriage was waiting for them outdoors. Moments later, Honoria was just stepping into the Greys' carriage when she glimpsed Philip and Mr. Dawson hailing the servant to fetch their own carriage. They were dressed very stylishly in similar bottle-green coats, and Honoria noticed just how well Philip looked when he was not contenting himself with the loose attire of a country gentleman.

Her heart began to race in anticipation as they pulled up to the assembly room where the ball was to take place. After all, she had one last card to play: the romance of a candlelit ballroom and the dance itself. Men and women in coats and dresses of all shades of green poured in through the doors, and the light of chandeliers spilled out onto the cobblestones outdoors. Inside, the assembly room was full and noisy, with crowds of people gathered in groups. The musicians were playing music that was too subtle to be calling the guests to dance, so they had not missed anything.

The crowd soon pushed them into close proximity until they were forced to seek out a space on the far end of the ballroom. Gus turned to face the couples lining up, and Honoria fell in his line of vision. She tried not to look conscious of his regard but hoped he was looking at her. Christine's maid had done well with Honoria's hair, and no other color suited her better than green. He did turn his gaze her way, and it seemed to stay there longer than was usual. But the focused regard only made her nervous, and she turned her head away, hoping he would admire her profile instead.

Philip found their group a short while later with Mr. Dawson behind him, and he bowed before her and Christine. "You two ladies are looking as fine as Lincolnshire can boast. I hope you will do me the honor of dancing with me, both of you." Christine shook her head about to respond, but he was too quick. "I apologize. You are not dancing. I had forgotten."

Honoria knew that Philip would turn to her next, but Gus, who had been staring at the crowds, snapped his gaze back. "Yes. A fine idea. Honoria, I believe I was here first, was I not?" She was torn between a sense of fairness to Philip that he had been the first to ask and a sense of exultation that Gus had at last noticed her. This was only enhanced when he said, "You *do* look splendidly."

"It is only now that you notice it," Philip muttered, and Honoria detected the note of annoyance in his voice that put words to the favoritism she hesitated to show and which also thrilled her. Was it possible that Philip had actually wanted to dance with her and hadn't asked out of duty?

"I suppose so, but never mind that. Listen. The strains of music are starting. Dance with me for this first dance," Gus said, tugging at Honoria's hand and in doing so, pushing all thoughts of Philip away.

At last. Honoria nodded and her smile felt so big it threatened to squeeze tears of joy right out of her eyes. At her side, Philip folded his arms as Mr. Dawson stepped up to Christine, prepared to engage her in conversation, and Honoria followed Gus on the floor.

As they took their places across from each other, she had a chance to feast her eyes on the set of his shoulders, and the brown hair that fell forward into his face. His dark eyes held hers, and it caused her heart to both freeze and take flight from one instance to the next. The music began, introducing the most heavenly dance she had ever experienced. Every time their hands joined in the steps, their gazes held and Gus's look was one of intent. He had invited her to dance at various country assemblies in the past, but this was different. He was truly noticing her for the first time, just as she'd known he would if only she was given the chance to capture his attention. *This is it. This is the beginning of the rest of our lives.*

When the final steps of the dance had them facing each other again, he slipped his arm around her waist and pulled her close. "We should spend more time in each other's company," he murmured, and Honoria only hoped that the stalks of hope that bloomed in her heart did not cause her face to turn an unbecoming red.

She had forgotten to answer! Honoria's heart was racketing about violently, and she could only nod her head and squeak out a, "Yes!" *This is the most perfect day of my life,* she thought as he led her to the edge of the dance floor, and they each gave their formal curtsy and bow. *I will remember it forever.*

CHAPTER 12

Philip stood on the sidelines watching Honoria dance with Gus. He knew it would not be entirely comfortable for him to dance, although his burns were healing more each day. But the pull to invite her was too strong, and he did not appreciate being cut out. Dancing with Gus made her eyes bright, but she seemed too shy to turn them in his direction. Philip couldn't help but contrast that with how she was with him. When he spoke to her, she had no difficulty in meeting his gaze. It was surely because she did not view him with any partiality. He was coming to regard that as a shame.

The couple turned and pivoted around one another, and Honoria laughed when a young man in the set went the wrong way. Once let loose, her laugh was natural and free, but then she clamped her lips tight in a gleeful smile when Gus looked at her, as if fearful of showing too much of herself.

Philip doubted the wisdom of having brought up Honoria's feelings for Gus when they had walked together after lunch. He couldn't claim it was any of his concern but had only wanted to protect her. She deserved so much more than to have the dubious attention of a man with a wandering eye, even if that man was his friend. Honoria deserved to be a man's sole focus. After all, what other woman of his acquaintance would march off to gather blackberries instead of sending a servant to do it—or carry healing tinctures with her and know how to use them? He had heard stories of her successfully healing some of the poorer people in the village and could readily believe it.

At some imprecise point in their reacquaintance, Philip's appreciation for her had turned into admiration. She had ready humor; she had resolve. Wherever she was in the room, her presence pulled to him like a magnet. And he could feast his eyes all day long on the way her full lips parted in a smile. It was perhaps more than admiration.

Now he feared his realization had come too late. From what he could observe, Honoria was still lost in love with Gus, who was finally beginning to open his eyes to what was before him. Philip supposed it was about time. He just hoped Gus would treat her with the respect she deserved and not flip his attention to some other woman who happened to win his regard in that moment.

Mr. Reid, the gentleman farmer from Horncastle, was present and talking to someone Philip recognized from past assemblies. He had not yet had a chance to speak to Mr. Reid about his opinions on the irrigation project, but he was confident enough in Mr. Mercer's observations to begin. He and his engineer had already discussed how they would divert the water as soon as the canal and dikes were finished, agreeing that Coates would begin testing without delay.

The two men gestured for Philip to join them, and he came instantly, thankful for an excuse to sit the dance out. His introduction to the unknown gentleman, a Mr. Fines, proved to be fruitful as Mr. Reid hinted that Philip had an English Thoroughbred stallion that might be of interest as a sire. Mr. Fines was possessed of a breeding farm for Thoroughbreds near the border to Scotland, and he was willing to travel for any stud that showed promise. They arranged for a meeting the following month when he would be coming through Lincolnshire on his way to London.

Afterwards, when Mr. Reid and Mr. Fines went off in search of a drink, Philip came to stand at Christine's side.

Theo had played the gallant without cease as he danced with one woman after another. He looked as though it did not tire him in the least, and on the contrary that there was nothing better he liked to do. Philip had not missed the fact that his cousin tended to invite those women who were overlooked by others. He should emulate such chivalrous behavior but contented himself with talking to Christine, a different form of chivalry.

"I hope you do not mind not dancing," he said when he noticed her tapping her foot in rhythm to the music.

"I do mind a bit," Christine admitted, meeting his gaze. "But even if society did not dictate a period of mourning, I would have wanted to observe it. My mother deserved that. It's just ... dancing is so lighthearted, and it removes the pressure to think of something witty to say."

"How much I can empathize with that sentiment," Philip said, thinking that although he was not an exceptional dancer, he was perhaps more skilled at that art than conversing when it came to women. His gaze drifted back to Honoria and settled there. As much as he had always felt at ease around her, he could not help but think he had not put his best foot forward in their conversation earlier that afternoon.

"Honoria is in good looks tonight." Christine's eyes were turned away, but he quite thought he detected a hint of mischief in her voice. Perhaps he had been staring at her too openly.

He let a moment pass before he agreed. "She is." And not daring to see how much Christine had discerned of his feelings, he kept his eyes trained on the crowd in front of him, focusing on no particular couple, until the dance ended and Honoria's partner brought her back to Christine's side.

Seizing the opportunity that fate afforded him, he lost no time in bowing before Honoria. "You have promised me a dance, and I believe this is as good a time as any. That is ... if you are free?"

Honoria put her hand on Philip's arm, leaning into him affectionately in a way that fed him with hope. "I am." She followed him onto the floor, and they took their places next to the other couples, waiting for their set to begin.

Philip applied his mind to what might be a good—and safe—topic of conversation that did not involve asking her inappropriate questions about the state of her heart. But in the end, he did not need to drive the conversation. As though she could bear it no longer she said, "Did you not notice how Gus looked at me while we were dancing? I cannot think he is indifferent to me now." She flashed Philip a conspiratorial smile that put dimples in her cheeks and a pang in his own heart.

The music began, and Philip held out his arm, giving himself time to think of how to respond. He walked the three steps forward before turning in time to the music. "It is difficult to think anyone could be indifferent to you, Honoria." He felt her turn, startled, seeking his gaze. "You are surprised, but you should not be. Any man with eyes in his head can see what a handsome woman you are, and that the beauty does not stop there."

"Oh." A tiny furrow appeared between Honoria's brow. She looked up at him innocently. "Do you find me handsome?" Her dimples made a reappearance as though she knew she was putting him on the spot.

He had no hesitation in answering. "Very handsome."

She looked pleased, and when they had promenaded around the other couples and come back together, he elaborated. "But what I admire most about you is not something that can be found in a pretty face or what you wear. What I admire most is your noble mind."

Her brow knit as she appeared to digest this, and he was encouraged to elaborate. "I admire the care you take in healing people and your skill in doing so. I admire that you seem to be good at everything you put your hand to, and that it all comes naturally. Speaking of which"—he paused while they separated in the dance—"I've been meaning to ask you for that recipe for blackberry preserves. Not that I am going to be able to reproduce it myself. But perhaps I can find somebody in my household who can manage it."

"You no longer have any brambles, Philip." The sound of his name spoken in her soft, wry voice almost made him miss what she had said.

"Ah. To be sure." *Idiot.* Philip was having trouble directing an intelligent conversation. "I suppose it's all for the best since I have difficulty getting anyone in my house to do what I ask of them in a timely manner."

Their first set came to an end, and as another set formed, Philip and Honoria went over to stand on the sidelines. She faced him with an earnest expression. "You need to be firm with them. They should know that you are their employer and that if they don't do as you please, you might easily replace them with someone who will."

Philip raised his brows skeptically. "It is all very well and good for me to tell them. The problem is that I fear I *won't* be able to replace them, and therefore my threat carries little weight. Even if I could find servants who are diligent, the thought of interviewing and attempting to train new ones makes me want to flee to London."

"Well, Philip." Honoria kept her gaze on the couples dancing, ready to jump back in when it was their turn, though that would not be for some minutes yet. "I believe the problem lies with your housekeeper then. It is her job to oversee the maids. If she sets high standards in her own work and makes her expectations clear, the other maids will do as she requests."

"I agree." Philip whisked two cups of punch from one of the trays being passed around and handed one to her. "But my housekeeper does not set high standards in her work, alas. I had hoped Theo would bring his sister to keep house for me, but it was not to be."

"That's a shame." Honoria sipped at the punch, her gaze roaming around the room, then turned her eyes to him. "But surely your housekeeper can be spoken to. If I were to have a conversation with her, I would ensure that she carried out her work as she should."

Philip laughed. "I believe you."

Their second set was beginning, and Philip had the pleasure of taking her hand carefully in his and leading her to the dance floor where they continued their steady conversation of little consequence but of great enjoyment. At the end of the second set, they bowed before one another, and he was given one of Honoria's full smiles. He was satisfied with the evening's work—happy with himself that he had been able to tell her what he thought about her. Perhaps those little seeds might take root, and her heart might be turned his way. It might be enough even to overcome a father's aversion.

His satisfaction was short-lived. As soon as they rejoined the sidelines where Christine stood, Gus came up to Honoria and grabbed her hand. "Dance with me again. There is no one at this ball so charming as you, I daresay." She flushed with pleasure straight up to her roots and raised her eyes very significantly to Philip's before setting her hand in Gus's.

Blast him. Gus might be his best friend, but Philip had no generous thoughts to spare for the man today. He watched Honoria take her place opposite Gus, her figure set to advantage in the trim green dress, and her expression lit with what he could only call adoration. She had a look in her eye when she was with Gus that he did not see anywhere else, but he wished he could be the one to put it there. It was time he quashed these hopes that had seemed to crystallize for the first time today. If she were really so partial to Gus—and it was now seeming as though Gus were partial to her as well—who was Philip to stand in the way?

Having finished another dance, Theo swiped a glass of champagne off the tray of a passing servant and walked up to where Philip stood. "I've barely seen you dance," he said by way of greeting.

"While you have not stopped."

"Amazing. They've managed to chill the champagne." Theo

peered into his glass. "How can I resist when the women outnumber men? I don't wish to see anyone neglected."

"You always did have too tender a heart." Philip set an affectionate hand on Theo's shoulder, then removed it. "Although I cannot believe I'm uttering such a namby-pamby thing as that."

Theo jerked his chin in the direction of the doorway where Mr. Northwick had just entered. "What do you think of him? The widow's brother-in-law?"

Mr. Northwick scanned the room as though searching for an acquaintance. Philip was not sure he would find any here apart from their own party, and it would be difficult for him to seek introductions without knowing anyone. However, he appeared to know some of the merchants, because he went over and shook their hands. So, apparently Northwick did know people in Lincolnshire.

"I don't know what to think. He seems a genial fellow. I have nothing to say against him. And yet ..."

"And yet there's something you don't like," Theo concluded. "I am of the same mind. I believe it is the way he treats Mrs. Northwick. There is something overbearing in his manner towards her that I cannot approve of. He seems to have some hold over her, treating her as though she's a juvenile. And what is even odder is that in his presence she appears to be too afraid to say anything."

"All that from a brief conversation at the picnic?" Philip asked him, eyebrows raised.

"I'm an observant fellow."

Philip folded his arms, and silence fell between them as they both watched the crowd. He couldn't refrain from speaking what was foremost in his mind. "Gus has been showing a pointed interest in Mrs. Northwick before tonight."

"Gus!" Theo's tone had turned as close to something like disgust as someone of his temperament could produce. "As much as I'm fond of him, he has a new infatuation every month. The last thing Mrs. Northwick needs is someone like him muddying the waters of her life."

"You have something there," Philip replied. But he was thinking about Honoria. He could only hope that if Gus had indeed set his sights on her that it would be long-lasting. He did not want to see her crushed by infidelity.

They continued to watch from the sidelines, as though they were no longer participants of the ball. There was something impressive about a room full of people all dressed in various shades of the same color. It had never ceased to strike Philip, and he could remember Stuff Balls over the years in every spectrum of the rainbow if he searched his memory far enough back. His gaze skirted the crowds and returned to Honoria as she danced. Gus stared at her in open admiration, and she looked bashfully away. The sight goaded. They didn't seem to have a whole lot to say to each other.

"So, we are to head to your sister's tomorrow?" Philip asked, ready to turn his thoughts elsewhere.

Theo smiled and bowed in acknowledgment of a young lady's greeting. "So you are still to come? I had almost thought you would back out at the last minute. But I am glad to hear it."

Philip answered, his eyes still trained on Honoria, her hand clasped in that of Gus's. "I suppose, apart from the irrigation project, there is nothing pressing to hurry me back to Horncastle. So let us go."

CHAPTER 13

After having danced with Gus the second time, the rest of the night passed by in a dreamy haze. At one point, Honoria caught a glimpse of Mr. Northwick weaving his way through the crowds at the assembly, which pulled her out of her pleasant reverie. *The baby! How is he?* She was also struck with a strange sense of relief at seeing Mr. Northwick there. If he was at the assembly, it meant he could not be imposing himself upon Arabella. Although why she should think of it—or him—in those terms she could not say. It must also mean that little David was doing well enough that his uncle was not needed. He found a circle of people to talk to, and she soon dismissed Mr. Northwick from her mind as she had something much more pleasant to consume her thoughts: Augustus Grey loved her at last.

They stayed at the ball until the wee hours, and she lost count of how many faceless gentlemen invited her to dance. She had eyes for only one. All too soon, it was time to take the Greys' carriage back to the inn and, sitting in the dark, she allowed herself to peek at Gus, only to find that his eyes were on her. Neither spoke about what had happened that evening, but Honoria knew he felt it as she did. Christine was quiet as usual and had not seemed to notice the earth-shattering event happening right under her very eyes. Her brother had at last fallen in love with her best friend.

As the carriage came to a halt at the inn, Honoria took Christine's hand and squeezed it. "Thank you for accompanying me." As an afterthought, she asked, "Did you enjoy yourself tonight?"

"Very much." Christine did not elaborate, but Honoria was accustomed to her friend's reserve. Gus climbed out first, then helped her out of the carriage before bowing over her hand and planting a kiss directly on it. A thrill shot through her.

She would have to find Christine the next day and pepper her with questions about what he said after they had parted for the evening. He could not hold back from his own sister his newly discovered feelings, surely? They were too close for that.

It was only as she approached the door to her room that she again remembered David's fever and, with a guilty twinge, wondered how he was. Inside, the room was dark, apart from the glowing embers of the fire. Finding a fresh candle, she got the wick to light and looked around.

Arabella lay asleep on the bed, fully clothed. In the adjoining room, the nurse was also asleep in the chair, so Honoria stepped over to look at the baby. His forehead was cool and damp to the touch, and the fever appeared to have left him.

In their bedroom, she woke Arabella gently. "You should get undressed. You will be more comfortable."

Arabella stretched and then came to with a start, getting up from the bed and hurrying into the bedroom. She must have come to the same conclusion because she returned looking relieved and began untying the back of her dress before dropping the laces. "Allow me to assist you, and then you may assist me. I do not wish to awaken my maid. She stayed up late enough as it is."

Honoria turned and allowed Arabella to unhook her dress, her thoughts still full of the evening.

"How was the ball?" Arabella asked when the laces to Honoria's stays were also undone.

"It was wonderful, although I regret you could not enjoy it with me." Honoria loosened the rest of Arabella's laces, then began to change into her nightshift. "It seems vastly unfair that you should miss it when I owe my presence here entirely to you."

"Think nothing of it." Arabella yawned and climbed into the bed. With her loose nightshift and hair braided to one side, she looked like a young girl. "However, I hope you will not be too disappointed if we return home directly rather than staying the two days as planned. I cannot help but think that poor David would recover more thoroughly in his own bed, even though he must endure some discomfort to get there."

"Not at all," Honoria replied after only a slight pause. This would mean she would not get to visit Lincoln in Gus's company. But perhaps he would wish to cut short his own stay as well so that he might accompany her back to Horncastle. This led to memories of the delicious sensation of dancing with him. "My most pressing wish has been granted, after all."

The thought crossed her mind as she climbed into her bed next to Arabella's that this must be what it was like to have a sister. She had never spent the night with a friend, even with Christine. There had never been any need, for she had always been accompanied by her parents when she went away. Her toes were sore from dancing, and she wiggled them in the cold sheets. "Did you send for the doctor in the end?"

Arabella curled on her side under the covers. "He said we had done all that was right, and he did not entertain any fears on David's account. It was enough to satisfy Mr. Northwick, who did not think either you or I capable of caring for David who is, after all, the heir."

"How little faith he has in women," Honoria murmured. She would have said more but she fell asleep before she could.

When she awoke the next day, the sun streamed in brightly. Arabella was already tending to David in the next room, who did indeed seem to be doing much better. The nurse kept trying to shoo her away, but Arabella remained steadfast until David had been dressed. Only then did she allow Nurse to give him some of the porridge that had been prepared for him.

When Honoria saw that Mrs. Billings had things well in hand she said, "Shall we not go down and see what can be had for breakfast?"

"Yes, do let us." Arabella put on a warm spencer over her cotton gown. "Nurse, please see that David takes some milk as well." Mrs. Billings gave the barest nod in response.

Once downstairs, they discovered that they were amongst the last of the guests to arrive, and Honoria scanned the room eagerly for a sight of the dark locks she adored, her heart thumping in anticipation. Philip and his cousin sat on one side of the room and appeared to have nearly finished their breakfast, while Christine and Gus sat at the table adjacent to theirs. As soon as he spotted them, Gus leapt to his feet and Honoria smiled even as she grew breathless. What attention he was showing her! She fixed her gaze upon him as they moved forward.

"Good morning." Gus bowed deeply with a broad smile and pulled out a chair, reaching his hand out for Arabella to escort her into it. "We sorely missed you last night, Mrs. Northwick. How is your son? Morning, Honoria."

Arabella murmured something in reply, and Honoria stood for a moment longer, waiting. When at last she saw that Gus was not going to pull out her chair, a stab of disappointment rose up in her so sharp it stole her breath.

The other gentlemen had also stood when they arrived, and now Philip stepped forward to pull out a chair for her. "Please have a seat. May I bring you something from the side table?"

Honoria turned her eyes his way, blinking against the tears that threatened to form. Through sheer will she summoned a fleeting smile. "Good morning, Philip. Yes, would you be so kind as to bring me some bread? That is all I shall take."

He bowed and went over to the sideboard to fill a plate for her. As he selected a roll and reached for the pot of butter, she blinked at him, then looked away when he turned and met her gaze. Her bewildered mind attempted to assess what was happening. Gus had rejected her after everything they shared. He had completely forgotten their two dances and treated her as though she meant nothing to him.

Philip, on the other hand, was steady. He was a friend to her, and it had only become increasingly evident in the past weeks. On a purely physical level, he was pleasing to look at. His shoulders had filled out in the time since she had known him. They were broader even than Gus's, and she experienced a sudden proprietary urge, as if those shoulders were for her to measure and appraise—although, of course, such a thing was ridiculous. Her mind had become muddled with disenchantment.

Thankfully ignorant of the surprising turn of her thoughts in his direction, Philip brought the plate to her, a look of warm understanding in his eyes. She dropped her gaze to what he had selected for her. There was a thick slice of dark rye bread, a white roll, and a piece of sourdough. He had also chosen a selection of jam and butter and arranged it to make a pretty display. She looked up at him in mute thanks.

"Coffee?" he asked.

Her smile came more naturally as she lifted her hand to take the knife. She would no longer be a fool but would show her resilience. "No. Tea, if you please." He turned a teacup over on its saucer and reached for the teapot that was sitting on the table just out of her reach. He poured a cup for her and set it in front of her plate. She glanced at him, then down at the miniature crock of jam, not trusting herself to speak.

To her right, Gus and Arabella carried on a stilted conversation. His interest in her was pronounced—even more so than what he had favored Honoria with the night before. She saw that now. But Arabella did not appear to relish it. As Honoria buttered her bread, she directed her attention to her left where Mr. Dawson drew Christine out in conversation as he always seemed to do. Philip had picked up his newspaper, but he occasionally answered or smiled at something that was said. More than once, she glanced in his direction, considering, and if their gazes met, he smiled at her before looking away again.

When breakfast was over, the party split up and Honoria went to help Arabella make ready for their departure. The rest of the company would be staying in Lincoln to visit the cathedral and the shops, but Honoria was no longer disappointed to miss it. On the contrary, she was glad she would not have to witness Gus fawning over Arabella. It was time to rip out the stitches of that fantasy and embroider something new. They were ready to leave by two, and Mr. Northwick, who had not made an appearance at breakfast, was waiting for them by the carriage.

The ride home was quiet. Arabella seemed preoccupied, and neither the nurse nor her maid spoke, which meant that Honoria was left to her own thoughts. David appeared much improved and except for a slight tendency to be fussy, suffered no obvious ill effects from his fever.

Honoria's thoughts turned back to Gus and his cavalier treatment of her after the particular attention he had shown her last night. As the day went on, she became fully indignant. Her affection for him had suffered a fatal blow. It was one thing for him to pay her the careless attention of an older brother—a paragon out of reach—but it was another thing for him to treat her with so little regard when they had danced together on such intimate terms. She was ready to put such childhood hopes behind her.

What struck her, however, were the odd thoughts she was having in parallel about Philip. It wasn't attraction, at least not one that came with the force she had felt for Gus. It was quieter than that. Simple and modest. All he had done was to fetch her a plate of bread, but in doing so, he had come in the guise of a hero. Observing the lack of respect shown to her, he redoubled his own efforts to lift her up. Did he have any interest in her, she wondered, or was he simply being noble?

By the halfway point, Honoria feared she was not being a good traveling companion and searched for a topic of conversation. "I was glad to see Mr. Northwick arrive at the ball last night. I took it as a sign that David was doing better, since he had no fears in leaving him."

Arabella pulled her gaze from the carriage window and carefully smoothed out her skirt with gloved hands. "I urged him to go. I told him that David would be just fine under my care, and that there was no reason he should miss the ball. Nurse supported me in this. However, he did not leave until the doctor assured him he could do so."

Mrs. Billings had folded her hands against her chest now that David had finally dropped off to sleep. Upon hearing this, Honoria pursed her lips in disapproval. "A man has no reason to be in a lady's bedroom to whom he is not married, even if he be the boy's uncle."

Arabella turned a grim smile to Honoria. "That is precisely what I told him." The conversation ended there, and this time Honoria allowed it to drop.

With no plans to pause for a leisurely picnic, they arrived at Arabella's house late in the afternoon, where she arranged for the carriage and her own maid to accompany Honoria home. A little less than an hour later, as the last of the sun dipped below the trees, the carriage drove into the small courtyard in front of her house. Her mother's face appeared in the candlelit window, and Honoria mumbled a hurried thanks to the maid for her services. She did not wait to be helped out of the carriage but ran to the entryway to hug her mother.

Mrs. Bassett pulled back to look at her with a concerned smile. "You are home a day early. I hope that all is well?"

"Yes, only little David had a fever so we did not stay to visit Lincoln. I've missed you, Mama." She linked her arm through her mother's and lent her support as they walked toward the drawing room. Her mother leaned heavily on her cane with her other hand.

"I have news," her mother said with such significance that Honoria turned her head to look at her. "However, that will have to wait. Let us ring for tea. And, of course, I will wish to hear all about the ball first."

As impatient as Honoria was to hear the news, she knew her mother would reveal nothing until they were settled comfortably. She helped her to sit in the drawing room, then went to the kitchen to greet Cook and ask for tea to be sent. When these preparations had been made, and the hot water was brought at last, she took a seat beside her mother.

"How was it, my dear?" Mrs. Bassett reached over and tucked a lock of hair behind Honoria's ear.

"The ball was much that I'd hoped it would be ..." Honoria hadn't decided how much she would share with her mother, but she finally decided to confess what had long been her most cherished desire. "But there was one element of disappointment."

She stared at the teapot, her lips twisted, and when she did not go on, her mother replied with a careful, "Oh?"

Honoria sighed, then leaned forward again to stir the leaves in the teapot just to give her hands something to do. "I've not told you this, Mama, but I've long hoped that Augustus Grey might one day notice me as a man notices a woman. Well, last night he finally did. We danced twice, and I seemed to have caught his regard."

She fell silent and poured tea she no longer wanted. Her face must have spoken volumes because her mother prompted her. "But ...?"

Honoria reached for her mother's hand and held it. "But the next day he was back to treating me as though I were nothing more than a little sister. He devoted all his attention to Arabella Northwick at breakfast. He scarcely bid me farewell when we announced we would be leaving a day early."

Her mother gave Honoria's hand a gentle squeeze. "Your confession does not surprise me. But, despite this, I must say, I cannot think Augustus Grey a good match for you. Oh yes, he is as handsome as can stare and he has a friendly, genial disposition that must always please. I think your father would be satisfied if he were to turn his attention to you, given his prospects. And then, of course, there is the added bonus of his being the brother of your best friend."

"So you understand ..."

"I do. But I've had ample chance to watch him grow and interact in town, and he does seem to have something of a wandering eye. Perhaps he just needs a few more years, but at present he does not seem to be a man ready to settle down. Or perhaps he has not met the right woman. As much as it pains me to say it, I don't think that woman is you, my dear. And I would not wish you to become attached to someone who was not completely devoted to you."

Honoria pondered her mother's words. It was painful to hear, although perhaps less than it would have been before the ball. It seemed, now that she had begun the process of mourning what would not be, the change would be swift.

She thought back to Philip's consideration toward her at breakfast and wondered if that was more in line with what her mother wished for her. She would not bring *him* up, as she did not want her mother to become hopeful about the match. And she certainly did not want to fight a battle with her father, who would have something to say about Philip Townsend as a marital prospect. At least, she did not want to fight for it when she had no idea if his treatment of her was a symptom of deeper feeling. It was true that it wasn't the first time he had appeared in the guise of a hero. He had saved her, quite literally, from the fire. And he had seemed to trust and appreciate her ministrations afterwards. But that could be something any friend might show for another whom he had known his whole life.

"I am sure we will have more to discuss on this topic, but let me tell you my news," her mother reminded, drawing Honoria's gaze to hers. She had forgotten that her mother had something to tell her. "Your brother is to be married."

"Married! That cannot be!" Samuel hardly seemed old enough. And if Gus was considered to have a wandering eye, her brother had an even worse reputation for it. At home, he was always flirting with one pretty girl after another. And now to become a husband? She could not picture it.

Her mother went on. "That was the thick letter I had from

your father when you left yesterday. He wrote to tell me that when he arrived in London, Samuel seemed to have matured overnight and was eager to present his betrothed to your father. She is a Miss Barbara Goodall, and from what your father said, she is a pretty, docile thing. He thinks she will be a good match for your brother."

Honoria's mind was running through all the consequences. "They will be married here, I imagine. We must start planning the wedding breakfast. Where will they live?"

Her mother smiled. "Now, that is the best news of all. They are coming back to Horncastle to stay, and they will live with us while your father readies the smaller house attached to the mill. They will reside there until the time comes for them to take up residence at Weeton. That way we can show Miss Goodall—Barbara, I suppose she must be to us—how the house should be run. After all, she will one day be its mistress."

Honoria's smile faltered. She had not thought about that. Her brother's wife would be mistress of Weeton Hall. How she loved this house. It would not be easy to cease running the household the way she was accustomed. Even worse for it to be run under the hands of a stranger who did not know it and love it as she did. Could she trust her brother to choose the right woman for the task?

Her mother bit into a jam tart that she had put on her plate. "I must not forget to tell you that a boy came from Gracefield Park tenancy to inquire after you. His mother is ill, and I promised you would come as soon as you returned."

Honoria was instantly diverted. "Oh, is it Mrs. Reedsby? The boy is about this high, with hair like straw?"

"I believe it to be him. He said you would know."

"Yes, his mother runs to the bilious condition. It is time that I return to see how she is doing." This brought her thoughts back to Philip as Gracefield Park lay on the other side of the public road that crossed his estate. She selected her own roll, deciding she would worry about Miss Barbara Goodall becoming Mrs. Barbara Bassett when the time called for it.

CHAPTER 14

Philip was shown around Leicester, where Theo's sister Mary lived, but that did not take up more than a day or two of their time. They could ride—and did so more and more as Philip's burns finally started to heal—but as Mary's husband was not a landowner and spent his days as senior banker in a counting house, there was little sport to be had. In the end, they mainly had cards and a few social engagements to entertain them.

Theo was uncharacteristically silent, and Philip darted glances at him when they sat with his brother-in-law over port. Gone were the quips and jokes that were to be expected when conversing with him. Instead, when he was spoken to, he would look up as if coming out of a reverie and give some vague answer. The only clue Philip could gather as to this unusual behavior was from the comment Theo had let drop about the widow at the ball, and another one upon their arrival. He showed unusual vehemence over the way he perceived Mr. Northwick to have treated his dead brother's widow. And since it was so unlike Theo to take up a cause that did not directly concern him, Philip could only assume there was some interest in the widow on the side of his cousin.

Philip left his seat beside Theo, who was staring at a book, and went to stand by the window of the library. There was activity on the street in front of their town residence, although it was set back a ways, giving a degree of privacy the less fortunate would not have. A portion of the sky was visible over the rooftops of the narrow houses on the other side of the street, and he looked up at it, wondering if Theo stood any chance with Arabella. Gus had also shown marked interest, to Honoria's dismay. He hoped there would not be a battle between his two friends. They had taken leave of each other with more reserve than usual.

He went over to the side table to pour himself a drink, then walked back to the window to resume his examination of the thoughts that had taken over his mind since he'd arrived at his cousin's house. He had not left Lincoln with a strong idea of his intentions toward Honoria. He knew only that it would be a shame if Gus were to win her over when she deserved more devotion than what his friend was capable of giving. As there were not as many social engagements in Leicester as promised—Theo's sister being newly in the family way and feeling ill and lethargic—it left Philip with too much time on his hands to think.

In a series of flashes, he remembered the way Honoria cradled his hands as she cared for them, the frozen look on her face when he had asked her about her feelings for Gus, and her exquisite form in the gown she had chosen for the Stuff Ball. He attempted to dismiss those nudges. But when tantalizing images of the curve of her lips or the way wisps of hair curled around her face persistently intruded into his thoughts, he finally had to admit to himself that he had become something of a hopeless case in her regard. And if Gus had not seized the chance that had been thrown to him when Honoria gazed up at him with such adoration, then Gus was a fool and did not deserve to win her. Perhaps Philip might.

PHILIP SWAYED in the carriage as it took a turn east out of the innyard in Sleaford and started forth on the last day of his journey. The rhythmic clop-clop sound made by the horses was soothing, but it did not speed him forward as fast as he would have liked. A full week had passed in Theo's company before Philip realized in which direction his intentions lay, and he came to the hopeful conclusion that he might still have a chance. He allowed only three more days to pass before he decided he no longer wanted to wait to find out if Honoria was willing to pledge her troth to him. He might not be dashing, but he would be loyal.

It was an easy matter to explain to Theo. He had simply told him he was preoccupied by the irrigation project and wished to return and oversee it. He and Coates had agreed that the engineer would begin diverting the river this very week before the Waring typically underwent its seasonal surge. If Philip hurried, he would be home in time to watch the event unfold. Theo understood readily and released him of his promise to stay for the full two weeks, saying that it was probably best that he returned to his affairs in Newark-on-Trent in any case. Now, Philip was back on the road in Lincolnshire and quickly approaching Boden House.

The crisp air coming through the windows of the carriage brought the scent of more burning leaves and branches. The scent of home. It was a cool October day—although warmer than it had been the week before in a teasing reminder of the forgotten days of summer—and the trees were at their most glorious, displaying their remaining leaves in all colors. As his carriage drew near to where the public road crossed his land, Philip became aware of a splashing sound that grew louder as the wheels turned over the road. The ground visible from his window was soggy, as though it had been raining for a week straight, although he was fairly certain they'd had the same weather in Horncastle as they had in Sleaford.

He lifted his hand to tap on the roof of the carriage so he might stop and investigate but then hesitated because he wasn't sure what he could do about all the mud. The wheels began to turn more slowly as the road dipped and the ground grew muddier. Frustration struck as he took in this perplexing condition. If he had been on horseback, he would have been in a better position to examine the conditions of the road that bordered his land. But he was left with his carriage and no spare horse. An unpleasant suspicion came upon him that the problem lay with his irrigation project.

He held on to the leather strap from the ceiling of the carriage, contemplating the worrisome sight when they passed an object on the side of the road. His gaze registered Honoria in his field with her tilbury fixed in the mud while she tried on foot to encourage the horse to move forward. The rush of excitement at seeing her again, and sooner than expected, was rudely tempered by the sight of her, covered in mud, now attempting to dislodge the large wheel. He pounded on the top of his carriage for it to stop and leapt out before it came to a complete standstill.

"Honoria!" He ran two steps to the edge of the road, before sliding and trying to regain his balance.

She tilted her head to look at him, her eyes flashing with fury. "Is this your doing, Philip?" She gestured with her free hand to the muddy swamp that had once been his field. "Was it your brilliant idea to flood the public road and your field while draining half the river?"

Philip felt heat rise to his chest, both from the sight of her glorious face and her rebuke. "Of course, it was not my intention to turn my field into a swamp," he said, picking his way across the field toward her. His boots squelched in the mud and threatened to stay put with each step. "And as for diverting half the river, I assure you that is not possible. The dikes have gates in place to prevent such a thing happening." The flimsiness of that argument in wake of his surroundings was not something he would contemplate.

He finally made his way to her side and stood facing her, then looked at the empty tilbury. "Why have you no servant with you?"

"This again?" Her eyes flashed as she turned them up at him. "In ordinary times, a woman may drive herself in the country without threat of being accosted or having her wheels fastened in the mud."

She was really angry, and Philip had enough common sense to know he should not make it worse by attempting to protest. After all, it was entirely his fault. Had he not left his field in the charge of someone he scarcely knew? Then he went off on a pleasure trip and had not been here to oversee the project himself. He thought he could trust the man, but now he would have to hunt down this supposed engineer of his.

Honoria took one step toward the carriage, and in doing so lost her half-boot. She toppled forward, and he darted to catch her waist before quickly bending to retrieve the boot for her. It was at this proximity that he finally noticed what a state she was in, with hair plastered to her neck from exertion, and the mud and water seeping up her gown all the way to the bodice. She must be freezing.

"Please allow me to help you," he said, his voice strangled from guilt and alarm. He did not wait for her answer but swept her up in his arms and carried her toward the main road, her boot in one of his hands, where his carriage was waiting. Each step was a slipping hazard, but he forced himself to walk straight and steady.

"Philip! Put me down. I will walk." Her tone expressed outrage, but he ignored her. He could not help but notice both how cold she was and how good she felt in his arms. He hugged her more closely as he climbed up the slight incline to the road, telling himself it was to keep her warm.

His servant had jumped down and opened the door to the carriage, and Philip placed Honoria in the seat of it, regretting that he had no blanket in the carriage to warm her.

"Jim, you see to Miss Bassett's horse. Cut the traces if you cannot untangle them and leave the carriage for now. I'll drive and will meet you back at the Bassetts'."

The sky was overcast and reflections of the clouds shimmered on the pools of water that lay on the ground. Jim turned and picked his way through clumps of grass whose stalks were visible to where her horse stood patiently. "We'll need more men to dig out that carriage, we will."

Philip nodded, though Jim had already turned away. He would have to find a solution for how they would get the carriage out of the mud, and one for how to drain the field. He turned his attention back to the more pressing matter. Honoria sat on the squabs, shivering and looking past Philip to Jim as he unhitched her horse.

"You are freezing." His throat ached with the consequences of his oversight.

She did not deny it, and he removed his jacket and wrapped it around her. "I only wish I had a rug in the carriage to warm you, but it's not cold enough for that yet. I will get you home as quickly as possible." When she did not reply, he asked, "Is your father home?"

"He is to return in two days." Honoria continued to shiver even under the coat he'd placed around her shoulders, and he could have kicked himself for putting her in such a situation.

"I suppose it's for the best then. I'm sure he would gladly tear me apart limb from limb if he saw you in such a state."

A smile touched Honoria's lips that felt to Philip like a mark of grace. "I have no doubt that he would."

He turned to climb up on the box seat, but Honoria stopped him. "How do you plan to put the field to rights again? It will not be easy to drain it."

Philip came back to the doorframe and looked in at her. He sighed as he set one hand on the top of the carriage and leaned his head against it. "I have no idea. I only know that something must be done. I suppose I will have to drain it in much the way they drained the fenlands. Digging further canals on the border and closing the dikes."

There was a streak of mud on her pale cheek and he wanted to wipe it off, but he resisted offering a touch that would not be welcome. Despite her pale cheeks, Honoria was a woman of vibrant colors—with thick hair a man could run his fingers through and bright green eyes one could get lost in. *That* was not helping him to think clearly, and he forced his expression to be severe. "By the way, what possessed you to go off the road and into the field?"

She turned her face to him and opened her mouth in indignation but then paused to reflect and answered without rancor. "The field appeared to be drier than the road when I first left it. This part of the road is at a decline and there was a pool of water at the bottom of it. I was trying to avoid having my carriage get stranded."

Philip shook his head, hiding the depth of affection he was coming to feel for her. "It's always safer to keep to a road made of packed dirt than it is to drive into a field that will only absorb the water, turning the ground to thick sludge."

Honoria trained her eyes forward, avoiding his. Her prim lips and wry voice spoke volumes. "Well, obviously I do not need you to tell me that *now*."

Philip's grin turned sheepish. Here he was chiding her for having made a foolish decision when the blame was set wholly upon himself. He reached into the carriage and took her hand in his. The cold of her fingers seeped through her gloves and his. "Forgive me, Honoria. It is my fault entirely that you are in this predicament, and I cannot tell you how much I regret it. I will see that all gets put to rights and will pray that no harm comes to you from the cold and damp."

She met his eyes for the first time and smiled, giving his hand a small squeeze. "Well, you are forgiven entirely."

He hadn't deserved such quick and complete exoneration, but he rejoiced in it. There was a spring to his step when he climbed to the box and took up the reins. His servant had already unhitched Honoria's horse from the carriage and had brought her to the road where he waited. Philip turned the carriage around, and Jim began walking behind him leading the horse. It would take him close to an hour without a saddle.

In a much shorter time than Jim, they reached the gates of the Bassett home. One of the servants came through the door at the sound of their carriage, and Philip called out to him. "Is Mrs. Bassett able to come? Your mistress has had a problem with her carriage, and although she has come to no harm, she is cold and will need to be seen to as quickly as possible."

The carriage door opened and Honoria stepped out, his coat still wrapped around her. "No, do not bother my mother. She cannot walk easily. I assure you I will be fine." She began to remove his coat from around her shoulders.

"Keep it," he said quickly. "At least until you are inside. I can do without it."

She looked at it and touched some of the mud that had stained the front of the coat. He wasn't sure it would ever come out. "I suppose you are right. In any case, it must be cleaned. I will see that it is done before I return it to you." She paused, "That is, if you will not be too cold when going home. Perhaps a muddy coat is better than none at all."

Philip held out his elbow for her and pulled her close, not feeling any of the cold at that moment. "I will not need it," he said as another servant hurried forward. Philip asked the man to stand at his lead horse's head. He wished to have some time alone with Honoria.

The front door stood open, and he ushered her into the hall which was empty of servants. Taking advantage of this unexpected boon, he leaned toward her and said in a low voice, "If I may, I would like to come tomorrow to see how you are."

She lifted her large green eyes to his, assessing him. He could not resist the pull any longer and reached over to his coat that she was wearing and pulled his handkerchief out of the inside pocket. "Forgive me. You have ..." He reached over to wipe the mud from her cheek with infinite gentleness, as close to a caress as he dared. She stood immobile.

At last she answered, her voice husky. "That is very kind of you, but I am sure there is no need to make a fuss."

It took a moment for her words to register, then another moment to decide he wouldn't be put off for want of courage. "Then I would like to come tomorrow just to see you."

Her eyes widened, and awareness flooded her features. There were no servants hovering, but still she whispered. "Are you saying you wish to pay me court, Philip?"

He flicked his eyes behind her at the sound of someone's approach, and leaned in to murmur, "That is precisely what I am saying." He lifted her hand and placed a kiss on it then squeezed it, dropping it just as a lady's maid rounded the corner.

"Miss! We didn't want to worry Mrs. Bassett, but you were a long time away. She is resting now—*oh*!" She hurried forward when she noticed Honoria's appearance.

Philip stepped back to let her reach her mistress. "Please see that she has hot water brought up as soon as it might be arranged. She had the misfortune to have her carriage become lodged in my flooded fields."

"We shall see to her right away, sir." The maid put her arm around Honoria in a protective gesture and moved forward.

Honoria looked back over her shoulder at Philip with something like a shy smile on her face. He held her gaze for a precious instant before she was led out of sight.

CHAPTER 15

On their way up the stairwell, Honoria and her mother's maid passed Maggie, who was coming down with a bundle of dirty clothes to be laundered. Perkins ordered for hot water to be brought up, and Maggie hastened her steps. When they entered her bedroom, the maid helped Honoria to remove her clinging wet and muddy clothes, then wrapped her in a blanket. She sank into a chair and waited until Maggie and a scullery maid brought in the copper tub and began filling it with kettles of hot water, followed by buckets of cool water to achieve the right temperature. In the warmth of the room, her feet and hands began to burn as the circulation flowed through them again, and Maggie chattered on about how lucky it was that belowstairs had been about to begin the washing and had hot water at the ready.

When the preparations were finished, Honoria dropped dried lavender buds in the water and allowed Maggie to help her slip into the copper tub. Then she ordered everyone to leave her, saying, "Take this coat to be cleaned, will you? I would like to return it to Mr. Townsend in good order."

"Ay, miss." Maggie took the coat, along with the muddy gown and pelisse before closing the door quietly behind her. Honoria swirled her hand in the hot water and watched the lavender buds spin then float back to the surface, allowing a smile to touch her lips. Philip Townsend had declared his interest in her. *Philip!* She would have to find out when his heart had shifted in her direction. She couldn't even begin to think when and if her own heart had changed. It was too confusing after so many years of loving Gus. But she could not deny that there was both attraction when his face hovered close to hers and feelings that went deeper than that as she thought about his honorable behavior that was— above all—consistent.

The fact that Gus had so quickly switched his interest to Arabella after showing Honoria a most flattering attention at the ball had been a disheartening blow, and even Christine had sat her down for tea in the week that followed their stay in Lincoln and advised her in no uncertain terms to set her sights elsewhere. "My brother is not the kind of man who appears capable of settling down with one woman," she had told her. "I hope he might prove me wrong one day, but I do not want my best friend to suffer from his lack of constancy."

You deserve better, Christine had said. And Honoria believed her. The two weeks after the ball were a time of grieving the loss of what would never be. She had too much self-respect to continue to offer her heart to someone who would never value it.

She dipped her head under water to wet her hair then reached for the lemon-thyme soap, biting her lip to keep the smile from making another appearance. It was really so unexpected. Here was Philip, whom she had never considered in the light of a suitor pursuing her. Now that she thought about it, he had never shown anything but the utmost gallantry toward her. He was gracious and kind when she had trespassed on his property, although she supposed she must have expected such behavior from him or she never would have dared to go in the first place. He had saved her life ... Honoria ran her fingers over the slight scar on her leg, which was now white and smooth, and minimal.

He had even noticed her crushing disappointment after the ball, and he got to his feet to serve her breakfast. Honoria reached again for the soap and began scrubbing away the mud from her arms, replacing the memories of cold and disappointment with warmth, soothing scents, and a calm joy.

The next day, Honoria selected a gown of soft beige lawn that she felt made her skin glow. She sat in companionable silence with her mother, her smile ready, stitching the family initials on a tablecloth that would be a gift for Samuel's bride, while her mother performed an inventory of the family silver. More than once she darted her gaze to her mother, wondering if she should tell her that Philip was coming to see her—and why. The sound of carriage wheels arriving through the gates reached them through the latticed windows, and she almost got to her feet, but then feigned concentration on a tricky knot in her embroidery. It would not be seemly for her to appear too eager to see Philip by rushing out of the door at the first sound of his arrival.

"Jeffrey, come get the horses! What does a man have to do to get some assistance in his own house?" Honoria and her mother exchanged a startled look, and Honoria shot to her feet, then ran to the door and into the courtyard.

"Papa! You're home early." Instead of the joy of return that she had expected to see on her father's face, his expression was tight with annoyance.

She came to his side as he handed the reins to the footman who had come running from the stables. "Come in, Papa! Whatever is the matter?" She kissed him on the cheek and pulled him toward the house.

"It's that bumbling, idiotic neighbor of ours. I should have known that Townsend would father a son who is just as much of a fool as he is. The sapskull has actually attempted to divert the Waring. He's turned his entire field and the public road back into the fens. And what's more, I will eat my hat if that addlepate has not succeeded in lowering the capacity of the mill by draining half the river so that there's nothing left to turn its wheel."

Honoria's head went light as she listened to his tirade, and she attempted to think how best to answer him. "Papa, come inside, and I will make you comfortable."

"And what were you doing in his fields?" He rounded on her. "Don't think I didn't see our tilbury there, fixed deep in the mud."

Her mind grasped at possible answers, but she was saved by the arrival of her mother at the front entrance, whose face was wreathed with the joy of his return. Honoria tugged a warning on her father's arm.

"There you are, Mama, but we were coming. Are you sure you should be walking?" She leaned in to whisper to her father. "Remove your scowl, please. Mama has missed you so much."

She needn't have given him the warning, as her father was already smiling and striding toward his wife to envelop her in his arms. They held each other for a long moment, and Honoria moved past them into the house to give them their privacy. She hoped her father would postpone his talk with her until after he had had some tea and was a good deal calmer.

Having gone to the kitchen to oversee the tea platter—ensuring it was filled with all the delicacies her father loved best—Honoria entered the drawing room behind their cook. Her father had already been coaxed into a much better humor, and she took that as a good sign.

Mrs. Sands set the heavy tea tray in front of him. "Welcome home, sir."

Mr. Bassett responded agreeably, all traces of his former ill humor gone. He was not a cantankerous man, but when something set him off, he would explode like a thundercloud, and then just as quickly put his good mood back in place—like the sun upon its return. She sat and prepared tea the way her parents liked, adding bread and ham to her father's plate, along with sweetened biscuits. She would have to escape and warn Philip not to come today and could only hope he would not call this early. It was impossible that she depart so soon after her father's arrival.

"Is there anything else you need, Papa?" she asked, resigning herself to staying until he had had his fill of domesticity and escaped into his library.

"No, this is quite nice." He set his plate down to take his wife's hand, smiling at her fondly. "What do you both think of Samuel's wedding?"

"I was never more shocked in my life," Honoria answered promptly, causing her parents to laugh. "It is true. He has never shown the slightest interest in settling down. I simply cannot picture it."

"Well, you are young yet," her father said fondly. "One day, you will also desire to be wed, although such a thing must be far from your thoughts." He bit into his ham and bread and chewed, while Honoria stared at him, stunned. Did he not know she was nineteen? She looked away when he turned his gaze upon her.

"Tell us more about Miss Goodall," her mother said, a smile hovering on her lips. She had not missed Honoria's indignation and had surely understood the cause for it.

Her father told them everything he knew, which was that Samuel—in a move most unlike his urbane self—had speared a small plum on his plate at Gunter's and the unobliging fruit bounded from the plate to Miss Goodall's back. He was so mortified, he sought an introduction at the next ball, and after one dance decided it was fate.

After Honoria and her mother had peppered Mr. Bassett with questions he could not answer, they allowed the conversation to drift to how the committee talks had gone and how he had entertained himself in London. As soon as she thought she might leave without suspicion, Honoria told her parents she was going for a walk while there was still sun and promised she would not stray far.

They nodded, and she grabbed her bonnet and tied it as she fled the house. She hoped to find Philip at the juncture where his field had been flooded, knowing that without her carriage it would be too far to walk all the way to his house— besides the fact she had no good excuse for visiting him. It would raise the eyebrows of every one of his servants. They might not be diligent, but they would know how to draw conclusions.

She was in luck. Honoria had not even reached the field when she saw him on horseback heading in her direction. As soon as he spotted her, his face split in a broad smile, and she stood still in anticipation, her heart warming at the sight of him. A longing to be close to him filled her as he drew near—to be in his arms as she had been the day before, when he had carried her.

"I was just on my way to see you." Philip swung down from his horse and took both her hands in his.

Honoria swallowed at the tremor of excitement that went through her as he looked at her. It was almost as though he wished to devour her. It was the first time she'd ever been on the receiving end of such a look. All she'd ever known until now was dashed hopes and patent disregard.

"That is why I came to find you." Her voice came out breathless, and she made an effort to strengthen it. "My father has returned a day early."

Philip stilled at the unwelcome revelation, but then he rallied. "This is very good news. Let me not waste any time in going to him and making my intentions known."

Honoria was already shaking her head before he had finished his sentence. "No, that is just it. You cannot see him—at least not today. He is in a thundering mood and not fit for company."

"Very well then. I will wait." He frowned, linking his fingers through hers, causing her to forget some of her urgency in the breathlessness that followed his gesture. Did he realize he was holding her hands in such an intimate way? Philip brought his gaze to hers. "But do you know what has upset him?"

"Unfortunately I do. He saw your flooded fields, the state of the public road, and the fact that our carriage is still firmly fixed in the mud—"

"Ah, blast. I have not yet been able to remove it. I've needed to call for more help." He looked down and absently rubbed her gloved hand, his frown lines becoming pronounced. Honoria had trouble focusing with the way he stroked her hand—had trouble breathing.

"And he's not only angry about the carriage and the public road." She pulled her hand away. It was too distracting. "He is convinced that you have diverted the river in such a way that has weakened our mill's production."

Philip glanced at her, his eyes serious. "I assure you, I did not. I would never do anything to harm your family. I sought advice before attempting such a large venture. It is true that when Coates abandoned the project in my absence, the resulting flood perhaps led to a weakening of the current. However, now that all the gates have been closed, the river is back to what it once was. It is only that I must now take care of the public road and drain my own fields. But that should not affect your father at all."

Honoria's heart softened at Philip's plight, and she wished somehow that she might help carry his burden. He was trying his best, and it was not easy to surmount so many difficulties. "I believe my father will soon see that the diversion has not affected mill production, at least not permanently. However, I think you must know that my father is particularly sensitive to correct behavior between neighbors. That is why our fathers were at such odds. He did not appreciate the way your father carried on projects that would affect the village without consulting his peers, such as excavating for the mine. He feared it would both be an eyesore, and that it would attract a different sort of population to this part of Lincolnshire."

She spoke apologetically, knowing that this admission did not paint her father in the most gracious light. "I suppose it did not help that your father hinted that my father's parentage was inferior."

Philip closed his eyes as he shook his head. "I am sorry. It was very wrong of him. And then of course the mine was dry and that was almost worse, for the estate did not gain the income it so desperately needed."

"And I am sorry it did not work out as your father had

hoped." Honoria remembered Mr. Townsend's sad demise, having died when the mine collapsed on top of him during one of his visits. She was filled with the desire to support Philip, to lift him up. "You are not your father, however. And ... and if you did decide to speak to my father, it would be with my full support."

"Is that so?" Philip lifted his eyes to hers and his gaze stilled. He touched his fingers to her cheek just below her jawline, and she waited for a long, breathless moment, until he stepped closer.

"May I ...?" he whispered.

The sound of approaching hoofbeats reached them, and Philip quickly dropped his hand and took a step back, a look of frustration on his face. Honoria did not dare to turn and see who it was, knowing her heightened color would reveal more about her current state of emotions than she wished to.

"Coates!" Philip shook his head in disbelief. "He dares to show his face here."

In another few moments, Mr. Coates had reined in, and he swung down to approach Philip. "Mr. Townsend, I owe you an apology. But before you chase me off your land, as I'm sure you have every right to do, please allow me to explain."

Philip had turned fully, placing Honoria behind him as though to protect her from the stranger's gaze. "Go on then."

Coates lifted his hands as though to clarify. "Just after we opened the pipes to divert the water and were in the critical stage of controlling its flow, I received an urgent summons from my wife that my daughter had contracted scarlatine and was in danger of her life. Upon learning of it, I could not delay my departure. I left the project in the hands of Tom Hull and the team, but I had misplaced confidence in them."

He glanced around at the destruction of Philip's field and frowned. "Once the workers did not have the man paying their salaries in front of them, they became more interested in the alehouse than they were in earning an honest wage. As soon as my daughter was out of danger, I learned about what happened and came as quickly as I could. And now, if you will trust me to repair what has been done, I know where to find a new team of workers, and we will build the trenches necessary to drain the field."

Mr. Coates turned to Honoria who, now fully recovered, stepped more fully into view. He pulled off his hat and bowed. "G'day, miss. I hope you'll pardon my intrusion."

Honoria acknowledged him then turned away and met Philip's gaze with a soft smile. "I can see that you are occupied, so I shall leave you now."

Philip glanced back at Mr. Coates, then at her, his features filled with regret. "I will come tomorrow," he said. "And I hope to see you then."

CHAPTER 16

P hilip spent the rest of the day with Coates, discussing how to solve the dilemma of the flooded fields. When asked, Coates estimated that there had probably been some decrease in the production at the mill, given the amount of river water that had drained out. The gates had not functioned as they ought to, causing the disaster. However, he was confident that the mill should now be working up to speed, and any ill effects would not be permanent. Surely, Mr. Bassett would see that. Philip returned home at the end of the day, his thoughts divided on whether the measures they'd discussed to drain the field would be enough and whether he stood any chance at winning Mr. Bassett's approval for his suit.

By the next day, Philip had come to the conclusion that if he wished to face Mr. Bassett confidently, he would need to oversee the new team Coates had put in place. When he arrived at the field, the workers were already busy digging trenches on the periphery that would allow the excess water to drain. At the very least, Mr. Bassett would not be able to reproach him for being slow to find a solution.

Coates took Philip to inspect the dikes, explaining apologetically that the gates that were constructed had been no match for the force of the river in high season, and that the problem would need to be rectified before they attempted the irrigation again. When Philip was confident of the progress, he had the men pause their work to extricate the carriage from the swampy field and bring it to the public road. There he hitched his own horse to it and drove it to the Bassetts'. He would return on horseback.

It was early afternoon when he arrived at Weeton Hall, and a servant came out at the sound of the carriage. Philip alighted and handed him the reins. This was soon followed by the arrival of Mr. Bassett himself.

"Townsend," he said in a curt manner that did not bode well for Philip.

"Sir, I am returning this carriage with my apologies." Philip paused for a moment to think how best to explain. "I had my men pull it from the earth this morning. The whole thing was terribly unfortunate, and I take full responsibility that my failed irrigation project caused your daughter's carriage to be entrenched in the mud."

"So I've heard," Mr. Bassett said, studying the tilbury critically. "And you've returned it to me covered in mud." He went over to examine the body of the carriage. "And there is a nick in the wood here. More like a gouge."

Philip should have taken the carriage home to clean and repair it first and was now realizing his error in having rushed to speak to Mr. Bassett. He was hardly going to win him over with such a lack of courtesy.

"Again, my apologies. In my haste to bring the carriage to you as quickly as possible, I did not stop to clean it. However, I can have my servants come and do that for you—or I can bring it to Boden, then return it tomorrow in good order."

"There is no need." Mr. Bassett signaled to his footman to unhitch the horse. "I see you have your saddle and are equipped to ride home without needing our assistance. You may be on your way."

Philip removed his hat and held it between his hands as

though it held his courage. "Sir, if you will spare me a few minutes of your time, I would like to have a word with you."

Mr. Bassett paused in his tracks and turned to glare at Philip under a lowered brow. He seemed to be seriously considering whether he should go with his first instinct and deny the request or whether he should grant it. At last, his good breeding won out. "Jeffrey, take Mr. Townsend's horse here and give it some water and whatever else it needs. He won't be long."

Mr. Bassett turned and strode toward the house, gesturing with a wave of his hand. "Come with me, then."

Philip could hardly believe he had been granted an interview after his initial reception, and he followed Mr. Bassett into the house. They walked directly into the library, and he was not granted a fortifying glimpse of Honoria.

"Have a seat." Mr. Bassett sat across from Philip, and although he did not offer any refreshments, Philip was encouraged that he was not made to remain standing while he made his request.

"Sir, this has already been said, but I wish again to apologize for the mishap that involved your carriage—"

"—and my daughter," Mr. Bassett finished.

Philip's pulse began to jump. "Yes, your daughter. It is concerning her that I wish to speak to you."

Mr. Bassett's scowl grew more pronounced. "What possible connection could you have with my daughter?" Although his tone could only be described as menacing, there was nothing for Philip to do but continue, now that he had already begun.

He planted his feet more firmly on the floor and placed his hands on his knees. "Sir, I want to speak to you about your daughter, because I wish to pay her court with a view to marriage."

Mr. Bassett's eyebrows now rose almost to his hairline, and he stood suddenly, causing Philip to leap to his feet. "You wish to court my daughter." He stated this in disbelief, then after a brief pause, added in a raised voice, "You realize what a foolish thing you're asking of me? You have no hope of gaining your wish."

139

Philip had known Mr. Bassett was angry—had suspected he would not entirely look upon the suit with favor—but he did not expect such vehement disapproval. After all, their mothers had been friendly. They were of an equal social standing, and in marrying him, Honoria would remain in the same village as her family.

"I do not quite follow." He forced his hands to remain still at his sides, making an effort not to fidget or pace in his agitation.

"You do not follow," Mr. Bassett repeated with awful irony. "Your father and I never saw eye to eye, and in fact I never liked the fellow. Your estate is barely earning enough income to sustain itself—if it's not already falling to ruin from debt. There is still that eyesore of a mine on your land, well in view of the public road and *my* property. You've just flooded the road, and had the audacity to divert the river without my consent, lowering the production of my mill." Philip was tempted to defend himself on this subject but knew better than to interrupt. When Mr. Bassett had drawn breath, he added, "What bacon-brained notion leads you to believe you could ever hope to win the hand of my daughter?"

Philip stood up straight. "I thought you would wish for your daughter's happiness. We share an attachment. There is a ... *a tendre* on both our parts, and I thought—"

"A *tendre*! What father would give away his only daughter for some imagined attachment? A foolish father indeed, and I am not he. No, it is for the women to think about feelings and for the men to think practically. Even if I had not had an aversion to your father—may God rest his soul—I could never give Honoria away to a man who was barely solvent."

Philip was struck mute by the oppressive barrage of accusations. He could not deny the facts, despite working hard to get his estate in order. And he could not defend himself from anything Mr. Bassett said, except perhaps the mill, but it did not seem the right moment. His estate in its current condition would hardly satisfy a father who was a stickler for results—never mind that Philip was certain he would turn things around.

And with a wife like Honoria at his side, there was simply no way he would fail.

"I hope I might prove myself in time then, sir. I am making steps to improve my estate. I am in the process of increasing the stables, and I'd irrigated my field with the hopes of multiplying the crops there—which would bring more business to your mill, I might add."

"I refuse to marry my daughter off on mere plans. Nor do I want to marry her to the son of a man who sank his fortune into an empty mine which grates my nerves every time I see it. No, sir. It is better to give up any pretensions toward Honoria, and I say this for the good of you both. I trust you understand me and will not think to darken my doorstep again with your talk of plans and attachment." Mr. Bassett opened the door and held it, putting an end to the conversation.

Reeling from the harsh words, Philip's voice abandoned him. He gave a stiff nod and put on his hat, managing a, "Thank you for your time, sir" before making his way outdoors. He found his horse ready and swung into the saddle, leading him out of the gates at a walk. As soon as he had the open field in front of him, he gave Poker-Up his head. They both needed a good run.

PHILIP SPENT the rest of the day in his library with a book on his lap. When he finally came to his surroundings and realized he had not turned the page for the past hour, he closed it and set it on the table. He had hardly moved from his chair, and the servants seemed to have noticed. Mrs. Mason treated him with more kindness than usual, bringing him tea without being summoned.

He couldn't believe his hopes for Honoria were over before he could prove himself. It was vastly unfair of her father to refuse even to consider the idea. How could Mr. Bassett say with such certainty that they would never be a good match? Here he was, unable to—as her father put it—darken their doorstep with his presence. How could he convince Mr. Bassett he would be as good a match for Honoria as the man could hope for? And if Philip couldn't see her, how would he ever find out whether she were willing to submit to her father's decree?

As the day grew into night, Philip turned Mr. Bassett's threat over in his mind, and it suddenly dawned on him that he had not precisely given his word to obey. It was true, at the time he had been too distraught to answer. But what that meant was that he had not exactly *promised* he wouldn't come—which meant he would not be breaking his word if he went to see Honoria and learn what she thought about the matter. He just didn't know how he would accomplish this since he was not to go to the front door.

The longing to see her grew in intensity until he began to pace. It grew until an idea took root. He quite thought, from those rare visits his mother made when they were children, that her room was on the south side and within easy reach. There was a brick wall not too far from that side of the house where her bedroom was located. If he were to get to the top of the wall, he could then lean over to the side of the building, grab the vines that grew there, and make his way up. There was a grotesque sculpture of a medieval goblin or some such thing cut into the stone that would allow him to gain the first foothold, and then he could climb the rest of the way on the vines and knock on her window. If indeed it were still her window.

It was a daring idea, but it might be his only chance to learn how she felt. He just *had* to win her hand. What good was a rambling house and estate if he lived in it alone? It just wanted a little courage, and his prize was within reach.

Philip waited until there was no longer a sound heard in his own household. It was well after midnight when he saddled his horse again and rode to Weeton Hall, stopping at a line of trees just on the edge of the property where he would not be heard.

"You stay here and wait for me." He tied his gelding to a tree and rubbed its neck. "I shall not be long."

The air was crisp, and there was little moonlight when he

went over to the wall. He blew on his hands, then grasped the protruding bricks and began to climb, relying on the missing chinks to gain a hold. At the top, he straddled the wall and peered around the property but spotted no one. There were no lights on anywhere in the house that he could see, so he leaned over and caught the vine on the side of the wall. The bark and remaining red leaves were more slippery than he'd expected, but he managed to get a foothold on the sculpture and continue his climb. As he neared the window, he wedged his top boots in a notch where the vines intertwined, but it was not enough of a hold and he slipped. He clung to the vine more securely until he had regained his footing, thinking wryly that he should have worn his dancing slippers, then climbed the rest of the way until he reached her window.

I cannot believe I'm doing this. Pray heavens let it be her room. He rapped softly on the window, not wishing to scare her. But when he waited and Honoria did not come, he knocked again a little more forcefully. In the next minute, he saw a flash of white at the window, followed by a vision of her red hair and pale face peering through it. Her eyes widened in surprise, and she lifted the sash.

"Philip! What are you doing here? My father would absolutely kill you. And I mean that quite literally. Come inside quickly." She tugged on his arm. He did not need any further encouragement and hauled himself over the ledge into the bedroom that was warm even with the fire burning low. "You must not let a servant catch sight of you, or we will both be in the suds."

She closed the window, and he stared at her in silence, only a foot away from her. His heart began to pound. It was only at that instant that he realized the impropriety of what he had just done. He had known such a visit would be improper but convinced himself that they had known each other their whole lives and were, for all accounts, mere friends. Yet, there she stood, more beautiful a woman than he'd ever seen in his life, the long thick waves of her hair falling loosely around her shoulders and her nightshift settling not much below her knees. He blushed in spite of himself, thankful for the dark.

"I will just get my dressing gown." Honoria hurried over to it and slipped her arms through the garment, tying the belt around her waist as she returned. Her eyes were round as she whispered, "Tell me, Philip, what is it? What caused you to come in the middle of the night at great risk to us both?"

"Forgive me. I am now realizing the idea was mad. I was driven by my need to see you." Philip rubbed his face, burying it in his hands for a moment. "Your father told me never to darken his doorstep again, so I wiggled around the promise by darkening a window."

This admission was met with silence and he looked up. Honoria was staring at him in shock before a laugh escaped her. "*That* is mere form, you realize."

"I do." Philip took a step backwards and held up both of his hands. "I promise you will receive no harm from me."

"I know it," she answered softly, waiting for him to explain himself. It was not such an easy thing to do now that he was standing before her.

"It came upon me suddenly, but I suppose it is the way with men when they meet the woman they hope"—Philip stopped when his voice cracked, and he swallowed—"when they meet the woman they wish to marry. But my hopes proved to be in vain, for your father has said no."

"I suspected such a thing," she said, even more softly. When he looked more closely at her face, despite the dearth of moonlight, he thought he saw traces of tears. "I heard my father ushering you into the library. Afterwards, my father said nothing of the matter to me, and that told me everything I needed to know. If he had approved your suit, he would have spoken to me."

"I will wait. I would wait for you until you came into your majority, if you were willing," Philip said. He could not touch her, would not compromise her in that way, so he held his hand

144

to his breast instead. "I would never presume to ask you to go against your father—"

"Despite coming into my bedroom in the middle of the night?" she said in teasing irony.

He let out a soft groan. "Not my best idea. I shall not make a practice of it. But if you thought I might have a chance at winning your heart, I would do everything possible to win your hand. Even if it meant waiting for years."

Honoria regarded him with a tender expression, her feet bare and hair flowing freely around her shoulders. Her arms were relaxed at her side and her face soft. Everything about her invited a kiss. Philip took another step backwards and grabbed the window ledge to remind himself that he should not be here.

"You already have, Phil," she whispered.

Philip's mind struggled to catch up. He had been so busy imagining what it would be like to taste her lips that he couldn't make sense of what she was saying. "I already have ... what?"

"You already have won my heart."

The whispered words echoed in the dark silence. He heard only her breath and his own, his feet rooted to the ground. In the shadows, their gaze grew in longing until she glided directly into his chest and put her arms around him. She lifted her face and went up on tiptoe, placing her lips on his.

He was stunned. Stunned. It took only a fraction of a second before he returned her kisses with all the suppressed passion of a man for whom the gates had been opened. Her dressing gown was satiny soft, and he skimmed his hands along her ribs as he ran them up her back, then lifted them to cradle her face, his fingers tangling in her hair. If her gown had felt like satin, her cheeks were somehow even softer and so fragrant as he breathed in her scent. He let his hands linger there. But then caressing her face left her too far from him, and he had to reach down and pull her closer to press his lips on hers with a hunger he had never known—

Philip shot away like a bolt and bumped into the window. His chest was heaving, and his eyes were wide. Honoria opened her eyes slowly, as though coming out of a dream. She didn't speak.

"I ..." Philip grabbed the window frame behind him. "I would like to say that there will be no more nighttime visits while we wait for your father's approval. This was one of my"—he shook his head and moistened his lips—"one of my less inspired ideas."

Grasping at any gallant instinct he had remaining, he bowed. "Good night, dearest."

Opening the window, he swung his legs over the ledge, making sure he had a good grip on the vines that kept him from plunging to the ground, then climbed down enough so that his head was level with the window. She had come to it and looked down at him, her hands resting on the sash and a smile tugging at her lips. He returned it before looking down and beginning the shaky descent that would bring him to the safety of firm ground. But really—he thought he might not plummet to the earth if he fell.

He might just fly.

CHAPTER 17

Honoria watched Philip climb the rest of the way down, stretch his feet over to the wall and leap to the other side without a backward glance, before she slid the window shut with a muted sound. She went over and sat on the bed, her unseeing gaze fixed on the darkened window. A sudden violent shiver had her slipping her feet under the covers and clasping her hands on top of them.

Her lips still tingled from the unexpected kiss. She could scarcely believe she had been the one to instigate such a thing, but in that earth-shifting moment there had been something about his presence that drew her like a magnet. There was also, she had to own, a degree of curiosity that had prompted her to make such a bold step. What would such a thing feel like? Now she had a glimpse of understanding as to why so many rules were set in place to keep propriety between a man and woman before marriage. She grinned suddenly and turned to bury her face in her pillow in a mixture of embarrassment and delight.

Philip had done right in warning her there would be no more nighttime visits, and now that she herself knew the danger of early intimacies, she would be much more careful. She rolled onto her back and touched her lips in wonder. Nothing, however, could keep her from dreaming. She was determined to marry

Philip without delay now that she knew what an exhilarating thing his kisses could be. The sensation of his lips on hers was magical, but it was not just that. It was his strong hands holding her close as if he could not bear for there to be any separation between them. And the look in his eyes when he broke away from her—one of alarm as though he had not quite acted the gentleman. There was another look there, and it was that one she adored. It was a look of hunger—of danger. One that said there was much more in store for her. She could feed on that look for a very long time.

Honoria exhaled in a soft sigh and tried to fall asleep, but it was impossible. To think she had almost thrown her heart away on Gus, whom she now felt she scarcely knew, despite having him in her life every bit as long as Philip. As a man, he must know about such intimacies and it seemed he was ready to exchange them with just about any woman. Sharing such a kiss with him would not have left her feeling the same way, of that she was sure.

Even when the physical sensation of cold and excitement died down, and the memories of Philip's face near hers began to fade, her mind was unceasingly restless. It did not take long for her to come to the realization that her first thought had been deceiving. She could *not* live on that look for so many years or even months. No, she could not bear to have her marriage to Philip put off until she came of age. She would have to find a way to convince her father. He *had* to come to see Philip as a worthy suitor. It was time to turn her thoughts to how she might help Philip assure his future prosperity enough to convince her father to accept.

Although Honoria did not fall asleep before the wee hours of the morning, the knowledge that something significant had happened, and a heart bursting with excitement woke her up the next day well before the morning was advanced. She rang for Maggie to come and dress her, wondering as she stared at her reflection in the glass if something looked different about her— wondering if it could be seen on her face that she was a woman kissed. No. Upon staring long enough, she thought not. A woman was allowed her secrets, after all.

When she entered the breakfast room, her parents were both there, and her mother was in the act of folding a letter. "Good morning, Honoria. This is late for you."

"I had trouble sleeping," she replied with perfect truth, taking her seat at the table. The next part was less truthful. "I could not stop thinking about Samuel's wedding. Do we have an idea of when it is to take place?"

"In fact, the letter I was just reading came from Samuel. And before I forget"—her mother pulled a folded paper from the stack and pushed it toward Honoria—"this also came for you from Mrs. Northwick, and it has been franked, which means she must not be at Thimbleby. The news I had from Samuel is that he, his betrothed, and her parents are arriving in two days. It is a most fortunate thing that we are ready, for the letter was delayed and it has left us with little time to prepare." Mrs. Bassett paused to sip her tea, then continued. "The Goodalls will be staying with us until the wedding and have expressed a wish to discover where the young couple will be spending their early days of marriage, which I suppose is only natural."

Honoria took the note from Arabella and tucked it under her plate to read later. She was conscious of her reluctance to meet Samuel's intended and wondered why this should be so. The only conclusion that came readily was not one that showed her to possess an abundance of Christian charity: she did not want a stranger to take up residence in her home, be it only for a short time.

Mr. Bassett wiped his mouth and set the napkin beside his plate. "I have already seen that the banns will be read beginning this Sunday, but I must speak with Mr. Grunden about having the house near the mill ready. His wife has promised to organize a thorough cleaning. It's a good thing we decided to have the roof repaired last summer." He turned to his wife. "As soon as our Honoria here is married off, you and I should think about removing to that house. It's a comfortable size, and there will be fewer stairs to trouble you. Samuel and his bride will want to settle into Weeton without an overly long delay, and I am not so partial to it I cannot be happy elsewhere. What think you, my dear?"

Mrs. Bassett glanced at her daughter before replying. "I must confess I am not in a hurry to see Honoria married off and making her home elsewhere, but you are perfectly right in saying that the smaller house will suit us very well."

Honoria summoned a smile and looked down at her plate before reaching for the teapot. It was apparently not just having a stranger in residence she would have to accept. She had not considered what it would be like to be displaced from her own home by her brother's marriage, although apparently such a step would not take place until she was married. How generous!

It would have hurt much more had she not had a prospect lined up, and perhaps she could turn this to good account. Yesterday, Honoria could not be entirely sure that Philip had broached the matter with her father of courting her until he came to deliver the news that night. But this seemed such a convergence of moments it was impossible for her to remain still.

"Papa, speaking of marriage guests. Philip Townsend came to speak with you yesterday." Honoria stopped short and reddened. She had been on the tip of confessing to him that she knew what had transpired, but it would mean revealing that Philip had paid her a secret visit. And not only would that inspire her father's wrath toward both of them, it would be the final nail on the coffin of any potential betrothal. "What did he wish to speak to you about?"

Mr. Bassett sent his daughter an unusually severe look under his thick, ginger-colored eyebrows. "So, you know about that meeting, do you?"

Honoria refused to be nervous, although she could not quite command her limbs not to quake under the table. "Yes, I saw him through the window when he came, and as I had some inkling that he was to speak to you, I suppose I was able to discern why. However, you never breathed a word of it ..." She let the sentence dangle. It was unlike her father not to take her into his confidence, especially for something that concerned her so nearly.

Her parents exchanged a look, then her father picked up his napkin and crumpled it in his hand. "Philip Townsend came to speak to me concerning matrimony to you, my girl. As I was sure that no such arrangement could do you any good, I had no hesitation in turning him down."

Honoria glanced at her mother, whose gaze was on her teacup. She could not tell if her mother was against the idea or not but hoped she would speak up in Philip's favor. "Yes, Papa. But you have not given me a good reason for why. I know there was some animosity between you and his father, but his father is no longer here. Philip is our closest neighbor, which means that in marrying him, I would remain near to my family. I thought such a thing might please you."

"You mean you would have a chance to sponge off your parents when he can't pay the tradesmen's bills," he shot back, and the unexpected harshness in his tone and words hit Honoria like a brick.

"Father, how you can think such a thing of me? I—" She could not finish the sentence as her throat had closed off the possibility of further words.

"Harold." Mrs. Bassett's gentle voice carried an unmistakable warning.

Mr. Bassett stared at his wife for a moment, blinking, then stood and reached across the table, squeezing Honoria's hand. "Forgive me, my daughter. My anger is directed toward Townsend. I did not mean for it to be directed at you."

He resumed his seat and continued, "He is simply incapable of supporting a wife. Even if I had not had a falling out with his father, who you must know was one of the most thoughtless, havey-cavey men I have ever had the misfortune to meet, I would still have an objection to the marriage. I cannot see my only daughter setting up house with a man who will not be able to provide all of the elegancies to which she is accustomed."

"But surely Philip's situation is not so dire as that," Honoria protested. "And with a practical woman at his side who is capable of housekeeping and managing expenditures ... Would that not be exactly what he needs to make his mark in the world?"

"I simply cannot make that sacrifice," Mr. Bassett said with finality. He glanced at Mrs. Bassett and a current of unspoken communication passed between them. "And your mother supports me in this. You must put the idea of Philip Townsend out of your mind." He got to his feet. "If you'll excuse me, I need to go meet with Mr. Grunden, especially now that the Goodalls are to arrive so soon. I would not wish for Samuel's bride to suffer a check at her first glance of her new home." He walked over and kissed his wife on the cheek and then quit the room without further ado.

"Honoria—"

"Mama, at what point did you decide that Philip and I would not suit? There was a time when you hatched a scheme with Philip's mother for our future. And now that I wish it—"

"But that is just it. How could I have supported you against your father when I did not know you wished it? You haven't spoken a word to me about Philip. The only guess I had about your feeling was my firm belief that he would never have dared approach your father if you and he had not come to some sort of agreement first."

Honoria ran her finger around the blue border of her empty plate. "The feelings came about suddenly, and I did not notice him at first because I was blinded by my feelings for Gus. Philip is kind to me. When Gus ignored me after the ball, he came to my rescue and brought me food. He ..." She very nearly said that he had saved her life, but she stopped herself. It was better that her parents remained in ignorance of what had happened. "He is interested in my welfare, and there is kindness in his eyes."

The words were too feeble, but she could not make them stronger. A flash of Philip's kiss sprang up suddenly, reminding

Honoria that there was more than kindness in his eyes. But this was not something she could tell her mother either.

Mrs. Bassett pushed her teacup away from her. "If you'll just help me to stand, I wish to go to the drawing room where the linens are waiting for me. I must begin embroidering initials on the sheets for the newlyweds. You've done a beautiful job with the napkins."

Honoria got to her feet and went over to help her mother, unable to hide her despondency. As she gave her arm in support on their way to the drawing room, Mrs. Bassett said, "Let us give your father his way in this for now. We have your brother's wedding to think about first, and you are young, my dear, though you do not think so. Let us see if your feelings do not change in a year or two and whether Philip is constant. If both of these things remain unchanged, nothing will prevent you from being married after that. I will speak to your father myself."

Honoria did not trust her voice and gave no response as she opened the door of the breakfast room to usher her mother through the Great Hall. A year or two! She was certain she could not wait that long.

TWO DAYS LATER, her brother arrived as promised, just as the sun reached its peak overhead. His hair was longer, nearly reaching his shoulders now in blond waves. He was slightly stouter and had grown whiskers, which gave him more the appearance of a man settled and grown. Even without these physical changes, the care he took in helping his betrothed out of the carriage showed him to be a changed man.

Honoria and her parents stood at the door of the house to greet them, and Mr. Bassett went forward first, shaking hands with his son and giving a kiss on the cheek to his future daughter-in-law. An older woman appeared at the door to the carriage, and he stepped forward to assist her and then her husband. "Welcome to our house, Mrs. Goodall, Mr. Goodall."

Samuel bussed Honoria on her cheek. "Come meet Babs. Babs, this is my sister, Honoria. You must use your Christian names. And this is my mother." Mrs. Bassett greeted Barbara, then turned to the girl's parents while Honoria smiled at her brother's wife-to-be.

"I wish to offer you congratulations on your betrothal and hope you might be happy here."

"I thank you." Barbara, whose clothing and deportment portrayed a woman given to considering appearances, looked up at the front of the house and allowed her gaze to roam around the small courtyard in front. "I had understood the house would be bigger."

Honoria hoped her brother had not heard such a thing, for he would be disappointed. She could detect no spite in her tone and could only wonder what had prompted such a remark. And what would Barbara think once she saw the house where they would be living following their honeymoon? That was only one third the size of this one.

As the crowd made their way toward the house, eventually settling in the drawing room, it did not take long for Honoria to form the opinion that Mrs. Goodall, a faded woman who had the tendency to mumble, was not the driving force of the family but only answered, "You are very right, my dear," to whatever Mr. Goodall said. Barbara had more color in her features and a stronger presence than her mother, but Honoria could not read her easily. Their first meeting offered no instant connection between them, though she hoped it would come.

Mr. Goodall had a more commanding presence than either, and whatever hair he lacked on the top of his head he made up for with whiskers that overran his round, polished face. "Bassett, it is very good of you to host us during our stay here. I am sure we are both eager to have the young people married off."

Samuel looked with affection at his bride, who had lapsed into silence after her remark about the house. Honoria hoped she wouldn't let Samuel ride roughshod over her. But then, Samuel seemed inordinately pleased with his choice. He had been careful to take her hand in his and assist her even over the tiniest ledge on the threshold.

"Honoria, why don't you take Babs on a tour of the house?" he proposed. "I will take her around myself, too, of course, since this is to be her home one day. But I wish to show Mr. Goodall that fine stretch of hunting we have in the woods near the Waring."

"Samuel," Mrs. Bassett interrupted gently, "Do not you think everyone will wish to have tea first?"

Samuel opened his mouth as if to object, but after one look at Mr. Goodall he appeared to reconsider. "Oh, I suppose some tea and something stronger would be in order. Mrs. Goodall, my sister will be happy to show you to your room if you would care to rest afterwards."

Mrs. Goodall shot a timid look at her husband and murmured something that sounded like an assent.

"We plan to have the wedding the Thursday after the last banns are read," Honoria's mother said. "I know the young people will not wish to wait, and that should give everyone who has decided to accept the invitation a chance to travel here."

Mr. Bassett waited until the ladies had been seated before taking his chair. "And we will bring the couple to visit the home where they will live until they eventually take possession of this house." He turned to Barbara. "I am sure you will find it a snug lodging." Honoria was not sure snug was the description most likely to please, but Barbara's expression revealed nothing.

When they had finished having tea and rolls with blackberry jam, the men went to visit the woods and Honoria left Barbara with her mother while she showed Mrs. Goodall to her room to change. "I hope you will be comfortable here," she told the woman. "If you need anything, you have only to ask."

"You are very kind." Mrs. Goodall's humble reply was accompanied by a sweet smile. Honoria had missed it in the earlier introductions.

She returned to take Barbara to visit the house, leading her first to the library. "You must have seen this room when we first came in. These latticed windows are a favorite of mine. I often come here to read."

Barbara looked around politely. "I am sure Samuel would like to have his privacy in the library. I hadn't thought I would spend time here myself." She blushed suddenly. "I mean, of course, when we one day live here."

Honoria let the comment pass and led the way into the Great Hall. "This is where they used to hold banquets in the seventeenth century." She lifted her hand and gestured to the balcony that surrounded the hall on all four sides. "And that is where our bedrooms are. I shall take you to yours afterwards. You will have one adjoining your parents." She waited while Barbara looked around. "Do you not like to read?"

"I am not a great reader," Barbara admitted. "I much prefer spending time in the garden."

Honoria gestured forward as they neared the corridor on the far end of the dining hall. "Let me take you to the kitchen, which is right this way. Do you see the stained glass window in the corner there? It is a favorite of mine. Here, in this room, is the undercroft, where we store our root vegetables. And as you can see, this is my apothecary," Honoria said, not a little proudly.

While Barbara took this in mutely, she added, "I am glad to hear you like spending time in the garden. I believe you will not be disappointed when I show you all of it. There is a fountain in the back at the end of a stone pond, and two very old oak trees in the walled garden beyond that. The yews on our property are hundreds of years old, and are much admired. Sam and I used to race under them when we were children." Honoria gave a smile of encouragement and touched Barbara's arm. "I am sure the gardens will flourish under your touch."

"Oh," Barbara faltered. "I am not so sure ... I do not mean to say that I am an avid gardener. But I do like to walk in the gardens, and I do like shade." She turned as the cook entered the kitchen from the door leading to the outside.

"Mrs. Sands, meet your future mistress, Miss Barbara Goodall. She is to be Samuel's bride." As the introductions took place and the cook asked questions of Barbara, who confessed not to know the first thing about organizing a dinner, Honoria began to feel sorry for her brother and to worry whether Barbara would be capable of running the house. *She will naturally need some advice. I will assist her in every way I can.*

When Honoria was finished showing the kitchen and surrounding rooms, she brought Barbara to her bedroom and to a few of the rooms that were not currently being occupied. She then led her up into the attic where there were stored various articles belonging to the house from centuries past—copper bed warmers, a broken spindle, silk dresses a hundred years out of date. It had always been Honoria's intention to put the attic to order and sort the trash from the treasures, but she continually found other more pressing things to do.

Barbara appeared to be overwhelmed by the chaos that was in the attic, so Honoria gestured toward the wooden stairwell. "It is a bit dusty here. You need not ever come up if you do not like it. I scarcely do. But let us go outside. On our way to visit the garden, I can show you the birds we have in cages." Before Barbara's visit, she had been excited about her reaction to the aviary, as everyone who saw it thought it quite wonderful. But having now met Barbara, she tempered her expectations.

Outside, the long, walk-in cages held a great variety of plain and exotic birds, with cockatoos, birds of paradise, lorikeets, and golden pheasants alongside the pigeons, quails, parakeets and turtledoves. Barbara refused to enter the aviary.

"I am not altogether comfortable with birds," she admitted. "I am afraid they will latch onto my hair and not be able to be freed. I cannot bear the flapping of their wings near me."

"No matter," Honoria said, but inwardly she was beginning to feel oppressed. It would take some time to help Barbara feel confident in her role. More than that, she had a sinking feeling that her beloved Weeton Hall would fall to someone who was not up to its measure.

"I will bring you to the flower garden," she said. "There, we may stop and cut fresh blooms for the table."

CHAPTER 18

The week following his visit to Honoria's bedchamber was a maelstrom of torture and bliss. On one hand, Philip knew with certainty how Honoria felt about him. Her kiss had unlocked a door into paradise. And if he could possibly have been in any doubt about his own feelings—which he assuredly was not, or he would never have approached Mr. Bassett—the doubts would have been put to rest by the eager way in which he had responded to her advances.

The obstacle, and one which caused him no small degree of torment, was the fact that it would be a long couple of years if he truly had to wait until his fair Honoria reached her majority and then won her father's approval. He would do it, of course. There could be no question about that. His own situation reminded him of Jacob, who worked for Laban for seven long years, but claimed because of his love for Rachel it felt like only a few days. Philip could relate to such a sentiment but could not say with any confidence that waiting years would seem like days.

And what was more, it had been a full week since he had been granted a glimpse of her. She had not come to his field after the nighttime visit, and he began to doubt whether he had only imagined the kiss. Now that Mr. Bassett had returned, and with the wedding occurring at their house—he had had the news from Christine—it might be some time before he would see her again.

It was time to pay a visit to the Greys. It had previously crossed Philip's mind that he might meet Honoria there, and he certainly hoped he would, but that was not what drove his steps. He had known a strange reluctance to see Gus after having declared himself to Honoria. But such a meeting was not something he could put off forever.

At Farlow Manor, the servant who answered the door directed him to the field behind the house where, he explained, Mr. Grey was in the process of culping wafers with his new pistols. Philip walked through the sitting room and the corridor next to the kitchen that led to the outside. He spotted Gus at the far end of the walled garden, his target on one side and he on the other.

Gus remained focused, and upon his approach, Philip gave notice so as not to startle. "Afternoon, Gus. Are those new pistols?"

Gus had been inspecting the loading device but he looked up upon hearing Philip. "It's you, is it? I haven't seen you since you returned from touring Nottinghamshire with Theo. Yes, do you like them? The handles are ivory inlaid, and with the silver barrels I think they're my prettiest pieces yet. But I've only been toying with them, and I'm not so sure about their accuracy. I'm afraid this one is slightly inferior." He handed it to Philip for inspection.

"I study the accuracy first thing before getting caught up in how shiny a pistol is," Philip retorted in something like his old tone.

Gus flashed a grin and checked Philip playfully on the shoulder. "Braggart. Even you make mistakes at times."

The pistol had a good weight to it, and he handed it back in silence. They had fallen into the comfortable practice of old friends, although Philip had built up an imagined tension between them in his mind because of Honoria. He had not come with any firm ideas of broaching the subject, but it suddenly seemed imperative that he do so. Gus was, after all, a friend of long date.

Gus went back to examining the loading device, and Philip knew he had to begin what he had come to say before he lost courage. "I thought you should know that Honoria Bassett and I have come to an understanding, although I must own that it is not with her father's approval."

Gus had lifted his arm and squinted at the target, but at this he lowered the pistol and faced him. "You and Honoria? What sort of an understanding?" He did not look entirely pleased, and Philip could feel his own defenses rising.

"An understanding in the traditional sense, of course. We wish to marry, but may very well have to wait until she reaches her majority. I could not convince her father to accept my suit."

Gus frowned at him. "I'm surprised. To be truthful, she has always favored me. I thought you knew that. I don't know what possessed her to switch her allegiance so easily to you."

Philip forced himself to take a steadying breath. "Well, it might very well be the fact that you had your chance to pursue her, but you did not take it. You gave her marked attention the night of the ball and completely ignored her the next day at breakfast."

Gus set the pistol down on the table the servant had laid out for him and folded his arms. "No good comes in forcing a man to make up his mind too soon. She is young, and I have not long been able to think of her as a viable candidate. There was time enough to decide if she was the right one for me. Well, there would have been if no one had rushed the matter."

There was an unspoken accusation that he had stolen a march on Gus, which raised Philip's hackles even more. "What of Mrs. Northwick?" When Gus did not respond, he added, "I was made to understand she was the one who'd caught your interest. You certainly have spoken enough of her of late and very little of Honoria."

Gus's mouth was set in firm lines. "She has left. The house was shuttered when I went to pay a visit, and the servant was not able to tell me when she would return. As Mrs. Northwick did not think to apprise me of her removal, I can only assume that whatever interest I had in her was one-sided. But you! You should've let me sort out how I felt about Honoria since it has been many years that she has been holding out for me."

Philip could take it no longer. "Gus, you've been my closest friend since childhood, but sometimes you're a cad. What right have you to toy with Honoria's feelings that way? Either you are certain of your interest in her, or you refrain as a gentleman from engaging her affections. You do not get the right of first refusal just because she liked you before she did me."

Gus scowled. He picked up the gun and cocked it to empty the bullets before slamming it in the case next to its twin. "If you think I'm a cad, perhaps you have no interest in continuing our friendship."

Philip almost laughed but caught himself in time. It would not be taken well. "Don't be daft, man. We cannot throw away a lifetime of friendship for a girl for whom I've been brought to the point of declaring myself and for whom *you've* never had more than a passing interest. Let it go, and let's shake on it. Confess that you were never serious about pursuing her."

Gus hesitated for a long moment, then reached out and shook Philip's hand. He did not speak as he finished packing his two pistols in the leatherbound case and snapped it shut, and Philip did not force it. They would get through this, but Gus needed a little time to allow his pride to recover.

They walked back toward the house, and a servant hurried past them to close the table and bring it inside. Gus tucked his pistol case under his arm as they walked. "When did it begin?"

Philip searched his memory, a smile hovering on his lips as he answered. "It began, I suppose, when I found her on my land picking blackberries. I hadn't seen her since my return, and she struck me as being grown. And then, of course, that unfortunate incident of the fire brought us together. I discovered in her a gift for healing which I admired, and I suppose I discovered her charms as well."

Gus led them through the gate and past the stables into the house. "Fair enough. It is true, she is a taking young thing. But I'm not sure she would've made the right wife for me. I suppose no one will do for me except a woman with a bit more mystery than one I've known my whole life."

Philip clapped his hand on Gus's shoulder without attempting to offer empty words. He was just glad they had gotten through the worst of it. Any thoughts he had on the mystery of Honoria Bassett and what her kisses were like he kept to himself.

When they entered the house, Philip heard Christine giving directions to one of the servants. Gus led the way in, and as Philip stepped into the sitting room, she smiled at him before finishing her instructions. "Philip, I have been waiting for your visit. I hear some form of congratulations is in order."

Philip was struck with a mild sense of alarm. What if he had not had a chance to speak with Gus first? Following quickly on the heels of that reaction was one of pleasure. Christine's words meant she had spoken to Honoria, and that she had not wavered in her feelings. However, he had to stay sober about his prospects. "I fear your congratulations are precipitous. I was just telling Gus here of my plans, but as they depend on Mr. Bassett for the next two years at the very least, it is too soon to accept any well-wishes."

Christine beamed at her brother. "It is very good news, is it not, Gus? Our two closest friends are to make a match, whether it is sooner or later. "

Gus did not return the smile. "Just don't go spreading it about the countryside. It would cause only harm for Philip and Honoria with her father still opposed to the match."

Christine leveled a gaze at her brother. "I am not such a simpleton. But rejoicing with the man himself and my own brother can hardly be compared to spreading it about the countryside." She turned to Philip. "Come and have a seat. Honoria was here and went off again to visit a tenant she is caring for and

162

has promised to come back when she is finished. I expect her at any moment."

Philip's pulse jumped at the thought of seeing her, and he took his seat, glad for the distraction. He could not deny that had been one of the motives behind his plan to visit today, besides the more pressing one of speaking with Gus. It might be the only place they could meet freely, as long as her father did not get wind of the plan.

"Well, it appears the widow has taken flight," Gus said to no one in particular when they had all sat. "Does anyone have news of her removal?"

Christine stood when the servant entered carrying refreshments. She removed her book from the table in front of her and allowed him to set the tray down. "Yes, as a matter of fact, Honoria mentioned having received a letter from Mrs. Northwick. She said she was to return to London for a stay of indefinite length but that she would surely return. She excused herself for not having made the call personally and hoped that Honoria would be glad to receive her when she returned."

"You never told me that," Gus said. "Here I was wondering where she had gone and when she might come back, and you knew all along."

"Well, you can't expect me to read your mind. If you'd asked me, I would've told you." Christine prepared plates of food and handed one to Philip and another to Gus. "I hope you will soon come out of your sullens, Gus. We might no longer have any visitors if they have a glimpse of your long face."

Once again, Philip had to catch himself before laughing outright. Christine was certainly not timid around her brother. There was a knock, and he turned to look through the window panes alongside the door and spotted Honoria's outline. He stood, eager for his first glimpse of her since that night in her bedroom. The footman opened the door to admit her.

"Mrs. Rossine has delivered herself of a fine girl," Honoria said, upon entering. She stopped short when she saw Philip, and with a touch of color in her cheeks added, "Oh, Philip. You are here."

The hint of a smile lifted Christine's lips as she ushered Honoria to where they were sitting. "I had some tea brought up. It has begun to be chilly outdoors, so why don't you have some to warm yourself? We were just speaking of Mrs. Northwick."

"Oh yes." Honoria turned worried eyes to Philip. "We are both wondering if her flight is not somehow related to Mr. Northwick's constant presence on the estate—and she so far from society in Thimbleby. She must have felt safer somehow in London."

"I hope she will indeed be safe there," Philip said in all sincerity. He truly pitied women who were at the mercy of their circumstances, forced to live subdued in a world where it was easier to be a man.

"What did Mrs. Rossine name her?" Christine asked.

"Bertha." Honoria smiled. "The shining one."

"Did you assist in the birth yourself?" Philip asked, wondering how far her talents for healing went.

"No, it was Mrs. Pokely. To own the truth, I would like to do so, but my mother has requested I wait until I, myself, am married." If anything, at these words her color rose further, and Philip was conscious of Christine's knowing smile directed his way.

"What do you think of Samuel's choice of a wife?" Christine asked her, and the conversation drifted to her first impression, which Philip thought a good one, although he could not discern any great initial attachment between Honoria and her future sister-in-law. She spoke of the family's plans for the wedding breakfast, and by the time they had exhausted this topic of conversation, the teapot was empty, and they had consumed most of the cake and all of the fruit.

"Gus," Christine said as she stood, "Why don't we find something to do and allow Philip a few moments with his intended. I am sure the opportunity presents itself rarely enough."

Gus lowered his brows, then lumbered to his feet. "I suppose I can clean my pistols."

Philip stood suddenly, hesitant to take Christine up on her very tempting offer. He imagined they would be safe in daylight, in someone else's house where there were no closed doors to the drawing room, but the sudden urge to be outside with her came upon him. He quite thought they might walk around the closed gardens, where there were plenty of gardeners to serve as chaperones.

"Honoria, if you have warmed yourself enough and would not mind returning outside, perhaps we might take a stroll in the gardens." He turned to Christine. "That is, if you do not mind."

Christine paused in her steps and gestured toward the kitchen which led to the back door. "Not in the slightest."

Honoria retied her bonnet and slipped into her brown cloak. They walked outside together, where the picturesque view of two golden chestnut trees embracing the stable tiled rooftops met their sight. He kept his hands behind his back as they strolled along the grass path that led under a stone arch through the brick wall. On the left was a small orchard where there remained only a few apples on the trees, the rest having already been harvested. On the right were beds of late-blooming flowers of mixed color and style. And ahead were the plots of earth that formed garden beds that had been left to seed.

"I am very pleased to find you here today. In fact, I came with the hope that I might see you." Philip squeezed his fingers together behind his back to keep them from reaching for her.

"And I you." Honoria glanced sideways at him, offering him a shy smile.

"I cannot tell you how happy the prospect of our future together makes me. A man can live on such hope—even though it seems very hard to wait." He turned to her suddenly, afraid to have given her cause to fear his steadfastness. "But you must not think that will trouble me. I meant what I said to you when I declared myself. Even if we have to wait until you are of age, I will not tire of waiting, for I can contemplate no one but you at my side."

"The day after you came," Honoria said, lifting her face as the wind caused leaves to scuttle across their path, "I broached the matter with my parents. My father remains dead set against the match, and even my mother said that we must wait until Samuel's wedding is finished and then wait still another year or two." She turned worried eyes his way. "A year seems interminable to me, much less waiting the two years until I am of age and however much longer it will be until I can persuade my father to let me go with good grace."

Philip grew tired of there being such distance between them, and he held out his arm. She tucked herself into his side, curling her fingers around his elbow, and he placed his own hand on hers, pulling her close. "What are two years out of a lifetime?" he asked. "Do not trouble yourself on that score. The only thing that continues to preoccupy my mind is that I should not like your father to have such a low opinion of me. I cannot ask him to give his only daughter away in marriage—even should you be old enough to make up your own mind—to a man he does not respect. If you think there is anything I might do to improve my situation, please do not hesitate to let me know."

Honoria tilted her head toward his shoulder for a brief instant as if communicating the affection she dared not show— as though laying a confidence. "He is troubled by what he fears to be your insolvent estate, and he is angry about your decision to divert the river. I am not sure he would have been happier about the irrigation scheme had you broached the matter with him first, though."

She stopped, and it allowed Philip to confirm this. "I don't think he would have given me his blessing. And no matter how much I seek his good opinion, I could not give up something I thought would help my land—and which truly did not affect his estate in any material way—on the chance I might garner his approval. In truth, I hardly think he would like me any better if I had."

"Probably not," she agreed.

They continued on the path slowly, following its circular bent that would bring them back to the house, and he felt pleasure to his bones that she appeared in no greater a hurry than he was to end their time together.

"I believe he still holds some animosity regarding the mine that caused the initial falling-out between your father and him." She looked up at Philip suddenly, as if struck by a thought. "I must own that the way the mine was excavated is not so pleasing to look upon, and it can be seen from the public road. Perhaps we might do something about that."

Philip treasured her words. *We might do something about that.* It had been a long time since he'd had anyone close enough for such a sentiment. "I have been avoiding that mine since my father's death. But maybe it is time I see if anything might be done to make it less of an eyesore and less of a potential danger. Very well, I will give some thought to it. I wish I might be at your side for your brother's wedding."

"I wish it too." Honoria leaned into him again, and he could happily grow used to such affection. "It is to be held in two more weeks. I will likely be called upon to do a great many things to prepare, so I may not see you until after it has taken place."

"Perhaps when the wedding is over ... that is to say, the morning after the wedding is held, as an example"—Philip shot her a look—"we might meet by chance at the same time on the field near the public road."

"As it happens, I might very well need to go in that direction on that particular day," she said with a smile. "After all, I will need to check on Mrs. Reedsby, who lives along that road." They had returned to the back door of the Greys' house, and Philip stopped to face her. He lifted her hand to his lips and pressed a kiss on it.

They entered the house just as the Mercers arrived through the front door and were removing their cloaks for a visit. Mrs. Mercer raised her eyebrows at seeing Philip and Honoria enter together from the garden, but this soon turned into a warm smile of satisfaction. Philip did not stay and risk the questions that might come, instead taking leave of his friends. His purpose had been achieved, after all. He had cleared the air with Gus about his interest in Honoria, and he had seen the woman herself. Barring a sudden change in heart from Mr. Bassett regarding his suit, the day simply could not be improved upon.

CHAPTER 19

Honoria filled the bowls of water in the aviary, allowing one parakeet she had dubbed Wink to sit on her shoulder. "No, you may not come out with me, dear birdie. You know that all too well. It's a cruel world out there, and I could not bear for you to become dinner for a hawk." She closed the door securely and walked toward the house as she removed her apron. She did not know what would become of the aviary if Barbara did not care for it. But she would not think about that just now.

That week, Honoria had enough to occupy her that her thoughts did not stray too often to Philip. At least, she did not have the luxury of pretending to set a stitch or read a book while dreaming of him. She was constantly doing. The most consuming of these tasks was to give orders for which meals would be served with which removes that Cook would ply their guests with every day. She hired a girl from the village to come and help, for they were unaccustomed to hosting for extended periods of time, and it had proven to be more of a charge than they had expected.

For the first two days, Mr. Bassett had taken pains to enter into discussions with Mr. Goodall but, when he found they had little in common, soon remembered urgent things to occupy him on the estate and in the village. It was left to Samuel to entertain his future father-in-law, which he did by bringing him to the house by the mill that they would occupy following the honeymoon. There they discussed at length the improvements Mr. Goodall thought it necessary to put into place. Unfortunately for Samuel, Mr. Goodall's enthusiasm over what sports could be had at Weeton soon waned, and all efforts were focused on house improvements. Led by his love for his betrothed, Samuel entertained all of his suggestions with the proper feeling of a man who was to marry Mr. Goodall's daughter.

Early in the Goodalls' stay, Honoria's mother had forced herself to be active in seeing to the needs of their guests, but she soon realized the error of her ways when she was no longer able to stand without help. She then had to resign their care solely to Honoria's charge, with the reminder to assist Barbara in adjusting to her eventual role. Normally, such a thing would not fluster Honoria, except that Samuel's intended had an unexpected stubborn streak and seemed ill disposed to accept any guidance in learning the running of a household that was foreign to her. This puzzled Honoria almost to the point of annoyance.

When she thought to demonstrate the best way to store the root vegetables in the undercroft, tucked in boxes of peat moss, Barbara had heard that sand was better. Honoria was mystified as to how someone could expound so confidently on a matter over which she had never overseen herself. And she was further at a loss to understand how it was that someone who'd expressed fear at the prospect of creating menus with Cook and presiding over a table could maintain such staunch ideas about where to place the white soup and whether carp or trout should be served alongside quail, based on the expert advice from a London friend. As Barbara remained unbending on domestic affairs, Honoria was forced to accept her own diminished role in the household.

So as not to offend her future sister-in-law, she found herself secretly preparing menus to give to Cook, instructing her to propose the ideas to Miss Goodall but to let herself be guided by her future mistress should Miss Goodall have a different idea. As obstinate as she was with Honoria, Barbara accepted all of Cook's ideas with complacency, and in the end, Honoria was able to order dinners that would be in season and available. In the meantime, in order to gain a measure of the freedom she so desperately desired, Honoria insisted she be allowed to attend to the wedding breakfast herself so that she might present it as a gift to the betrothed couple. Only through this argument was she allowed to have her way.

Day after day passed in this silent battle of wills, and it was not long before she was knocking on Christine's door, looking for a little solace. They were sitting in the tidy drawing room that was now perfectly in order under Christine's capable touch, and Honoria found great relief in unburdening her heart.

"I suspect Miss Goodall is attempting to establish her place and not finding it easy," Christine said, her gaze fixed on the tiny paper cuttings she was making for an arrangement to be placed in the family sitting room. "You must not find it surprising that you present a formidable example to follow. I'm sure once she settles into her role, she will become more accommodating."

"I hope for Samuel's sake it is so." Honoria toyed with a scrap of paper, then grinned suddenly. "On the other hand, it might be just the thing he needs to take him down a peg or two in his conceit."

Christine laughed, and Guinea looked up from the ham bone he was enjoying at his mistress's feet. "The third banns were read yesterday. You must be looking forward to the day of the wedding when you can at last see the happy couple off on their honeymoon."

There was not a hint of unkindness in her tone. Yet, she had been friends with Honoria long enough to understand how much it pained her to be forced to give way in her own home to someone who was so new to the role. With Mrs. Bassett unable to move about freely, Honoria had long held the unofficial post of matron of the household.

"They will go on their honeymoon, but eventually they will

come back," she grumbled, before thinking the better of it. She had only one brother, and she was determined to have an ally and a friend in his wife, even if it meant biting her tongue. This forced her to amend her words.

"But she is only right in wishing to assert herself. If I were in her shoes, I would not want my husband's younger sister ruling the roost once I came to stay. I wish I could say with any truth that I do not envy her position and that I'm willing to hand it over gladly. But you know me too well and will see that for the falsehood it is. In truth, it pains me to give up my role. I have always loved Weeton Hall, and now I have to leave it. My father envisions Samuel and his bride settled in our house before the year is out and no longer deems it necessary to wait for my marriage. He wants a more manageable arrangement for my mother, so we will be taking the smaller house near the mill after only a few months to allow Samuel and Barbara to adjust to married life. I am coming to see what little place a woman has in a home that is not her own. We are nothing without marriage," she added with despondency.

Christine tucked a loose strand of hair into her chignon before focusing her efforts back on the design her thin blade made upon the paper. "I suppose I would feel the same way had I not some lurking fear that my brother will never marry and I shall be forced to play housekeeper to him in his old age. I assure you, this scenario had not played any part in my childhood dreams for my future."

Honoria smiled at her and shook her head. "You must be jesting. There is not a chance in the world that you will end up an old maid. You are the loveliest, most capable, and kindest woman of my acquaintance, and you will make a fine wife to some lucky man."

Christine sighed. "One would think so, but as much as you fight against your father's restraints, I can only wish my father were still here to look out for my future. I am left with my brother as guardian until I am of age, and he is an indifferent one at best. I am not sure he can see past the end of his nose to consider looking out for a husband for me."

Honoria examined the tiny, perfect paper butterflies Christine was cutting. Even the wings were detailed. She felt for her friend, fearing she had spoken only the truth. "What did you think of Mr. Dawson? Philip's cousin."

Christine did not take her eyes off her design. "He is a fine young man, and we held conversations of interest, but I never felt anything more for him than what I might for Philip. And I'm quite sure he harbored no deeper feelings for me. No, I am doomed to old-maidenhood, I fear."

Honoria stretched her legs out and set her elbows on the armrests of her chair. "We are both of us in a sad state, are we not? You without a ready prospect, and I with a perfect one of whom my father will never approve."

"There is only one remedy for it." Christine glanced at Honoria with twinkling eyes. "Queen cakes," she exclaimed, leaping to her feet. "I will see to it and ready the tea platter."

Honoria smiled at her, buoyed by her friend's cheerful outlook on their circumstances. She stayed behind, applying her thoughts for once, not to Philip and her own predicament, but on what man might have his eyes opened to Christine's virtues. There were so few eligible men in the vicinity, but perhaps Thomas Moreland might possess a hidden vein of fascination. True, he was not the most voluble of men, but maybe he became as animated as Christine when in intimate company.

A sound brought Honoria's head turning toward the door. Gus strolled into the room and froze when he saw her. They had crossed each other's path since her understanding with Philip had been made known, but it had always been in the presence of Christine or the servants, and they had exchanged no personal words on the topic. She wondered if he would say something now and hoped he would not.

"You look as fine as a five pence, Honoria," he said, taking the seat Christine had vacated. He picked up his sister's penknife and fingered it, his gaze on her.

His compliments and regard no longer affected her in the same way they once did, and she was able to answer without constraint. "Why, thank you. Christine has just gone to fetch some queen cakes. She has worked wonders in this room, wouldn't you say? Everything is in perfect order." When he did no more than nod, she added, "How are the affairs on the estate? Christine said the tenants had been much neglected in your absence."

He pursed his full lips as he picked up the blade and turned it, then set it back on the table. "It is true. Our extended time in Bath did not help in that regard. I'm working with my new steward on reviewing the tenants' leases, some of which will not be renewed. But I shall not go into further detail on the subject, for I know such a thing must bore a lady."

She looked at him seriously. "It does not bore me. I visit the tenants and help them with their ills, so of course their futures must be of interest to me. And Philip talks to me about the affairs on his estate."

"I don't know why Philip bothers. There is only one domain for a woman, and it's inside the home. It is not to be giving advice on matters she can know little about." He glanced up to see her eyes fixed on him. "I can see that you take objection to my words, but you must see that it is so."

"If we women know little about such things, it is only because the matter has been kept from us. It is not because we lack the intelligence to understand it." Honoria forced herself to be calm.

How was it she had never seen Gus for what he was? There might be a woman for him, but it could never have been her. She had been swept away by a childhood infatuation and over the years had become blinded by it. She only hoped that—had Philip not opened her eyes to something better—she would have been able to resist Gus's charm before it was too late.

As if he had read her thoughts, Gus folded his arms and swiveled in the chair toward her. "It is to be Philip, then? Are you certain of your choice?"

"Quite."

Honoria was not given time to say more because Christine returned with the queen cakes. Honoria was quickly discovering that as mistress of the house, Christine's tea platters were unparalleled. She had no qualms about turning up her sleeves and making the cakes herself, and if she had not been away for the past three years, she would be renowned for them throughout Horncastle.

"Gus, you're here. I will fetch another cup."

"Never mind. I will leave you both. I have things I need to see to." He brushed past the tea tray and left without further words.

Christine watched him leave. "He'll recover." She stirred sugar into both cups of tea and handed one to her.

Honoria took a fortifying sip of the scented tea, weighing her words. "Gus would never have made a good match for me, I now realize."

"I will refrain from repeating that I've told you so many times. I will only say that I'm glad you realize it and that you are spared a marriage that would have brought you little happiness. I love my brother, but I am not unaware of his failings. It is better that I accept them for, apart from my uncle, he is all I have left and it would not do for us to have a rift." She sipped her tea, then set the cup down suddenly and tightened her lips. Guinea paused in his culinary occupation, then jumped up on the sofa next to her to lick her hand.

Honoria went to the other side of the sofa and sat near Christine, touched by the melancholy she heard in her friend's voice. "One of the Proverbs says, 'There is a friend that sticks closer than a brother.' Your brother is not all you have left, for you have me."

FOUR DAYS before Samuel's wedding, her brother surprised Honoria by cornering her in her apothecary to ask for a word in private. She set down the *bouquet garni* she had been preparing to give to Cook and gave him her full attention.

Samuel rubbed the back of his neck and stretched his lips in what looked more like a grimace than a smile. "I know you and Babs have not quite had the easy start I'd hoped for. She can be ..." He seemed at a loss for how to go on, as though he was loath to say anything about his betrothed that might be anything less than absolute praise. Honoria kept her face perfectly neutral.

"Well, what I mean to say is, Babs can be a bit stubborn about getting her way. But she only does that when she feels threatened. And you, dear sis, can be quite intimidating in how you run Weeton. She will be a good sister to you. I know it. Just ... don't pay too close attention to her little fits and starts, will you? She doesn't mean them."

Honoria couldn't help but be touched by her brother's efforts on Barbara's behalf, and it helped her to see more than anything else that he was well and truly smitten with his future wife. She would make every effort to keep their relationship a peaceful one.

"Barbara will make you a lovely wife. I will take everything she says in a spirit of goodwill and will respond in kind. You may count on it." If the fact that her brother sought her out on the subject was not enough to surprise her, his reaching over to pull her into an awkward embrace was. He gave a few clumsy swats on her back, then pulled away, his face a dull red.

"Well then. I must see to Mr. Goodall. I believe he is waiting for me." Samuel rushed off from that unusual display of vulnerability, and Honoria was left biting her lip to keep from smiling in case he gave a backward glance.

THE HEAVENS WERE PLEASED, it seemed, on the day of the wedding. They had been blessed with blue skies and a slight rise in temperatures that had recently threatened snow, and which made it possible for the bride to wear the dress of her choice. The gown in question had an open bodice, short puffed sleeves made of fur, and thin silk sleeves under it extending to her hands—this, as opposed to the heavy embroidered silk which constituted her other choice. She had been afraid the latter would be too stiff to be comfortable, and that it would make her itch. With this favored gown now a possibility, Barbara had explained to Honoria in one of her more loquacious moments, it meant that they would have good luck in their marriage.

Honoria had given up trying to fully understand the way Barbara's mind worked on a good many things, but she could readily understand her wish to wear a favorite dress. She was glad she had followed her mother's advice to purchase a set of gray silk gloves as a gift for the bride, which purely by coincidence, would be a becoming addition to her gown.

"Oh," Barbara exclaimed as she slipped the gloves out of the paper. "These are simply lovely, and they fit to perfection. However did you guess my size?"

Honoria smiled impishly. "I borrowed a glove that had been muddied, which you sent to be washed. I brought it to the glovemaker to have the measurements taken, and he was able to do it quickly enough that you didn't notice it was missing."

"It is a charming gift. I shall wear them today and think of you." She turned and enveloped Honoria in a brief embrace. "I do thank you for your attention."

Honoria warmed under her praise and the first sign of promise in their fledgling relationship. They might actually find things in common that would draw them closer.

She accompanied Barbara to where her parents sat in the waiting carriage and promised to see her at the church. The Goodalls would be departing Weeton Hall immediately after the wedding breakfast. Honoria's mother and father had gone ahead with Samuel, entrusting the last-minute particulars of the wedding breakfast to her care.

The carriage was soon gone, and she had no time to spare. In the kitchen, Mrs. Sands was busy with the small army of servants they had hired for the event. "I forgot to ask if the turtle had been delivered for the soup," Honoria called out over the din.

"It came just this morning, and none too late," was the cook's reply. "Do not overmix that batter, Laurette, or the cake will be heavy," she called out to one of the servants at the wooden table, whisking the contents of a large bowl.

"Excellent news." Honoria hurried up the stairs and ordered an extra set of wine glasses to be set beside each plate, then looked around, satisfied.

I had better go, she breathed. It would not do for her to spend so much time preparing the perfect wedding breakfast for the honored couple that she missed the wedding itself. She took one last glance at herself in the mirror to make sure everything was in place. Her hair had been curled for the occasion, with a wreath of white silk flowers woven throughout, and her mother's looped pearls hung from thin wires in her ears. She allowed herself a moment to stare in the mirror, wondering what it would be like to be a bride herself. With what she was wearing, she could almost convince herself she was one. Then her spirits plunged as she remembered that such a happy event might not be for ages.

The footman was waiting in the open carriage to drive her to the church, and she waved off his help and climbed into the phaeton. "Do make haste, Jeffrey. I do not wish to keep everyone waiting and have no time to spare."

He flicked the reins and they set out, turning right to drive over the little stone bridge that led onto the road around the small village, where they would reach the chapel on the northern edge. They could not take the more direct route as it was Market Day. At the sound of an approaching carriage coming from the opposite way, Honoria looked up in time to see Philip and held out her hand to stop the footman's progress. "Please wait a moment. I wish to greet Mr. Townsend."

Philip had seen her, and his eyes lit with surprise and plea-sure as he pulled his carriage alongside hers. He held out his hand, and she put hers in it for a brief moment. "Honoria! How fine you look. I heard the bells ringing from the chapel. It is Samuel's wedding today, is it not?"

"It is. I fear I am running late as I was seeing to the wedding breakfast details, but when I saw you ..." She stopped, blushing.

Philip's eyes spoke volumes, but he did not take her hand again. He would take no chance that a passerby should have something to remark upon, or that the servant could report back to her father. Honoria knew this, and yet it contributed to her melancholy. She wished to tell him about the wedding, and how long she found it to be before they, too, could have their chance at happiness. She could say none of this in front of the footman.

"I suppose I must not detain you," Philip said when no more words were forthcoming. "Christine and Gus will be there, I am told. I wish you will pass on my congratulations to the happy couple."

"I will," she replied softly. She hoped he had remembered their plans to meet the next day, but she would not remind him of it. With a nod, she signaled for Jeffrey to continue.

The wedding was solemn, with the curate's words resonating in the sparsely attended pews. Barbara's voice wavered when she repeated the vows, and this unexpected sign of emotion gave Honoria hope for their future. Despite her new sister-in-law's reserve, it did seem as though she was eager to find happiness in her marriage to Samuel.

When the vows had been exchanged and the new Mr. and Mrs. Bassett were pronounced man and wife, the elder Mr. Bassett took Mrs. Bassett and Honoria on either arm and followed the rest of the crowd down the center aisle of the chapel. "Well, Honoria," he said, his indulgent tones echoing in the empty church, "I believe it is time we gave thought to your marriage now. Samuel's wedding has only given me a taste for you to be suitably riveted."

Her heart leapt. *He has had a change of heart!* "I have thought of it, Papa, as I have told you. I am determined to marry Mr. Townsend."

Her father pulled the two women to a stop and stared at her

with raised eyebrows. "Him? I told you I would in no way countenance such a match. You shall have to look elsewhere."

"Now, Harold," her mother said, but she was interrupted by
the raised hand of her beloved spouse, who continued to try to
cow his daughter through his glare.

"I have always allowed you to have your own way, my girl. But
you must trust me in this. If I forbid a match with Townsend, it
is with good reason."

Honoria was determined that she would not give way to high
flights of emotion or tears. "You have always been a most excellent father," she began, in what she thought was a measured
voice. "You say you have indulged me, and it is true. But you
have also raised me to know my own mind. Philip and I will
make a good match. And we are determined to be wed, even if
we must wait until I reach my majority."

Her father opened his mouth to retort, but Mrs. Bassett laid
her hand on his arm and spoke in firm tones. "As important as
this discussion is, we must not keep the guests waiting. It is
Samuel's day, after all."

Mr. Bassett snapped his mouth shut and moved forward
again, bringing his wife and daughter with him, as the sounds of
conversation outdoors spilled into the church from the narthex.
"You are perfectly right, Mary. Very well. Once you reach your
majority, Honoria, I shall have little enough say in your future,
and you may spend it as you please," he said. "If you are still of
the same mind in two or three years, then we will visit the
discussion again."

This should have felt like a victory; after all, it was not an
outright no. But at the moment, two years was akin to a lifetime.
And her father's disapproval felt like a closing curtain on the
glimpse of something magical.

CHAPTER 20

Philip led his stallion under the shade of a silver birch tree on his field, the frozen grass crunching under his feet. When he left the shade to walk over to the newly dug trench that was being used to drain the field, the ground became less frozen, but his boots did not sink into the mud as they had during the flood.

The day was one typical of autumn, with an intermittent show of sunlight and a cool wind that seemed to promise storms at one moment and a brightening of the clouds and a calming of the wind the next. The climate seemed to match his present mood. Bright rays of hope for his future that were in the next moment obscured by the reality of his circumstances.

He lifted his head and cast his gaze across the field of grass and cropped stalks ready to be plowed and furrowed for the spring. It would bring in much-needed income. Although he did not agree with the idea of fixing grain prices, for he knew what devastation it caused to the working class, the law would help him out of his current predicament of insolvency and give him what was needed to get his estate into order. This thought naturally led to Honoria. As of late, his attempts to improve his fortune were more to win her than they were for his own sake.

Perhaps when he saw her today, he might place his arm around her waist. Perhaps he might even coax another kiss from her.

At his side, Crown Glory stretched his head down and nibbled on the stiff grass that had not yet thawed in the chill of late morning. Mr. Fines had made his visit as promised and was impressed with the stallion. Philip had him run through his paces and knew the moment Mr. Fines saw him jump that he was sold. He had since learned that the man was well renowned for his stock and even supplied Tattersall's. If the resulting foal sired of the Thoroughbred mare was anything like he expected, it would not be long before he had others requesting stud services. He ran his hands along the stallion's flank. "You're going to be a busy one." He grinned to himself, then wrenched his thoughts into a new direction.

The approach of a thin, wiry man whose build seemed familiar caused Philip to stop and peer at him. He was walking on Philip's land and heading toward the public road as though he had camped somewhere on the estate. As the figure drew nearer, he now had no trouble recognizing it as that of the navvy, Tom Hull. He had not seen him since the first team had abandoned the digging, and he was not happy to see him now. The last thing he needed was a vagabond squatting on his estate, especially one who could not be trusted to do the work for which he was hired.

"Hull, what are you doing on my land?" Philip watched him approach, brisk steps that were only slightly hindered by the short, bowed legs of the older gentleman.

It seemed he used all of the time it took for him to reach Philip to think of a suitable reply, because the navvy did not respond until he was in front of him. "I'n been looking around the field. The work of *these* new men here is fust rate. The fens is near gone."

"Yes, yes. But you were walking on my land without my permission. How did you get to the other end if you did not come by the public road? I've been here for over an hour."

Tom Hull shifted his gaze, avoiding Philip's entirely. "I figured you 'us i' trouble and my sperrit was lowered at the

182

thought. Arter I heared Coates ha' brought in some new men, I thought as how I might help."

Philip was aware that Tom had avoided his question and came to his own conclusions about what he was doing on the land. He was probably in between jobs and needed someplace to camp. The man smelled as though he needed a wash, though. His clothing and person were about as fresh as a bucket of rotten eggs.

He did not think Hull a bad character, however. Perhaps just a lazy one. "Why did you abandon the digging when Coates left? The other workers were not as experienced in the project, so I'm not entirely surprised they took off. But you—I would have thought you would have done what you came to do regardless."

Tom studied his cap, which he had pulled off, and rubbed at a stain that was beyond hope of being removed. "They chased me off, sir. One raskill let me know I 'us not welcome." At this admission, he looked up at Philip. "Truth be told, digging 'ull get tiresome arter a certain age, but I would hev kept at it, I would. I 'us the one as sent a message to Coates to say we're i' trouble."

This was news to Philip. Coates had never mentioned how he had learned of the project's failure. "I am much obliged to you then." Philip looked across the land, which was now draining as it should with the canals in place for the spring. There was no sense in revisiting the past. "If you don't want to dig anymore, what do you hope to do?"

As if sensing he was no longer under scrutiny, Tom put his cap back on and sent Philip a cheeky grin. "I allays thought to be a farmer. That 'ud be the life for me, 'twould. On'y my father 'us thrown off as a tenant, and I'd chanced to find a different line o' work."

As quickly as the idea came to Philip, he spoke it. He had afterwards only to pray he had not been wrong in his instinct to trust the man. "Well, you might be in luck. It just so happens that I'm going to have more land that I'll need tending to, and there are some tenant houses that are not yet filled. If that sounds like something that will interest you, come to the house next week, and we can sort out the terms. This will be on a trial basis, mind."

Tom's weathered face broke into a smile, and he bowed deeply. "Much obliged to ye, sir." He put his cap back on his head and nodded again before beginning to walk in the opposite direction toward the village, this time making his way along the public road.

Philip watched him start off, then with a sudden inspiration as to where he might have been camping, thought to send him a warning. "Hull!" The navvy turned, and he said, "If you should chance to be on my land again without my knowledge—which I am very sure you would not like to risk—stay clear of the old mine that is boarded up. It has collapsed once and lives were lost. I should not like it to happen again."

Hull looked thoughtful, sobered, and he nodded once. "Ay, sir."

The field was entirely too quiet. Philip was accustomed to the sound of men working here, or the occasional horse or carriage on the public road, but there were none, and the silence made him grow even more impatient for a sight of Honoria. He walked over to one of the basins in the canal to examine the water pooled in it. There was not much, as there was no plan to divert more of the Waring until it was needed. He lifted one of the gates in the dike to test the water flowing through. Then he dropped it back in place before the water level grew too high.

With half his mind listening for Honoria's approach, he occupied the rest with his plans for the future. The field had been properly drained by now, and the system for irrigation was in place to begin planting in the spring. If he had calculated correctly, the additional crops would bring enough income after two plentiful seasons for him to purchase a second stud horse. The investment in his stables did not give an immediate return, and he would need to look at all other sources of income in the meantime. But it was a start.

Good heavens, but he was impatient! *Had Honoria forgotten?* With the fields empty, Philip had nothing to do but wait for her to arrive, and he hoped she would come soon. He was thirsting for a sight of her. Leaving Crown Glory to nibble on the grass of his field, he crossed the part of the public road where his property adjoined the Bassetts' and sat there waiting for her to appear.

What he saw instead was a carriage barreling down the public road from the opposite direction, with Mr. Bassett driving it. His thick brow furrowed when he saw Philip, and he reined in.

"Townsend, you may have done what you wished with the river, but you will not sit on my property."

Philip got to his feet, nervous, guilty, defiant. "I apologize, sir. I was waiting for ..." He stopped before that piece of folly left his mouth, but Mr. Bassett finished it for him.

"You are waiting for Honoria." Philip met his gaze with a level stare, neither confirming it nor denying it, and Mr. Bassett frowned. "I thought I made it clear you were not to see her."

"You mentioned not coming to your house," Philip mumbled, knowing he had not a leg to stand on.

"Merely sidestepping the matter, sir, and you know it," Mr. Bassett thundered, bringing to mind his daughter's gentler tone saying much the same thing. "I want you to steer clear from my daughter, understood? Now, remove yourself from my property at once."

Angry and feeling much like a chastised boy instead of the man he was, Philip stood and crossed the public road over to his field. The frustration bubbled over, and Mr. Bassett was on the point of driving off when Philip called out. "You may try to separate us, but you will only end up driving a wedge in your own relationship with your daughter. If she has decided on me, she is unlikely to give in to opposition."

"*Oho*, you think so, do you? You think you know Honoria? Well, you may be sure that I've taken your measure. Do not think that you shall get a groat from me if you seek to marry my daughter," Mr. Bassett growled, lifting a fist. "She has nothing but what I decide to leave her."

185

"You must do as you see fit, sir." Philip walked over to Crown Glory and grabbed his reins. The horse seemed to sense his mood and followed him more docilely than was his habit.

He would not see Honoria today. Mr. Bassett would make sure of it. Embittered, he swung up on the saddle and watched the sight of Mr. Bassett's retreating carriage. Every feeling revolted at the idea of carrying on a secret alliance, but it was one thing to be obliged to wait until Honoria was of age before they could be married. It was another thing to not be able to see her at all. How could their attachment thrive under such circumstances?

In the distance, Honoria appeared on foot out of the clearing in the woods that led to her house. Seated on Crown Glory, he stopped to watch her, the stallion standing with remarkable patience, and he was able to witness her catch sight of both him and her father at the same time. She stopped and waited for her father to approach, her face revealing little that he could see from this distance. Mr. Bassett said a few words to her that Philip could not hear, and she rounded the carriage and climbed up next to her father and they drove off.

He gave a nudge to his horse, who needed no more than that before setting off across the fields at a canter, then at a gallop. If only Philip could outrace his impotent fury at Mr. Bassett's high-handedness and the dismal outcome to the day.

CHAPTER 21

Honoria cast a lingering glance after Philip before climbing into her father's waiting carriage. It took only one look at her father's face for Honoria to know she would not be speaking to Philip today. Or perhaps not at all for the foreseeable future. She had not taken her father for an ogre, but never before had she seen him so set against something she wished for. If there was a thing she was convinced was best, she had always been able to cajole him into seeing things in a favorable light so that he ended up agreeing to it. But in this—in the most important longing in her life, which was her future with Philip—he was impossible to move.

"I did not expect to see my daughter going against my express wishes to satisfy her own." Mr. Bassett's face was inflexible as he steered the horses down the road that led to Weeton.

Honoria looked down at her fingers clasped on her lap. "Papa, I cannot understand what it is you object to so much about Philip that you would forbid me to even see him. How can you have so little regard for what is important to me?"

Her father had set his horses at a spanking pace as they drove down the road, a sure sign of his agitation, along with his clenched jaw. "Well, you must simply trust me on this, my girl. I have had a few more turns around the sun than you have, and if I am fixed upon my decision, it is with good reason."

"So, that is it then?" Honoria's throat closed suddenly, and she had to fight to get the rest of the words out. "We shall have no further discussion about it? I had not known you to be so severe."

He glanced at her, and his tone softened when he answered. "I cannot relent—even if I thought him to be a husband who could provide for you, which I don't. There's something about the Townsends that has always set up my bristles. To think that old Townsend looked down his nose at *me* because I had not held this land for three generations and our family can boast of no crest. Fustian! I am every inch the gentleman he is—or was—and wealthier besides. I cannot have my only daughter wed to a man such as that."

"But Philip is not his father, Papa. Surely you must see that." She remembered how he had pulled away from her kiss that night in her bedroom—her private, sacred memory. "He's kind, and gentlemanly—"

"Even a man appearing gentlemanly can be a wolf."

"But he is not." Honoria was growing weary of insisting, her progress rather like water wearing away stone. "You knew that Mama and Mrs. Townsend were at one time keen to see us wed. If at that time you were so set against the idea, why did you not say so? Mama would never have spoken to me about it. I am quite certain I would have developed feelings for him anyway, but I would not have been fooled into thinking it would meet with your eventual approval."

"Humbug. I'm sorry to say it, but women scheme, and they may do so to their hearts' content. You know I love and esteem your mother, but in this I cannot agree with her. In this, she was wrong." They had crossed the bridge and pulled into the court-yard of Weeton Hall. Honoria felt that if she did not get him to see reason now, the subject would be closed, and she would never be allowed to open it again.

"Papa, please. I beg of you. Don't allow your prejudice to ruin my only chance at happiness." Her voice broke at the end.

"You are only nineteen years old," he replied, pulling the horses to a stop and turning to look at her. He lifted his finger and finished with quiet resolution. "Your chance at happiness will look very different in a year than it does now." Jeffrey came over to take the reins to the horses, and her father made a move to alight, putting an end to the conversation.

"I don't think so," Honoria said softly. She climbed down from the phaeton and walked slowly into the house behind her father.

"Honoria, is that you?" Mrs. Bassett called out to her from the drawing room, bringing her to its door. "Would you have some of that nettle tea made up for me? I am feeling particularly stiff, and it has been difficult to do the tasks I wish. If there is enough to make up a paste for my fingers as well, I would take that gladly."

Honoria momentarily forgot her worries. "Of course, Mama. I shall fetch what you need right away."

"What, are you pained again, Mary?" Mr. Bassett walked forward with a look of concern in his eyes, and he leaned over to kiss his wife on her lips. Taking her hands in his, he sat at her side and rubbed them gently. Honoria had a glimpse of the loving man her father was—a side to him it seemed she had not seen of late.

She made up the tea and the paste, which had thankfully not caused any irritation to her mother's skin but rather had shown to possess improving benefits. She brought them both to her mother, and her father stood when she entered the room to allow her his place. After she had seen to her mother, rubbing the ointment on her hands and elbows, she stood and turned to find her father looking at her.

He stepped forward and wrapped her in his embrace. "I hope you know I'm only doing what I think is best for you." Honoria did not answer him over her closed throat—she could not. But her tears fell. She returned his embrace, then left the drawing room in silence.

Alone in her room, she thought back to the quick glance she had had of Philip. She had been so looking forward to seeing him today and discussing what they might do about their own wedding. From where things stood now, it seemed that even waiting two years might be too optimistic when she would not be allowed to see him. How could she ask him to wait for that long with no encouragement? If she could not reconcile her father to the idea, she would have to let him go. It was the only kind thing she could do.

The beauty of the autumn day called to her through her window. Above the yew trees, the sky had turned from the dull, orangish-gray of late morning to the most beautiful color of purple in the far distance. It gave all the signs that a storm might brew, but it did not seem imminent, and there was enough sun to tempt her. A sudden gust of wind through the branches of an elm tree sent the leaves scuttling across the grass, and that decided it for her. The wind seemed to be blowing the storm in the opposite direction, removing its threat from breaking above their heads. In any case, Honoria suddenly needed to be outside. She could not bear to be in this house any longer.

Knowing her father would assume she was disobeying him by leaving, she did not warn him of her departure. It was only to walk off her distress and be healed by the fresh air. She was not planning to go to see Philip and assumed he would have left the fields after their failed rendezvous. Then again, if she did have a chance to stand before him, have her hands taken in his ... why, then, that was providence. It was not her disobeying.

Outside, the wind did indeed seem to be blowing the storm away from them although it blew hard enough to whip her cloak around her legs. At this time of year, they did not risk anything so drastic as a thunderstorm, so there was no harm in continuing. She hurried out of the courtyard before any of the servants could see her and went back over the bridge in the direction of Philip's fields, deciding at the last minute that she should walk along the public road toward her father's woods instead of the open field. That would remove all temptation to see Philip. As she strode forward, she breathed in deeply, allowing the exercise to ease her heart. Rather than torture herself with her imminent problem, she allowed her mind to relive the wedding breakfast—the looks that passed between the happy couple, the neighbors eating at their table and entering into lively discussions, then Samuel and Barbara driving off toward the Peak District, where they had rented a house for a few weeks for their honeymoon. Then she thought of Philip, who was alone.

Perhaps it was that more than anything else. She had a family, but he had no one. She wanted to be his family.

She had marched forward with her head lowered in thought, but as she crossed the public road, it impressed upon her that the direction of the wind had changed and was now bringing the storm her way. The air had grown suddenly chillier, and the black, low-lying clouds against the gray sky were more menacing than she had ever seen them. She quickened her pace even as the wind picked up, doubtful that she would reach the woods before it broke.

She was jogging now, her legs hindered by the skirt of her narrow gown. There was no one in sight. It seemed that everyone but her was possessed of some degree of sense that kept them indoors. Her heart began to beat in fear as a howling gust of wind hurled a thick broken tree branch beside her, nearly hitting her. She was a puny creature in the vast elements.

The rain began, the sparse cold droplets becoming tiny balls of ice that thundered down. Honoria threw the hood of her cloak over her head, lifted her skirt, and began to run as the wind launched more gnarled branches at her, and a large elm splintered at the trunk and fell on the side of the road. She fought against the gales of wind that flapped her cloak against her, which came with such strength it stole her breath. It would be impossible to make it home at this pace. She could only move forward toward the woods and hope to find shelter there.

The rain now came down in driving force, and she squinted

to see where she was going. Ahead, off the side of the road, was the dilapidated structure of the old Townsend mine, its entrance partially enclosed by a steep hill that ended with a sharp drop. She hurried toward it as the closest place for shelter. Even a piece of roof overhanging the entrance—if such could be found —would spare her the worst of the wind and rain. When she reached it, the door to the mine was partly open and, propelled forward by a sudden squall of wind driving the icy rain into her cloak, she stumbled into it.

The door clattered shut behind her and she blinked in the dark space, the sudden stillness both eerie and welcome. The rain and howling wind outside continued to devastate the countryside, but inside every breath was audible, and her sopping dress and cloak chilled her skin. A new burst of wind pulled at the door, which flapped open to reveal, in the weak light of the outdoors, some old lanterns hanging on the side of the wall, along with a tinderbox. She went over to the shelf and blew on her hands to warm them, then with some effort and fumbling in the darkness, got the match in the tinderbox to light and transferred it to the lantern.

Having achieved a source of illumination, she turned now to examine the inside of the mine. She wouldn't go far into it. After all, this was how Mr. Townsend had met his demise. But surely there would be a safe place to wait out the storm that was more sheltered than the entrance? On the right was a small room, where a dusty table was tucked in one corner next to some buckets and utensils that had at one time been in use. Ahead was a tunnel that led farther into the pitch black, and when she paused beside it, she was struck for the first time by a strange but familiar odor.

I know what that is! Honoria's breath quickened as she took two more steps into the corridor. *If I'm right, this could be the making of Philip's fortune.*

Now heedless of the potential danger, Honoria turned into the corridor, her steps coming faster as though propelled by the hint of peril. Perhaps if she hurried, there was a chance to verify her hunch before any harm could befall her. After today, her father would never let her step foot on the Townsend property again. This would be her only chance.

The light from the lantern bounced around the chiseled, dirt walls of the mine as she moved forward. She kept going until the tunnel branched off in one direction, but she needed only to direct her lantern that way to see a dissuading pile of stone. It was possibly here that Mr. Townsend had been mortally wounded. But it was too late to turn back now—Philip's fortune was at stake and it was too important. She continued down the main tunnel.

The sounds from the outside had now completely given way to the quiet dripping sounds of the interior. And the smell that had intrigued her and called for her to investigate became overpowering. Her heart picked up a notch as she inhaled the odor of sulfur, which was combined with a warmth that felt heavenly in the moment, but would soon make her wish to remove her cloak. She recognized that smell. It was the exact smell of the waters they had bathed in when they went to Harrogate.

As she continued toward its source, she noticed a bed roll tucked to the side of the tunnel along the wall, and for the first time began to think that perhaps she was not alone. A frisson of fear stole over her and made her want to turn back to the entrance, but the discovery of where the sulfur smell came from was too strong to deny. The implications were too important.

"Is there someone here?" she called out, hoping the tremor of fear in her voice would not be heard. There was no answer, only the sounds of humidity emanating from the walls of the mine. As she walked on, the dripping sound grew louder until she arrived at the place where the mine tunneled downward. She lifted her lantern to look around at the circular tunnel that constituted a small room and then cast her gaze down. In place of a gaping hole that led to blackness, there was water.

With a small gasp, Honoria reached down to touch it and found the water to be hot. Swirling her fingers through the pool, she then cupped her hand and sipped the water before making a face. The revolting taste gave her a jolt of pure excitement. This was the exact taste of the water in Harrogate. This was spa water. She leapt to her feet. She had to tell Philip instantly. *This* was how he was going to restore his estate. And this was how she was going to convince her father of his suitability. This discovery was as good as a goldmine.

Honoria turned to run back down the tunnel, no longer caring about the storm outside. The lantern caused shadows to jerk across the walls of the mine, but it did not hinder her, and she hurried on in determination. A sudden draught of air blew out the lantern, and before she could slow her pace, she tripped over some obstacle in her path. And then she was falling.

CHAPTER 22

The storm came over the countryside suddenly. There had been little hint that they could have such squalls of wind as to fell trees, but that was what Philip was seeing as he watched the storm unfold over the meadows. He began to wonder how bad the damage would be. He feared it would be extensive and that he would be hard put to find the ready in order to pay for everything. Thankfully, he had not begun to repair the vacant tenant houses and would therefore not be called to do it twice. However, there were poplar trees that spread their branches over the roof of the stables, and he could only hope they would not come down and break through the tiles. It took him only a moment's reflection to decide that the horses were safer in the stable, even with the threat of trees falling on them, than they were in the open pasture.

Curious as to what such a wind would feel like, he went to stand at the front door, opening it to step outside of the portico. One step on the stairs and the wind nearly knocked him over, causing him to inch his way backwards to the safety of shelter. It would be best if no one had been caught out in such a storm, for the rain was icy and punishing enough, but with the driving wind it could be mortal.

He reentered the house and caught a glimpse of his housekeeper scurrying by. "Mrs. Mason, be so good as to bring me some tea if you will."

He thought he heard her mutter a cross between an excuse and acquiescence under her breath. He was beginning to lose patience with her. "Was that a yes, Mrs. Mason?"

"I'll bring it as soon as I take this vinegar to the stillroom, sir."

His housekeeper disappeared from sight, and Philip went to stand by the window, where he watched the rain pelting down, blurring the image of the landscape. He wished he had a housekeeper who leapt to her feet to serve him rather than one he had to chase after. But he had it on good authority that it was difficult to find help, and he had no wish to add to his worries. He went to sit on the armchair, listening to the sound of the rain.

Twenty minutes had passed, and he was still waiting for the tea tray to arrive. All of a sudden, there was a pounding on the door that pulled Philip out of his seat. It resonated with the sound of urgency.

"Townsend!" It was indeed the voice of a desperate man. Philip thought he recognized it but he could not credit his ears. He strode over to the door and threw it open.

"Mr. Bassett," he exclaimed in surprise. So, his ears had not deceived him. Mr. Bassett was the last person he expected to show up on his doorstep. He made his way in the rain down those few steps from the portico and grasped the man's arm. "You must get out of the storm, sir. Let me have our footman see to your horse and carriage." The wind was pushing the tilbury at an alarming angle.

"Never mind about that. Honoria is missing. Is she here? Where is she?"

Philip had gripped the side of the portico for balance, and he pulled Mr. Bassett into its shelter. There he peered into his face in alarm. Honoria was out in this weather? "She's not here. I haven't seen her since she rode away with you."

"Well, then she's out in the storm somewhere." Mr. Bassett could barely speak against the wind. In front of the house, the tilbury lurched to the side again and the bay horse fretted, backing up in the harness. They needed to get the horse to the stables.

But the thought of Honoria in this weather made it difficult for Philip to breathe. He hoped she would have thought to seek shelter somewhere, but he did not want to leave that to chance. His mind rapidly spun over the possibilities. Even if the need was urgent to find her, they could not take Mr. Bassett's small carriage out in this storm.

"Come inside and let me run for Jim, sir." He called behind him into the house. "Mrs. Mason, you are needed. Jim!" As soon as the footman arrived, he told him to bring the carriage to Marcus in the stables and have the groom saddle his dray horse and gelding. Mr. Bassett's bay looked spent and should not be brought out again into the storm. When he had seen to these arrangements, he ushered Mr. Bassett into the sitting room.

After another glance through the window at his footman struggling with the tilbury, Philip made a snap decision to leave Honoria's father to assist. Jim did not seem to be having success battling against the wind with both the horse and carriage. "Wait a moment, will you? I will help my footman." He left the safety of the house, and if anything was needed to tighten his resolve to help Honoria, it was how difficult it was to make any headway against the driving wind. This was an antediluvian level storm.

Jim pushed on the side of the tilbury that was being beaten by the wind while Philip steered Mr. Bassett's horse, and like this they made it into the stables, where Philip relayed the orders himself to have the horses readied. The groom promised he would bring them as soon as it was possible, so Philip made his way back, finding relief from the wind in the shelter of the house's façade. When he arrived at the front door, he found that Mr. Bassett had come back outside and was now leaning against the wall inside the portico, his hands on his knees, as he attempted to recover his breath.

"How long before we may set out?"

Mr. Bassett was clearly worn through with exhaustion and

worry. His skin had taken on a gray pallor, causing him to look aged and feeble. Honoria would never be able to bear it if anything happened to her father. "Do come inside, I beg of you. I have asked my housekeeper to bring some tea, and we will get warmed up while the horses are being saddled. I give you my assurance that we will set out directly as soon as we have the horses. We cannot cover enough ground without them."

Mr. Bassett did not respond, but he followed him into the house again. Philip walked over to the set of stairs leading to the kitchen and called down. "Mrs. Mason, is the tea ready? I will need you to send up another cup." He figured it would be faster to call her than it would be to ring the bell. There was no answer and he turned to find Mrs. Mason walking toward him from the housekeeper's pantry.

"I will get that now, sir," she said, her tone a mix of defiance and fear.

He gritted his teeth in irritation toward the woman. She had not even begun to have the tea ready. "Never mind the tea. Just bring some brandy," he replied curtly. "And in the future, if you cannot have tea prepared when I ask for it, I shall have to wonder how fit you are for the role of housekeeper."

Philip did not stay to see her reaction but went into the sitting room where Mr. Bassett stood, dripping. He started forward. "Please let me take your coat and hang it before the fire." He was glad that he had seen to the fire himself because it was now a blazing roar, nestled firmly behind the new fender he had ordered. Mr. Bassett would need to dry off quickly before they set out again. And as he had not recovered from his shocked silence, Philip was determined to remain at his side as they searched for her.

"What led your daughter to leave the house?" he asked as they both stood in front of the flames.

Mr. Bassett did not meet his eyes, and to lower himself to communicate with Philip seemed a struggle almost beyond what he could bear. At last he said, "I cannot say for sure. We had words about her choice to meet you clandestinely, but I had not thought them harsh enough to precipitate her flight."

Philip wished to object to the word clandestine, because that was not at all what they were attempting to do. But then he remembered his nighttime visit and knew he could not proclaim his innocence. Instead he asked, "I must know, what led you to believe your daughter would come here when you had expressly forbidden her to see me?"

"I had hoped she was not lost to all sense of propriety," he grumbled. "But I could not be sure."

"As you can see, she is not." Philip strove for an even tone to cover his indignation that her father thought so little of her honor—and of his. The memory of Honoria in her nightshift and in his arms, while her parents slept in a nearby room, intruded most inconveniently into his conscience again, and he wanted to throw up his hands. He had no defense. "But if she were, I would not have encouraged her to remain here, sir. That is ... not in any other situation. In a storm like this, I must have given her shelter."

Mr. Bassett glanced over at his coat drying over the chair, then looked around the room. "It chafes me to remain here."

"As it does me," Philip said. "My groom will bring us my horses as quickly as he can. We cannot set out without them."

At that moment Mrs. Mason came in, carrying a decanter of brandy and two glasses. "That will be all," Philip said. He poured a small amount of brandy for Mr. Bassett, which he drank quickly.

He seemed to regain his strength from it. "I can't imagine where she could have gone. She likes to take walks and tends to stay to the woods for shade when it's hot and the open road for sun when it's cool. But I have ridden through both and have not seen a sign of her. What is keeping your groom?"

Mr. Bassett was right; the delay seemed excessive. Philip glanced through the window for a sign of him. The wind blew so hard across the garden and pasture beyond, it seemed as though even the thick trees were doubling over. At that moment, the large oak at the edge of his property lost a heavy limb, nearly splitting the tree in two. His immediate worry for Mr. Bassett's health was beginning to give way to the urgency of needing to be out looking for Honoria, despite the danger.

"Let me get my cloak," Philip said. He went into the stairwell and grabbed it from the hook underneath the stairs, and after Mr. Bassett had donned his own coat, they went outdoors where they made slow progress toward the stables. Philip just needed to calculate the best course. If they kept to the path along the woods, they were at risk of what might fall on them. But in the open meadow, the wind would hinder their progress to a degree that might be equally dangerous.

Marcus and Jim had the two horses saddled and were on the point of leading them both out of the stables. Philip took the reins of his gelding and said, "I think we should search for her together—even if we might be less effective that way. One of us may need the other's help."

Mr. Bassett did not object, and they mounted their horses and rode off toward where Philip's property met the Bassetts'. It was easier on horseback than on foot as long as they leaned forward to break the force of the wind. As they rode to the edge of his property in the direction of the public road, they called her name and tried to listen for an answer. It was difficult to hear their own voices over the wind.

"Honoria," they called again, but only the shrill whistle of the wind was their reply.

The rain came down unabated as their horses pushed forward at a walk. Up ahead, a small, dark form distinguished itself from the rain-soaked terrain. To Philip's surprise, it was Tom Hull making his way toward them, and with difficulty. "What in the world is he doing out in this weather?" he mumbled.

When at last Tom looked up enough to spot them, he began waving to get their attention but then bent over again as the wind almost knocked him backwards.

"Tom," Philip called out when he had reached him. "What

are you doing out in this storm? Have you seen Miss Bassett? A young woman—red hair, petite?"

"Just so. I know where she is," he called out, though Philip had to lean forward to catch Tom's words. "She's in the mine, she is. She's had a fall." Philip did not stay to hear more, but urged his horse forward, his heart full of panic. Where had she fallen, and how far? The mine was unstable. A gruesome image of her pale face struck by the falling rocks filled his mind.

It took them an unbearable length of time to reach the entrance to the mine, fighting against the wind. Its door swung on its hinges with sharp claps against the rocky exterior, and it looked as though it would not stay attached.

"Look out," Philip cried as the door tore free and catapulted mere inches from where Mr. Bassett sat astride his horse.

Philip swung down from the saddle and, with difficulty, led Poker-Up toward the entrance to the mine where there was a natural shelter from the gale, although not from the rain. In this space, the wind howled less fiercely, and he tied his gelding to an iron ring that had been drilled into the outside wall. Mr. Bassett followed suit and they both hurried into the mine through the wooden structure at its opening.

"Honoria!" Mr. Bassett called out, as soon as they had entered. His hoarse voice echoed through the tunnels.

"I am here," she answered instantly from the recesses of the mine. "Do not fret, Papa. I am well." Philip wanted to fall to his knees in relief. He was incapable of uttering a word. In a softer, muted voice he could hear her add, "Or nearly."

He rushed forward, listening to the sounds of dripping water from somewhere inside and unsure how to find her in such darkness. His foot bumped against something, and he almost fell but righted himself by throwing his hand out, where it met the slimy wall. A horrid smell of rotten egg permeated the entire place. What had happened to the mine? This was not something he had ever noticed when he used to come here with his father. Such a smell he would have remembered.

The dim light from the broken door at the entrance did not

extend far into the mine. Despite Philip's desperation to get to Honoria, he did not walk more than a few steps into the pitch black before he realized he would not get far without some sort of light. He began feeling his way along the side of the wall, growing accustomed to the revolting feel of it.

"There are lanterns and a tinderbox at the entrance," Honoria called out. "You will find me more easily with it. I do not want you to fall, Papa."

"It seems it is you who mean to rescue us, and not the other way around," Philip said, the relief that overcame him at last giving him his voice.

"Philip? Is that you? What are you doing here?"

"Let us get to you, and we will explain everything," Mr. Bassett called out as Philip hurried back to the lanterns. In his haste, it was impossible to get one to light.

"You're blowing on it too hard." Mr. Bassett dipped his hand around the tinderbox.

When at last Philip coaxed a flame to it and had transferred it to the lantern, he led the way forward, gagging under the smell that was emanating from the mine. He feared if they didn't get Honoria out of here quickly, she might suffer from the noxious odor. Now, led by the light that filled the corridor, they found her, sitting against the wall of the mine, her legs stretched out in front of her.

"There you are! Oh, my girl." Mr. Bassett fell to his knees beside Honoria. He embraced her, kissing her head, as Philip cast the light of the lantern beyond her, staring in disbelief at the sight. What should have been a mine shaft now appeared to be a large pool of water with the beams of light reflecting on its rippled surface. Where was the open tunnel leading down to the lower levels of the mine?

"All is well," Honoria said, patting her father on the back as he held on to her. "I have only hurt my knee, stupidly. And I suppose my head a little bit. I was running and the lantern went out. I tripped and knocked my head, but I think I was only out for a moment. I was mainly just dizzy. However, when I tried to get up and walk, I found it to be impossible. So I have been waiting here. I think there might be someone living here."

"I believe I know just who it might be," Philip said drily, bringing his full attention back to her. He would have to talk to Tom about trespassing, but for the moment he could only be grateful the man had led them to Honoria. His eyes held hers for a minute.

"Let us get you home," Mr. Bassett said, leaning down to lift Honoria in his arms. Philip moved forward to offer but pulled back when he saw his services would not be welcome. Mr. Bassett grunted as he began to lift, then set her down heavily.

"Oh!" Honoria exclaimed as she was back on the ground. "Are you hurt?"

Mr. Bassett said nothing for a moment, before gasping out the words, "I have hurt my back."

"Oh, Papa." Honoria looked at him in sympathy but could not go to him.

"It is nothing, but ..." Mr. Bassett's voice trailed away and he glared at Philip.

"If you will permit me, sir, I will carry her." He exchanged a look with Honoria, and her eyes sparkled. He hoped his own face did not reveal to Mr. Bassett just how much he was looking forward to holding his daughter in his arms.

Mr. Bassett grunted and grabbed the lantern, looking anything but pleased. He staggered forward, rubbing his lower back, and Philip leaned down to gather Honoria in his arms. She clasped her hands around his neck and kept her face tantalizingly near. Philip smiled at her as he followed Mr. Basset in silence.

"Careful you do not trip like I did," she said in a near whisper, her grin teasing.

"Ah. Thank you for the warning. The mine is dangerous," he replied. "You scared us both out of our wits."

"What in heaven's name are you doing with my father?" she whispered. "I was never more surprised in my life."

"He thought he might find you at my house." Philip set his jaw and looked down when Honoria gasped.

"Papa! I cannot believe you thought I would leave the house just to go to Philip's without your permission. I just went for a walk."

"We'll talk more about that, never you fear." Mr. Bassett's words echoed behind him as he marched forward in slow progress.

Honoria put on a look of weary resignation before bringing her gaze back to Philip and smiling. In a voice so soft he almost did not catch it, she said, "I could get used to this mode of transportation. I see you have no need for buckram padding in your coats. You seem to carry me with ease."

"You will not hear any complaints from me," he replied, inordinately pleased by her compliment.

"Sound carries in this tunnel. I can hear your words quite clearly," Mr. Bassett said as Honoria stifled a giggle then gave her own retort.

"Perhaps you ought to marry your daughter off, so you need not be troubled by her any longer."

Not deigning to answer, Mr. Bassett moved stiffly toward the entrance of the mine. As they neared it, Tom Hull stepped inside from the storm, panting at the effort of having reached it at last. Outside, the wind howled as heavily as before. Mr. Bassett nodded to Tom. "Obliged to you for leading us to my daughter."

Tom, drenched to the skin, touched his cap to Mr. Bassett, then turned to Honoria. "G'day, miss. I doubt you aren't feeling sorely. When I saw ye, you 'us senseless."

"Thank you." The hesitation in Honoria's voice showed that she did not fully understand how he had come to find her.

Pivoting so she could see the navvy, Philip explained. "This here is Tom Hull, a navvy who was digging the canal for me and who apparently also has been squatting in the mine. That misdemeanor ended up being a fortunate thing since, as soon as he saw your fall, he braved the storm to get help."

"I thought there might be someone here, but I did not see you," Honoria said, her brows furrowed.

"Ay, miss. I afeared I 'ud only frighten you. Thought your own people could help you better nor me." Hull said this with gentle respect, and Philip's trust in the man grew.

"Well, I do thank you, then." Honoria bestowed a smile upon him that had him ducking his head shyly.

Philip carried Honoria into the front room that had served as an office, where the wind could not reach them, and set her down gently near the table. After peering out to see that the horses were all right, he came back and sat on the floor beside her. He looked up at Mr. Bassett. "I believe we shall have to wait this storm out. We can't take Honoria out in such a wind."

Mr. Bassett did not reply but lowered himself stiffly to the floor, and Tom followed suit forming a cozy circle of four. Philip looked outside as the storm continued to rage. Dreadful though it was, he was feeling optimistically cheerful. Here he was, with Honoria at his side and her father sitting across from them—the way it should be. On terms of peace as neighbors ought to be. He could not imagine that he had won Honoria's hand so easily in the work of one afternoon, but it was a glimpse of possibility.

He folded his arms. "I suppose we shall have to endure the horrid smell while we wait, but I, for one, shall be glad to be rid of it."

"You will soon recant those words," Honoria replied enigmatically. "That horrid smell is the best part of today's adventure." Philip and Mr. Bassett both turned to her in confusion, and her expression could only be described as smug. "Your collapsed mine, Philip, has given way to a healing spring. This can be made into a spa that will bring people from all over the shire. And what's more—Mama is going to be able to use it without even leaving Horncastle."

CHAPTER 23

B oth her father and Philip turned to Honoria with looks of amazement etched on their faces, and it was Philip who spoke first. "Are you saying that this water has restorative properties like those in Bath? It seems too fantastic to be true. Do you think we can turn it to good account?"

"I think so. Of course, I know very little about such matters, but I believe the people of Lincolnshire would willingly pay for access to spa waters if it does not involve leaving the shire." She leaned back against the wall of the cave then shifted when it touched the sore spot on her head. Thankfully, the bump had not been too severe and she seemed to have avoided a headache. Looking at her father she added, "And, as I said, Mama would be the first one to benefit from it. Even for no other reason, I think we should see if it really does possess spa properties."

"How high and thick is that roof above the basin of water near where we found Honoria?" Mr. Bassett asked Philip, giving the first indication that he was seriously considering the idea's merit. The sound of rain continued outdoors and the wind pushed it into the entrance, but they were well protected in the room where they sat.

Philip turned to his right and peered down the black corridor they had come from, but there was nothing to see. "I don't know. Why do you ask?"

Her father trained his eyes to the ceiling of the mine, following its path over to the corridor. "You could never hope to earn anything unless the area was lit. No one will dare enter the place unless it is modernized. Besides, we cannot risk the mine having another collapse, particularly from the roof. You would have to replace the stone ceiling with a wooden one to give it less of a cave-like aspect."

"And perhaps add some glass," Philip suggested. Honoria studied his face to see if he had been affected by the reminder of the mine's collapse, but his reflective answer gave her hope that the negative memories from the past would be erased by the more hopeful future.

Tom, the navvy, had not given any evidence of having followed their discussion, but that was apparently a cover for a mind actively working. "We 'ud have to begin to dig from above, the same way as if we war digging a canal. The earth furst and the rock arter that. But it's summat as could be done."

Philip looked at him now with curiosity. "Do you think it's something *you* could do? Along with Coates?"

"Ay. Trusten I could," Tom said without any modesty.

It seemed the fact that this idea was actually a feasible one was beginning to dawn on Philip, for he met Honoria's gaze with a look of excitement on his face. As if on impulse, he reached for her hand and pressed it to his lips. "You are a gem," he said. "And apparently the maker of my fortune."

"Don't think this changes anything." Mr. Bassett scowled at Philip from where he sat across from them. "My answer is still no."

Honoria sent him a look of indignation, but the suspicion dawned on her that this was just bluster and she clamped her mouth shut. Her father would have to arrive at the decision that Philip was as worthy as she knew him to be. And he would— with a little help.

As the storm outside continued unabated, they deliberated

over how it might be possible to create some sort of a floor with benches in the water that would allow for people to sit in the hot springs, which were currently of an unknown depth. They argued over the merits and drawbacks of both wood and iron.

At last, the storm lost strength and the weather outdoors grew calm enough for Philip to carry Honoria to the entrance, where he set her down on a bench. Then he and her father ventured outside. The two horses stood docilely as though they had not just weathered a fierce storm; the sheltered area at the entrance of the mine had been enough to spare them the worst of it. Then Philip went over to talk to Tom, and she overheard him giving a rare trimming for having trespassed. But he softened at the end of his diatribe and thanked him for having led them to her.

With her father's back still paining him, he led the horse over to a large rock and climbed up with difficulty then turned his face to Philip. "We shall have to bring Honoria to your house first. Then I can drive her home in my carriage. I would be much obliged if you would lift her to me, Townsend." This was said in almost a cordial tone, and to make up for any softening on his part Mr. Bassett added, "Do not think I shall permit her to ride with you."

"I thought no such thing," Philip said, walking back toward Honoria and winking at her. Honoria's father waited on the horse, as Philip reached down and swept her into his arms. With his back to her father, he pressed a kiss on her lips and murmured, "Thank you. Our future is assured."

"I like to think so," she said, returning his grin and filled with more hope than she had felt in weeks.

He lifted her up to her father, who scooted back on the horse so she could hook her uninjured knee over the pommel. With his arms holding the reins around her, he placed a kiss on her head. Once they arrived at Boden, a servant came running from the house. Philip dismounted and handed the reins to him, then walked over to where she sat and held up his arms. Honoria allowed herself to fall into them, and he called over his shoulder,

"Help Mr. Bassett to dismount and then bring both horses to the stables."

"Ay. Will do, sir. We are that glad you've come to no harm." He led Philip's horse over to where her father sat astride and dropped the reins to assist him.

Philip carried Honoria inside and set her gently down on the sofa, then went over to stoke the fire as the room had grown chilly. Her father did not immediately follow, and she hoped his back was not paining him too much. While Philip was kneeling before the fire, the housekeeper entered the room, pulling back to stare at Honoria as though she were a trespasser. It was time someone reminded Mrs. Mason of her place. After all, the woman must earn no less than twenty-five guineas a year as housekeeper!

"Mrs. Mason, I will trouble you for some tea." She made sure her tone was cordial, but firm.

"The kitchen maid has gone off to see her family. There is no one in the kitchen to help." The housekeeper planted her feet as though she had no intention of moving for a mere Miss Bassett. Philip turned at his task and began to get to his feet, but Honoria forestalled him.

"Then I suggest you fan the fire and get a kettle boiling your-self," she replied in a pert tone. "It is the task of the housekeeper to see to such things. Of course, if you are not sufficiently skilled to run the household, Mr. Townsend has only to find a replace-ment. I am sure Mrs. Sands at Weeton will have no problem providing a recommendation."

A variety of emotions flitted across the housekeeper's face, ranging from anger to alarm, and she dipped a curtsy. "As you wish, miss."

When she left, Philip brushed off his hands and went to her side, his face full of affection and humor but his eyebrow lifted at her daring. She was compelled to say to him, "Honestly, if she does not improve rapidly there are others who are more worthy."

"Do you think it possible for her to reform?" He stared in doubt at the empty doorway the housekeeper had just quit.

"With the right mistress, perhaps. She must learn to show respect, or she simply cannot remain. A house *must* have a good housekeeper, or it will not be run well." This was a conviction Honoria held deeply, especially since she performed many of the roles a housekeeper might—not out of necessity, but out of pleasure. And while she would not want to be the cause of someone losing their position, there was nothing that gave her more satisfaction than putting a house to order.

Philip draped a blanket around her shoulders and sat across from her. "When you are mistress here, you shall take her well in hand."

"I certainly shall," she replied, as her father came indoors at last, moving slowly but without help.

"Honoria, we shall leave as soon as the carriage is readied, so do not think to become too comfortable here." Mr. Bassett remained at the threshold of the sitting room, and Philip stood, indicating for him to have a seat if he were so inclined.

Honoria looked at her father, not missing his signs of exhaustion. "I shall be ready as soon as I've had some tea, and you have had some as well, Papa. It has been a trying afternoon, and it will be beneficial to get something hot inside of us. Besides, it will be good for Philip's housekeeper to be put to proper use for once."

Mr. Bassett made a sound of dissent deep in his throat that sounded like a growl. "I am anxious to be off. Your mother will be fretting over what has happened to us both." However, he took the seat that was offered.

That brought Honoria swiftly to reality. In her contentment to have her father and Philip speaking cordially under the same roof, she had forgotten about her mother and how worried she would be. "I understand, Papa. We will leave immediately after we have had tea."

Mrs. Mason brought the tea tray with an celerity that gave Honoria satisfaction—and hope for the woman's possibility of redemption. The housekeeper even stooped so far as to ask, "Will you pour, miss?"

"I will." Honoria removed the lid of the charming teapot and poured in leaves from a copper tea canister. She prepared tea for everyone and, true to her word, did not dawdle over her own. No one was inclined to do so as Mr. Bassett appeared to be both worried for his wife and in some degree of discomfort.

At the sounds of the carriage pulling up, Philip and her father went outside to where Marcus was holding the horse and tilbury. He allowed Mr. Bassett the dignity of climbing up on his own, though it took him some time to do so. He came back inside to sweep Honoria up in his arms, then brought her out, where he set her in the conveyance at her father's side. She reached her hand out to caress his cheek before her father's watchful gaze brought Philip back to his surroundings and he stepped back.

"Townsend." Mr. Bassett stretched out his hand to Philip, and they shook. "I could not have found my daughter without you. For the moment, my answer is still no. But I will see how this project of yours comes along. That will give me time to judge if there's something different in you than in your father. I should not like to give my only daughter away to a man I cannot esteem."

"I understand that, sir." The humility in Philip's response touched Honoria to the core. Her father had insulted his father and him in one go, and he took it with grace and dignity.

She turned and waved at Philip as they rode off but then faced her father. "Papa, I am grateful that you are willing to reconsider my marriage to Philip. But do you not think you are being severe to him? He has shown nothing but good in his regard toward me."

Mr. Bassett kept his eyes trained ahead as though absorbed by his task of driving. "So far, everything Townsend has done is what I would expect of a gentleman. But those small services can still be deceiving. I should not like to give you away, only to find out when it's too late that your new husband is a rake. I could not forgive myself if I ushered you into an unhappy marriage."

Honoria did not answer. There was love and protection in his words, but she hoped she might prevail upon her father with

211

time to trust. He really did have a soft heart underneath his gruff exterior, and such a thing was not impossible.

When they reached Weeton, her mother came to the door immediately, her hands held to her lips. "Oh my heavens, I was so worried!" She did not attempt the few stairs down to the courtyard but held out her arms for Honoria. Mr. Bassett shook his head. "She cannot come to you. She has hurt her knee. Ah, Jeffrey, there you are. Have the goodness to carry Miss Bassett to the drawing room."

The footman did so immediately, and Honoria was soon sitting next to her mother, who reached for her hand. She leaned down and sniffed. "Your clothes smell terribly. We shall have to get you changed. I tremble to think of what adventure you must have stumbled into."

"*Such* an adventure, Mama. But perhaps I will wait until I have changed before telling you what it is that has caused that dreadful odor. It is good news." In her mind, she was already working out how a bathing area with fresh water could be arranged so the smell alone did not turn people away. They would likely need special bathing costumes that could be taken to be cleaned following their dip in the water. "And I must tell you how Philip found me."

"Did he?" Mrs. Bassett turned to her husband, who had come into the room.

Mr. Bassett clarified. "Townsend was with me, but it was one of his workers who discovered her. I will own, however, that if I had not gone to Boden House first, it is not likely we would have thought to look in the mine."

When Honoria had been brought up to her room to change, Maggie wrinkled her nose at the smell of her clothes. "We will have to wash your hair tonight, too, miss," she said, as she stripped her of her clothes and rubbed her with a towel to warm her.

Once she was clothed in fresh raiment, Jeffrey carried her back downstairs to the sitting room, where they had now received a visitor. Mr. Mercer was seated in one of the armchairs in the room with a drink in his hand. He stood when he saw her.

"Miss Bassett! I am to understand you had quite a rescue," he said, bowing and resuming his seat as soon as she had been set down on the sofa. "Your father has just been telling both your mother and me how it all came about."

"As exciting an adventure as I could wish for," she said cheerfully.

"I came by to tell your father about the storm's damage to the mill, which I happened to see when I rode by. But this news is eclipsed indeed by your exciting rescue." Turning to her father, he added with a benign smile, "You must be quite indebted to Townsend. This makes a second time he has come to her aid in a rather dramatic fashion. Although in the first incident, as I am sure you are aware, he truly saved her life."

Honoria's expression froze and she blinked, darting a glance from her mother to her father. Mr. Bassett turned his regard from Mr. Mercer to her. "I am not aware of to what you are referring," he said slowly.

Her mother chimed in, her tone puzzled and carrying notes of alarm. "Honoria, what is this?"

Sensing the tension in the room, a look of confusion crossed Mr. Mercer's face. "Ah. I believe I have let my tongue run away with me. But, miss, there is no reason you should keep your parents from what happened. Indeed, they should know of it."

He turned to her father. "While we were at Farlow Manor, an evening shortly after the Greys' return to Horncastle, your daughter's gown caught on fire—and quite dramatically, as I said before. The speed with which the flames sped up the skirt of her gown ..." He stopped and dropped his gaze to his hands. "I shudder to think of it. If Townsend had not thrown himself on top of her and beat out the flames with his hands, causing considerable burns to himself, I fear she might not be here today. He was very quick to act."

Mr. Bassett was silent for a long moment as he stared at his daughter, and she could read what was going through his mind.

He was reliving the memory of his sister's death. No one spoke, and at last he met her gaze. "Is this true?"

Honoria's heart, which had sped up at the unexpected turn to the conversation, now sank at the pain she saw in his eyes. She dropped her gaze. "It is. I didn't want to tell you. I didn't wish to resurrect frightening memories."

It seemed the implications were too much for her father, and he lowered his face in his hands. Her mother reached over to his armchair and placed her hand on his arm, and Mr. Mercer stood.

"Well, I shall not trespass upon your time any longer. I can see you have things to discuss that are better done without the annoyance of outsiders underfoot." He bowed to Mrs. Bassett who gave him a grateful smile of acknowledgment. Then he turned to face Honoria. "It was the right thing to do, you know—telling your parents. Secrets amongst family members always have a way of coming out." Then he took his leave.

"Why did you not tell us?" her father asked, lifting his head at last. "I shall have to invite Townsend over to thank him myself. I owe him a debt of gratitude that I can never repay."

"We do, indeed," her mother said quietly. After a small beat, she added, "But I think you might easily begin to repay it. The best way you could thank the man is to give him your daughter's hand in marriage." When his gaze remained fixed ahead, unseeing, Mrs. Bassett smiled at Honoria over Mr. Bassett's head with something of a conspiratorial look.

Honoria's heart began to hammer with excitement. She was tempted to speak and cajole, but silence would answer better. Instead, she turned hopeful eyes to her father and waited.

"Very well," he said, at last. "He may have my blessing. But the marriage will have to wait. It is not something we can rush. And I must first see to the damage at the mill."

The exultant feeling inside threatened to bloom and burst outward in a cheer. But, as Honoria knew her father was speaking as a man goaded beyond what he could bear, she bit back a smile and let him have his way.

"Yes, Papa," she said meekly.

CHAPTER 24

Philip walked aimlessly from the library to the dining room and then retraced his steps, wondering once again if Honoria had completely healed from her fall. It had been nearly a week since he had watched Honoria ride off with her father following the storm. After what had transpired, he didn't precisely despair of winning her hand even before the two years were up. That didn't make it easier to wait.

In other matters, all was going splendidly for him. He had received a letter from another prospective horse breeder concerning Crown Glory, and with the money he'd received from Mr. Fines to the same purpose, he had begun work repairing the stables. He met with Coates and Tom Hull together regarding the mine, and as they discussed the specifics of the proposal, he was growing confident that they would indeed be able to accomplish the task of turning the place into a spa that could bring in an income. And he had promised Tom a tenancy if he would first assist with the spa endeavor.

His grounds were ready for planting once they got through the winter, and he had engaged a new bailiff to oversee the tenants. Everything was looking up, compared to a few months ago when it was hard to imagine the estate running with anything approaching efficiency. Even Mrs. Mason had seemed to take the combined warning from him and Honoria to heart and was answering his summonses with a readiness he hoped would last.

The sound of a carriage rolling to the front of his house reached him in the dining room, and he began to walk to the entrance that led to the front drawing room. A stab of hope shot through him that it might be Honoria, although such a thing could hardly be likely. Despite all the recent improvements he was enjoying on his estate, he missed her. His house echoed with the loneliness of it. More than once, he'd wondered what the point was of doing all of these things on his estate if she were not there to share it with him.

A knock sounded on the door, and Jim went to answer it as he entered the room.

"I'm here to see Townsend."

Philip took in a sharp breath at the sound of that voice. Jim opened the door fully, and Mr. Bassett walked into the drawing room. Philip hesitated, wondering if he should bow or shake his hand, and when Mr. Bassett did not offer his own, he bowed.

"Townsend, I—" He glared at Jim, who had hung back with an unbecoming degree of curiosity, and who now quickly left the room. "I am to understand I owe you my daughter's life."

Philip could see no reason why Mr. Bassett was bringing this up now. "Well, we both found her, sir."

"No, I'm not talking about the other day in the storm. I've recently learned from Mr. Mercer that you risked your own life to put out the flames when Honoria's dress caught fire." Mr. Bassett glowered at him now, and it dawned on Philip that the scowling look hid deeper feelings that he did not like to reveal. "Your quick thinking and willingness to put yourself in harm's way resulted in my daughter being with us today. She suffered no serious burns to speak of, and I am to understand that you suffered worse."

Philip looked at his hands, which had white scars on the palms that would probably never go away. Other than the scars on his hands and thighs, there was no lasting harm. He would have done it again. "I thought you knew, sir. I did not realize she had kept this from you."

Mr. Bassett removed his top hat as he took a step toward Philip. "When I was a lad, my older sister had a like thing happen. I watched the flames catch, heard her scream ..." He stopped and allowed his gaze to rest on the window and the scenery beyond it. "I was too small to do anything, and she did not fare so well. Amy died as a result of her injuries. I believe Honoria kept silent because she wished to spare me the horror she must have known I would feel, and indeed *did* feel when I heard."

It made sense now. Philip had been led to believe that Mr. Bassett was aware of what had happened and still held a prejudice against him—not that Philip would have hesitated for an instant to save her even with no hope of ever gaining her hand.

In the silence that followed, Mr. Bassett glanced around the room, assessing everything in it. Philip followed his gaze and saw the shabby set of furniture as if for the first time. He could understand why Mr. Bassett hesitated. He could hardly prove himself worthy as a son-in-law with such a home as this.

"Well, Philip, I believe with everything that has transpired over the past couple of days, you deserve to win the hand of my daughter." Mr. Bassett scowled even more fiercely. "I will not make her wait until her majority or throw any other obstacle in your path. If you are still of the same mind—"

"Of course," Philip broke in quickly. "I am of the same mind. I have interest in no one but her. And, apart from the affairs of my estate, I think only of her. You have my word that I will care for her and protect her in the same way I've done in the fire, in the storm—until my last breath."

At these words, Mr. Bassett broke out into a rare smile, and Philip was finally given a glimpse of why he was thought so well of in the village. For the first time since he had known the man, Mr. Bassett looked approachable. More than that, he looked kind.

"I have wronged you, Philip, and I'm not ashamed to admit

it. I will be glad to welcome you as a son. Mind, we will not think about a wedding before the spring. We've just seen to Samuel's wedding and we will need to outfit Weeton Hall for them sooner than we had expected. We must end one season before we begin another." He held out his hand, and Philip wasted no time in giving his own to shake. The day that had started with such empty restlessness was now filled with promise.

"Honoria has been waiting these days for you to come by Weeton. I did not choose to make this visit to you until I had seen to some of the matters on my own land. But you may come to us as soon as you wish. Today even." He gave him a wry smile and something like a wink. "I am on my way to the mill, but you will find my daughter at home."

"Excellent. I will go at once." Philip thought perhaps that such eagerness did not become him, but he was beyond caring.

As soon as he had seen Mr. Bassett off, he had his own horse readied. It required no thought to choose his prized stallion. The Thoroughbred needed some exercise, and it matched Philip's own desire for exhilarating speed. On his ride over, at a stretch where there was no one, he laughed and called out a boyish, "*Woohooo!*"

At Weeton, he leapt down and handed his horse's reins to the groom there, then walked up the steps to the front door. He was ushered into the drawing room, where he found Honoria with Mrs. Bassett, and she sat up straight, an expectant light in her eyes.

"How do you do, Philip?" Mrs. Bassett greeted with a knowing smile.

Philip looked at Honoria, whose matching smile also reached her eyes. "I am very well, ma'am. In fact, I have never been better."

Mrs. Bassett turned to her daughter. "It is a beautiful day. Not so very cold, although it's almost November—and your knee is better. Why don't you take Philip for a short walk to one of the benches in the garden?"

Honoria set down her sewing and stood, walking toward him with only the slightest limp. "A most excellent idea. I will just fetch my cloak."

A few moments later, they were outside walking toward the fountain at a slow pace, and Philip took as much of her weight on his arm as he could. He did not want the pain in her knee to grow worse.

"Do you suppose the two of us shall ever cease to be candidates for a teaching hospital that they might gain experience?" Honoria's breath came out in short puffs as she laughed.

"Our successive injuries, do you mean?" Philip said, grinning. "We are quite the pair, the two of us. But then, at least one of us is a skilled healer."

He saw Honoria's dimpled smile at his side. "Thank you for believing in me, Phil."

Her quiet confidence and intimate use of his name made him breathe in deeply, throwing out his chest. She stopped and pointed to the alley of yew trees. "Let us go here. There is a bench where we may sit, and it is protected from the wind."

And prying eyes, Philip added to himself. They turned toward it and he pulled her close, stealing one hand around her waist. *The better to help her walk*, he thought. They entered the shade of the thick yew trees, with the gnarled branches above them, and moved toward the bench in the open center that was placed near two old oak trees. He helped her to sit and, instead of taking the seat beside her, knelt so he could look fully into her face.

"Miss Bassett," he said, a smile touching his lips. He should not be nervous. He was certain of her answer, after all.

"Mr. Townsend," she replied, her hands folded on her lap and her smile more gleeful than shy. It gave him courage.

He took her hands in his, his gaze steady on hers. "I have this very day been given leave to formally request your hand in marriage and could not avail myself of the opportunity quickly enough. Will you?"

"Marry you?" She tucked her chin so her eyes were level with his. "Yes, of course, Philip."

Yes! He quickly took the seat beside her and pulled her toward him. The bench was placed under one of the rare openings of the thick branches that allowed for a shaft of sunlight to fall upon her, and the clouds opened so that a ray did so at that moment. Her hair shone reddish-gold, and he thought her eyes would match the green of the trees in summer, although he was discovering that they seemed to change color according to the setting. He would have a lifetime to figure out exactly what color green they were. It was the lifetime that stretched before him that gave him courage.

"Will you allow me to kiss you then?"

A charming pink color bloomed in her cheeks, and the smile was now in her voice. "Yes, of course, Philip."

Sitting even closer, he lifted his hands to cradle her face and brought his gaze to her lips. She sat still, and her eyes grew soft as he lowered his head and placed his lips on hers, his heart pounding in his ears. She was his now, and he was entirely hers.

Spring could not come soon enough.

EPILOGUE

Theo Dawson handed Philip his hat before placing his own hat on his head and followed him out the door. They climbed into the tilbury, where Philip took the reins and drove around the circular path that led to the main road, their first few minutes of the drive done in complete silence.

"Mrs. Mason managed to set out a decent supper last night," Theo observed.

"Yes." Philip pulled on the reins to turn west along the public road. "It helps that Mrs. Branley takes pride in what she sends up to the table, and that provoked a hitherto dormant spirit in Mrs. Mason. A cook and housekeeper who are each eager to outshine the other, so that my house runs like a respectable gentleman's establishment? I never thought I would see the day."

"Honoria?" Theo lifted a gloved hand to secure his hat as the spring wind threatened to lift it off.

"Of course." The speed with which Philip drove his tilbury, while fast, could not adequately demonstrate how great his need was to see her. Today was the last day—the very last day—that they would reside in separate houses. Tomorrow was the wedding.

"I always thought she would be good for you," Theo said in a smug voice.

"I shall take the wind out of your sail by agreeing with you." Philip steered his carriage toward the village, the chill of the spring afternoon cooling his cheeks and threatening to seep into his cloak.

"Will all the Bassetts be there this evening?" Theo grasped the side of the tilbury as Philip feathered a corner.

Philip glanced sideways at him. "How little faith you have in my driving. No, they have decided to allow the younger set to have our fun. Samuel and Barbara will serve as the married chaperones for the event."

Theo laughed. "And next it will be you to serve such a role. My, how we have grown."

"Unavoidable," Philip replied as they neared the Greys' house. His short words and dry tone belied an excitement, an impatience, an absolute joy for what tomorrow would bring. His long wait was nearly at an end.

They pulled into the courtyard of Farlow Manor, and Gus's groom came to the carriage to take hold of the horses. Philip leapt down and, without waiting for Theo, walked to the front door, which opened before he could reach it.

Christine stood in attendance, smiling. She curtsied before him, then turned to greet Theo, while Philip looked across the room to where the fireplace was and saw her. Honoria turned, her gown an elegant corbeau-colored green silk. His eyes went to the fire behind her, but it was too mild to be of danger, and there was now a fender in place, too. She came toward him with her hands held out. He wanted to kiss her but contented himself instead with taking her hands in his and lifting them to his lips.

"Mrs. Northwick!"

Philip heard Theo's voice of surprise and, with Honoria's hands still in his, turned to see the widow leave Gus's side and come to face Theo, a timid smile on her face.

"I am surprised you remember me, Mr. Dawson," she said, curtsying before him.

"How could I forget?" Theo's broad smile stiffened as Gus came to join them.

Despite the proprietary gesture toward Mrs. Northwick, Gus seemed genuinely glad to see him. "Theo, I thought it might be years before I saw you again. And here it is mere months."

"I can't miss my only cousin's wedding." Theo relaxed and shook Gus's hand.

Philip leaned down to murmur in Honoria's ear. "I didn't know Mrs. Northwick would be joining us this evening, but I suppose it makes sense given that she traveled all this way for the wedding."

Honoria smiled at him in the way he was coming to depend upon. "I thought you would divine that she would come, of course, and would not need to be told." She leaned in to whisper, "Theo seems happy to see her again. How long will he be staying after the wedding?"

Philip did not respond to her observation about Theo's potential interest but answered the easier question. "It is to be a short visit, as you and I will be leaving directly after the wedding breakfast. As happy as he is to see Gus, I don't think he planned on making a prolonged stay just for him."

"*Hm.*" Honoria pursed her lips. "Then we shall have to invite him for a prolonged stay at a near date to see us."

Christine went over to Gus, and at a look from her, he held up his hand. "We would like to invite everyone to be seated for dinner." He then led them all into the dining room as Barbara took Honoria by the elbow and whispered something in her ear in a way that spoke of their increased affection since Samuel's marriage. Honoria smiled and nodded in reply.

Mrs. Northwick was seated on the opposite end of the table with Theo at her side, and Philip wondered if this was deliberate on Christine's part. Otherwise, as the one woman who was married and the one to be married, Honoria and Barbara had the places of honor on either side of Gus, and everyone else sat in what places remained. The footmen brought one dish after another into the dining room as conversation flowed freely amongst the group that had little reserve when together.

Honoria was seated on the other side of the table and at an angle from Philip, but he did not waste any opportunity to communicate with her with his eyes—laughter when Samuel said something Honoria would call "odiously conceited" and raising his eyebrows when Gus expounded on a winding tale of some sporting exploit.

The dinner went on like this in a happy dream. The early crops were in the ground of his new field, with plenty of space left over for corn and wheat as the weather warmed. The mine's transformation into a mineral spa for bathers wishing to benefit from the healing powers of the waters was progressing, as they carefully removed earth from above it. Coates estimated that they could begin welcoming the public in about another four months. And Philip was going to take advantage of their honeymoon trip to the Lake District to visit another stud horse near the Scottish border to continue his ongoing efforts to increase his stables. He caught Honoria's eye again across the table.

And he would marry her.

The gentlemen decided to forego the port and spend time with the ladies, so they could all end the evening earlier. Tomorrow would be a big day. Christine and Theo would serve as witnesses for their wedding, and in addition to the crowd present tonight and Honoria's parents, the betrothed couple would have the honor of a few older couples' presence at their wedding who had all known them from birth.

Philip allowed the conversation to flow around him as he waited for Honoria by the door to the sitting room. He tucked her arm in his, leading her into the room so that he might be seated beside her. When everyone had taken their places, another two hours were spent in a game of charades that had them all laughing, both from the silly antics and from the joy of participating in one of life's more festive moments. Samuel's wife Barbara possessed an unexpected knack for pantomime, and Mrs. Northwick was as carefree as Philip had ever seen her.

It was soon time to end the evening and for Philip to prepare for his last night on earth as a bachelor. Stealing a quiet moment amidst the activity, he led Honoria to an empty nook by the window, where they faced each other. He stared at her in silence, holding her hands in his. She spoke first.

"Is everything set for tomorrow?"

"Yes."

"So I have only to marry you," she said simply.

"Yes." He grinned, his gaze dancing from one perfect feature of her face to another. Honoria's eyes were brimming with the joy that mirrored his own.

"Well, then."

"Well, then," he repeated. He was not sure he would get a wink of sleep in the anticipation that coursed through him. He could hardly care. "I shall meet you at the altar, Miss Bassett."

If anything, at these words, her joy seemed only to increase. In full view of anyone who might be turned their way, Miss Honoria Bassett went up on tiptoes and kissed him fully on the lips.

"Mr. Townsend, I shall not fail."

AFTERWORD

My husband and I visited Lincolnshire in preparation for writing this book, and I would like to thank my wonderful reader, Rod Stormes, for the copious notes about the area, as well as the staff and volunteers of the national monuments in the shire who answered questions and gave us tours. Your stories and additional information were invaluable. The places in my book are only loosely based on these manors, but the collection we visited allowed me to have a better feel for what the various houses and gardens are like in Lincolnshire.

The house on Philip's estate, Boden House, was based on Gunby Hall. Honoria's family house is based on the medieval Ayscoughfee Hall, complete with the gorgeous gardens and magnificent yew trees. Arabella's house is modeled after Belton House, but as we arrived too late for an interior visit (alas), the inside is entirely imagined. And finally, Gus and Christine Grey's Farlow Manor is based on Alford Manor House, although their fictional property is greater and is not confined to the village where the house is located. I also moved Honoria's house from Spalding to Horncastle and stuck the Greys' house pretty close to Horncastle as well (in that imperious manner of writers of fiction, and to the consternation of readers who are local to the area).

We stayed in the Lea Gate Inn, whose sign in the small dining room, "Satisfying the Hungry Traveller since 1542" never ceased to charm me. My depiction of the Lincoln inn, where Honoria and Arabella stayed was based on the rooms here. The Stuff Ball, as you may have guessed, was an annual tradition, dating from 1785 through until about 1900. I also included some local terrain details, such as the fenlands and the Wolds. And in case you thought the mine-turned-spa too far-fetched to be believed, you need only look up Woodhall Spa to see that the idea was based on fact, although this did not occur until the Victorian era. We visited that charming town as well, although it is no longer a bathing town.

Finally, some period details. My idea for the series came from reading *A Gentleman's Daughter* by Amanda Vickery. I wanted to portray what life was like outside of London, particularly for gentlemen and ladies who were not members of the peerage, but who lived as landed gentry. What I learned from the book is that members of this set, such as the frequently mentioned Elizabeth Parker, were quite interested in the running of the household. Although they had servants (and often bemoaned their ineptitude but found them hard to replace), they got involved with the upkeep and maintenance of the house. Another fun fact: despite the somewhat strict mores of the time, Elizabeth's intended, Robert, paid her nighttime visits in her room before they were married, prompting Philip's daring attempt to see Honoria.

And lastly, from reading *Eavesdropping on Jane Austen's England* by Roy & Lesley Adkins, I learned about the frequency of fires. At times, it was below freezing *even indoors*, and people gathered close to the hearth to stay warm. It was not unusual for long garments to catch fire in this way, or for fires to be ignited from candles. The installation of fenders to protect the hearths began in the early 19th century. As much as it's fun to plunge into the world of Regency England, I think most of us can find reason to be thankful for modern conveniences.

Thank you for following along with my Lincolnshire stories!

The next up in the *Daughters of the Gentry* series is *A Stroke of Good Fortune*, to be released in 2023.

ABOUT THE AUTHOR

Jennie Goutet is an American-born Anglophile who lives with her French husband and their three children in a small town outside of Paris. Her imagination resides in Regency England, where her best-selling proper Regency romances are set. She is also author of the award-winning memoir *Stars Upside Down,* two contemporary romances, and a smattering of other published works. A Christian, a cook, and an inveterate klutz, Jennie writes (with increasing infrequency) about faith, food, and life—even the clumsy moments—on her blog, aladyinfrance.com. If you really want to learn more about Jennie and her books, sign up for her newsletter on her author website: jenniegoutet.com.

* Photo Credit : Caroline Aoustin

Made in the USA
Las Vegas, NV
22 August 2023

76418892R00139